Army vet Persephone "Perri" Morgan has big plans, as her custom leather leashes, saddles, and other pet accessories are the rage of dog and horse enthusiasts everywhere. But when murder prances into the ring at a Massachusetts dog show, Perri must confront a cunning killer who's a breed apart.

Accompanied by her bestie Babette and four oversize canines, Perri motors down to the Big E Dog Show in high style. Perri hopes to combine business with pleasure by also spending time with sexy DC journalist Wing Pruett. Until a storm traps everyone at the exposition hall . . . and a man's body is found in a snow-covered field, a pair of pink poodle grooming shears plunged through his heart.

Turns out the deceased was a double-dealing huckster who had plenty of enemies chomping at the bit. But as breeders and their prize pets preen and strut, the murderer strikes again. Aided by her trusty canine companions, Keats and Poe, Perri must collar a killer before she's the next "Dead in Show" winner.

Visit us at www.kensingtonbooks.com

Death by Dog Show

A Creature Comforts Mystery

Arlene Kay

LYRICAL UNDERGROUND
Kensington Publishing Corp.
www.kensingtonbooks.com

LYRICAL UNDERGROUND BOOKS are published by
Kensington Publishing Corp.
119 West 40th Street
New York, NY 10018

All Kensington titles, imprints, and distributed lines are available at special quantity discounts for bulk purchases for sales promotion, premiums, fund-raising, educational, or institutional use.

Special book excerpts or customized printings can also be created to fit specific needs. For details, write or phone the office of the Kensington Sales Manager: Kensington Publishing Corp., 119 West 40th Street, New York, NY 10018. Attn. Sales Department. Phone: 1-800-221-2647.
Lyrical Underground and Lyrical Underground logo Reg. US Pat. & TM Off.

First Electronic Edition: March 2019
ISBN-13: 978-1-5161-0930-2 (ebook)
ISBN-10: 1-5161-0930-9 (ebook)

First Print Edition: March 2019
ISBN-13: 978-1-5161-0933-3
ISBN-10: 1-5161-0933-3

Printed in the United States of America

*To Paula Hogan, friend, master leathersmith, and breeder of Winjammer's
Grand Champion Lord Byron*

Chapter 1

Road trips always rattled me. They carried me back to my army days in an airless transport truck, where I sat wedged between raunchy guys with mixed motives. I had to admit that they were expert practitioners of that international game—Russian hands and Roman fingers. In those times, a woman needed sharp elbows and an even sharper tongue to survive and thrive. Out of necessity, I had acquired both. They weren't a bad bunch. Like me, most of my fellow warriors were actually scared kids buoying their courage with a show of false bravado. As soldiers, we served our country and learned invaluable life lessons that strengthened us—if we survived.

Things were different now, of course, but those memories still hovered about the recesses of my mind every time I took a road trip. I closed my eyes and made a wish.

Please. Whisk me away on a magic carpet and make me vanish.

Naturally that didn't happen. We barreled down the highway in Babette Croy's superduper Class A motor home at top speed without missing a beat. Then, for the hundredth time that day, I wondered how in the world I would ever survive the coming week. Seven whole days in close quarters with my best friend and several thousand dog enthusiasts. The possibilities for mischief were endless.

"Are you okay, Perri?" The dulcet tones of seven-year-old Ella Pruett revived me and brought me to my senses. A mini-frown marred the sweet face of the moppet I had grown to love, flooding me with guilt.

"Of course. Don't worry about me. I was just dreaming." I winked to show her that everything was fine. Hunky-dory. Peachy keen. My trusty Malinois Keats and Poe immediately went on alert. They were canine truth detectors who could sense lies—particularly mine—at ten paces. That was their job during a three-year stint in the army, and retired or not, they hadn't lost a step. Most people confused Belgians like my boys with either German shepherds or shepherd/collie mixes. Nothing could be further from the truth, as police forces throughout the world now realized. Belgian Malinois are a distinct breed—streamlined, tireless workers with an unending appetite for action. I reached for them, looked into soulful doggy eyes, and gave each a nose kiss. In times of stress, nothing surpassed a furry embrace.

"Don't mind Perri, sugar. She's just a stick in the mud." Babette, my best pal and our designated driver, twisted around in the driver's seat and rolled her eyes, ignoring the threat of oncoming traffic and the blaring horns of outraged drivers. "I know," she said, "let's sing a song. Road trips are supposed to be fun. Look at it this way. By leavin' today, we'll beat the snowstorm and avoid all that nasty winter traffic. Plus, that gives us plenty of girl time together."

Babette was a guided missile—locked, loaded, and ready to fire. Fortunately, I distracted her by mentioning one of her favorite subjects: dogs. After all, canine competition was what had sparked our little caravan. Why else would two adults, one child, and four large dogs abandon Great Marsh, Virginia, and drive for six hours to the sooty embrace of the Big E Coliseum, also known as the Eastern States Expo Center, a carbuncle on the foot of western Massachusetts.

I didn't mind roughing it. Four years in the US Army had cured me of needless luxuries, but Babette was a different story entirely. My friend considered anything short of full cable, Italian sheets, and catered meals an unendurable hardship. Great wealth does that to a person, I'm told, although in my case it was strictly a rumor. My business, Creature Comforts, provided me with a decent livelihood and a satisfying creative outlet. I left the opulence to Babette and most of my neighbors in Great Marsh. That explained the luxury motor home. There were more modest models available, but Babette wouldn't hear of it. Second class was simply not in her vocabulary. This latest acquisition, the behemoth dubbed Steady Eddie, sported granite countertops, plush leather furniture, two steam showers, and accommodations for eight. At first, I'd been wary, but Babette surprised me. After all, not everyone could maneuver a metal monster through heavy traffic. My friend was petite but surprisingly adept at doing just that. Rule number one in the Croy friendship manual—never underestimate Babette!

"Miss your daddy, Ella?" Babette's coy tone gave her away. "I know Ms. Perri does."

Ella was the much-loved daughter of Wing Pruett, investigative journalist, hottie supreme, and my main squeeze. How to describe Wing Pruett? Sculpted features, thick dark hair, and a body most women (and men) could only dream about. No doubt about it. All six plus feet of my honey were as close to perfection as mere mortals could ever get. He was absent today but planned to join us later in the week after wrapping up his current assignment. He'd been uncharacteristically vague about the project, and that made me wonder. Despite Babette's prompts and none too subtle hints, Pruett refused to spill the journalistic beans. I surmised, however, that it had something to do with dog shows. That was a real puzzler. Wing Pruett, the man who fearlessly confronted evildoers of all stripes, was terrified of dogs. Cynophobia was the clinical term for an ailment I simply could not understand. Still, he had made great strides, mostly due to Ella and his interaction with my own menagerie. Few men would admit, let alone address, such a malady, but then Pruett was not most men. I missed him like crazy but kept that feeling to myself.

I turned toward my dogs to avoid Babette's scrutiny. Damn that woman. She sometimes knew me better than I knew myself. Truth be told, I missed Pruett every second that we spent apart. Simple logic told me that a country mouse like me was unlikely to hold his interest long-term, but raw emotion kept me firmly anchored to his side. After almost a year, things had only gotten better—for me at least.

"I see him every night on Skype," Ella said with that unassailable logic small children often use. "He blows kisses to me and Guinnie." Lady Guinivere, a champion pointer, was the love of Ella's life. "Ms. Perri too. Daddy always saves a kiss for her." I loved that child as if she were my own little girl. She wasn't, of course. She was the offspring of Pruett and renowned photojournalist Monique Allaire and had the black curly mane and soulful blue eyes to prove it. Monique was mostly absent from her life, but Pruett was the ultimate Mr. Mom. I knew that allowing Ella to join our merry band proved his trust in me, but it also conferred an awesome responsibility. That's what shattered my nerves and led to sleepless nights. Dog shows were busy places, and the Big E was cavernous—so many nooks and crevices where a little girl might wander off, get lost, or worse. Add a potential blizzard to the mix, and anything might happen.

"You won't go anywhere without me or Ms. Babette. Right, Ella? Remember. We promised your dad that."

She nodded solemnly. "I promise. Besides, Guinnie will protect me too." Her eyes shone as she stroked the pointer's silky coat. "And all the other dogs will help."

I crossed my fingers and took a deep breath. Babette and her border collie, Clara, were focused on agility contests. Babette was obsessed with winning agility competitions, and border collies—those bright, stealthy herders— won top honors in most agility contests. My friend tended toward extremes, especially in times of emotional stress. Since she had recently divorced the cretinous Carleton Croy, Babette was temporarily man-less, and a lonely Babette was a fearsome thing indeed. Thank heavens for the presence of an innocent child. That shielded me from hearing a litany of praise for Carleton's manly parts that Babette so desperately missed. She conveniently forgot that her ex had shared his largesse with any number of her friends and a few enemies as well. When it came to men, Babette had a fond but very selective memory.

Ella had her own dreams. She yearned to be a junior dog handler, a member of that select group of youngsters that dotted every dog show. After discussing the issue with Pruett, I promised to introduce her to some of the kids who participated in the sport. Fortunately, all juniors had to be at least nine years of age, so Pruett had two years to go before confronting the situation. Wing was ambivalent about animals, and I was certain that he hoped Ella's interest would fade.

"Remember," I told Ella, "I'm counting on you to help me with my store." I am a leathersmith by trade, an occupation that requires both creativity and precision. After careful study at art school and an apprenticeship with a master craftsman, I focused on designing products for the creatures I most loved. The majority of my customers were dog and horse fanciers, although lately I'd branched out to custom belts with mother-daughter themes. Any event at the Big E was bound to bring in a slew of business. Snowstorms and other weather mishaps encouraged even more potential customers to attend the show. They chose to brave the elements rather than risk a bout of cabin fever. That pleased me since by necessity I kept my eyes firmly trained on the bottom line.

The little girl beamed. "Yep. See, I got my belt on."

I nodded in appreciation of Ella, a truly wonderful child. I had never married, although I came close one time. Being childless wasn't a problem for me since my biological clock simply did not tick. Before meeting Pruett, I lacked the maternal gene, or so I thought. An affinity for animals came naturally to me, and my menagerie included two dogs, one cantankerous feline, and an ornery goat with bad manners and a temper to match.

Once Ella stepped into the picture, that all changed. At thirty years of age, I had finally embraced the role of child nurturer and caregiver. Go figure.

Babette slowed the trailer and pulled into a rest stop parking lot. "Let's take a break," she said. "I need to stretch my legs, and I know the pups could use some potty time."

Fortunately, we had the coach fully stocked with every possible type of provision, so food and drink were plentiful. Babette had made sure of that. After leashing the dogs, we stepped into the bright sunshine and walked toward the pet area.

"Heard they had some fireworks at last week's show," Babette said in a stage whisper.

I raised my eyebrows.

"Yep. A real dustup." She watched as Ella disposed of Guinnie's waste. "Yael Lindsay almost came to blows with that Bethany. You know her."

My goal was to sell products, not become mired in scandals. "Nope. Can't place either one."

Babette puffed out her cheeks in a pout. "Oh. You're no fun at all, Ms. Goody Two-shoes. Bethany is that slutty one. Slinks around the arena in super-tight duds that show everything and pretends to be a pet psychic. Don't see how that heifer can even move, let alone mentally communicate with dogs. Thinks she's the queen of agility too."

Something she said piqued my interest. "That's odd. Yael rules the pointer world with an iron fist. Strictly conformation events. Why would she bother with an agility person? Besides she's rather elderly for a fistfight."

"Aha!" Babette pounced immediately. "You know more than you let on. I knew it."

What could I do? I shrugged and gave her a guilty grin. Babette, master of trickery, had trapped me fair and square. "You know I steer clear of these feuds. At least I try to. Remember, I need to sell stuff to both camps."

Sales were a foreign language to my pal. She never even bothered to balance her checkbook, whereas I accounted for each penny with nuclear precision. Call it a legacy from my life as a foster child or just plain business acumen. Either one worked for me. Pip had always urged me to ease up and enjoy life without going overboard. Balance was his watchword.

I snapped a leash on further memories lest tears flood my eyes. Pip, my late fiancé, was gone. Had been these three years since melanoma had stolen him from me. He still resided with me in the home we'd shared, in the pets we both had loved, and in the memories I cherished. Those were the hardest things to suppress because I simply refused to. No matter where things went with Pruett, the late Philip Hahn, DVM, owned a part of me and always would. I told myself that he wasn't really gone. Pip had just left ahead of me.

"Hey, Earth to Perri." Babette tapped me on my forehead. "Stop mooning and get movin'. We've got a show to get to." She clapped her hands for Ella. "Right, Ella? Let's roll."

The remainder of our journey was uneventful, and we exited the Mass Pike and approached the Big E without incident. To my surprise, Babette had researched everything pertinent to parking and maintaining her motor coach right down to electronic and cable television hookups. Many dog show veterans chose the convenience of recreational vehicles over the rigors of motel life since upscale establishments banned or severely restricted dogs. The remaining "dog hotels" simply didn't measure up to Babette's high standards. Thus, the luxury coach—an inspired, if pricey, solution that paid dividends to me too. I groused about needless spending when my pal had purchased Steady Eddie, citing depreciation, inconvenience, and the numerous animal charities that needed the money instead. Opulence made me uncomfortable, a throwback to my hardscrabble childhood. Still, I was secretly pleased by the comfort and ease of our accommodations. Friendship with Babette conferred many benefits, and chief among them was sharing the spoils of wealth. Money aside, her loyalty and sweet nature were the primary attractions for me.

Although the Big E reserved a sizable area for large vehicles and trailers, choice slots close to the show venue were at a premium. I worried that our late arrival might relegate us to the far reaches of the fairground—Siberia, as the regulars termed it. If that were our fate, juggling dogs, leather products, and one lively child would present quite a challenge, especially during inclement weather.

Once again, Babette read my mind. "Don't fret, Perri. We've got a primo spot. I already arranged it." Try as she might, she couldn't hide the smirk that covered her pretty face.

"How'd you manage that?" I asked, mindful that a small child was within earshot.

Babette fluttered her eyelashes. "Charm and wit."

I crossed my arms. "What else?"

"Suspicious little twit, aren't you? Okay. You caught me. A well-placed bribe didn't hurt either. Just a generous cash gift to the guy in charge of the area." Babette stared me down. "Don't be an old prig, Perri. It's the American way. Once that snow starts, things will get crazy here."

"What's a prig, Ms. Babette?" Ella proved yet again that her hearing was exceptionally sharp.

Babette swung into a reserved slot closest to the show area. "Don't worry, pumpkin. Ms. Perri is just a stuffed shirt. We have to loosen her up."

Ella's big blue eyes sparkled. "My daddy says Ms. Perri is perfect."

Now it was my turn to blush and change the subject. I hated to acknowledge the firm grip that Wing Pruett and his darling moppet had on my heart. Orphans like me fear loss more than most folks. After being wrenched from my parents' arms and watching my fiancé slip away, I tried mightily to steel myself against further pain. Through a concentrated stealth campaign, Pruett had managed to penetrate those defenses and unleash my fondest hopes. Love does that to a body, but it's a deep and dangerous game.

"Come on," I said, dusting off my jeans. "Let's hook up this baby and walk around the grounds. I see a few familiar faces already."

Babette clambered out of the driver's seat and immediately made a connection. Our near neighbor, a muscular, middle-aged man with a thick crop of gray hair, held out his arm and helped Babette alight. She sized him up and went all girly on him.

"Why, thank you, kind sir. I can always use a little help." In true Babette fashion, she simpered. I really hated when she did that, but it was straight from the Croy playbook, with a bow to Scarlett O'Hara. Most men fell for it, especially when she showed her dimples. This guy was no exception.

I did a quick appraisal of Prince Galahad. He was tall, tanned, and neatly dressed in a pressed pair of jeans and checked shirt. There was nothing wrong with his body either, but I was more concerned with his motives. Call me protective, but Babette had zero judgment when it came to men. The unlamented Carleton Croy, husband number four, was an opportunist who was more interested in her bankbook than her loving heart. Similarly, any con man worth his salt would assess Steady Eddie and quickly realize the bucks that went with it. I leapt out of my seat, clutched Ella, and unleashed my dogs.

"Forgive me, ma'am. I should have introduced myself." Babette's admirer ignored me and kept hold of her hand. "Rafael Ramos at your service. Most folks call me Rafa."

Ramos's vehicle was a poor cousin of ours, a rusted Airstream that had seen better days. Naturally, Babette seemed oblivious to that as she zeroed in on our neighbor. I knew the signs and decided to immediately nip young love in the bud.

Babette was still in dreamland. "Rafa? Ooh. Just like the tennis player. That's fascinatin'!"

He shrugged and shook his head. "Don't I wish. Unfortunately, I'm not much of an athlete." His faux modesty aroused my suspicions. The muscles on this guy proved that he did some serious physical training.

"Hi, Rafa," I said, extending my hand. "I'm Perri Morgan, and this is Ella. Excuse us while we exercise our crew. We've got four hungry canines on board."

Ramos unhanded my friend and switched into helpful mode. "Of course. Be glad to help you with the connections on this big boy if you need anything. Sure is a beauty." He then proved that he was also a dog person. "Wow! Speaking of beauties, your dogs are phenomenal." He approached Keats and Poe with the palm of his hand open and lowered. When they acknowledged him, he patted their silky heads and did the same to Clara and Guinnie.

"Do you have a dog, sir?" Ella asked.

He bent down and smiled. "Call me Rafa, honey. And the answer is yes. My breed is standard poodles. Don't have any with me this trip because I'm judging."

"You're a judge," Babette trilled as if he had said "brain surgeon." The throb in her voice sounded authentic and probably was. "How excitin'."

Rafael lowered his head in an "aw shucks" routine. "I just love doing the show circuit. Being around beautiful dogs and lovely ladies—doesn't get much better than that."

"Guinnie is a Grand Champion," Ella said proudly. "She's almost at bronze level." In dog show parlance, there were five levels of Grand Champion, and Guinnie was new to that elevated crowd. She had bronze, silver, gold, and platinum levels yet to conquer, but that didn't concern me one bit. With Guinnie's perfection, Ella's persistence, and Pruett's pocketbook, no obstacle was insurmountable.

Rafa nodded. "I can see why. Didn't I see her written up in the latest issue of *Canine Chronicles*?"

Ella's smile was luminous. She nodded and reached down to give Guinnie another hug. In deference to the little girl, I hoped Rafa wouldn't probe any further. Grand Champion Camelot Kennel's Lady Guinevere had come to us under tragic circumstances that were best forgotten. Like most pointers, Guinnie was a gentle, loving companion with plenty of brains. The important thing was the immutable bond between Ella and her dog.

"Let me take these guys for a run," I said, whistling to my dogs. "Ready, Ella?" We loped toward the backfields, leaving Babette to her new suitor. I know from experience when to fade from the scene, particularly when it involved a man. Their animated conversation told me that our absence hadn't even been noticed. No surprise there. Babette was a loyal friend, but any presentable man with a pulse could easily turn her head.

Ella, on the other hand, saw only Guinnie and the other dogs. Her big blue eyes shone with happiness as she romped with our pack of pups. Loving animals came easily to most children, and I harbored grave suspicions about kids who felt otherwise. Indifference to animals was just plain unnatural—serial killer material.

A sudden cacophony of noise rudely interrupted my thoughts. I clutched Ella's hand, steering her toward the trees and to the left of the warring parties. Neither combatant acknowledged us, but I suspect that, in the heat of battle, neither of them noticed us either. To my chagrin, these disturbers of the peace were adults, grown women, not marauding teens. Yael Lindsay, a well-preserved sexagenarian with seriously teased hair and an eye-popping diamond ring, shook her fist. "You listen here, Bethany. I run this show. That means no shenanigans by the likes of you. Hussy!"

Her antagonist, agility master Bethany Zahn, was the seductress so vividly described by Babette. Maybe it was the black leather blanketing her from stem to sultry stern that gave Bethany away or the mane of unnaturally black curls that she twirled. Either way, she radiated sex appeal, snark, and a dollop of dominatrix.

"Run?" she sneered, hands on hips. "Honey, at your age you couldn't run if your life depended on it. Join a gym, why don't you? Better still, muzzle that horny hubby of yours. He's into agility in a big way, or so I hear." Bethany smirked at her own wit and sauntered off toward the show entrance without a backward glance.

I normally eschew gossip, but that little tiff fascinated me—until I recalled the urchin who clutched my hand. Ella Pruett trained her baby blues on me and asked, "Why were those ladies fighting, Perri? Daddy says that's not right."

Honesty was the best policy, especially when it involved a bright, inquisitive child like Ella, who was not easily fooled.

"Your daddy was right. Shouting never solves anything, honey. Some people never learn." I clapped my hands, causing Poe and Keats to snap to attention. "Come on. Let's run a race with these pups."

We sped down the field, trailing four dogs that easily outpaced us and leaving the snarling women behind. Canine quarrels were typically sparked by competition—dominance, food, territory, or sex. Humans were no different. Based on the scene I had just witnessed, one or all of those factors might have caused the dustup. I never dreamed that tragedy awaited us.

Chapter 2

I spent my time focused on business, relegating that catfight between Yael and Bethany to the dustbin of my mind. Selling my wares, satisfying customers, and making new friends—that was enough for me. I had neither the time nor the desire to indulge in blood sports at the Big E, especially with Pruett due to arrive any day.

Unfortunately, I forgot about Babette and her all-consuming interest in the affairs of others. She was all smiles when we returned, giving us a coy act that fooled no one, not even little Ella.

"You look happy, Ms. Babette," Ella said. "Where's your friend?"

Babette fussed with Clara's collar to avoid answering. When she raised her head, her cheeks were flushed with an emotion I was all too familiar with. Some people called it infatuation. When Babette Croy was involved, I called it trouble.

"Where is Rafa?" I asked. The Airstream looked deserted and more disreputable than ever.

"He had a meeting with the organizers," Babette replied. "He is a judge, after all. And guess what? Rafael lives in Spain part-time, just like the famous tennis player. He came all this way just to judge poodles. In fact, he's doing the Non-sporting Group too."

Ella dipped into her gear bag for Guinnie's comb. She hugged her pet and carefully groomed the pointer's silky coat. "Two ladies were fighting," she told Babette.

That let the proverbial cat out of the bag and activated Babette's scary senses.

"Oh?" She shot me a venomous look. "And you planned to tell me when?"

I shrugged, trying to resurrect my innocent girl-next-door persona. "No big deal. Just a difference of opinion between two adults who should have known better."

Babette put her hands on her hips and planted herself in my path. "Come on. Who were they? Don't make me beg."

Bargaining was one of my strong suits, and in this instance, it paid big dividends.

"Help me set up my shop, and I promise to tell you everything. Besides, didn't they schedule some kind of welcome reception tonight? We don't want to miss it."

Unlike me, my friend was a social butterfly. Nothing phony; it came naturally to her. I knew she would move mountains to attend the opening ceremony at the Big E. No doubt she intended to dazzle the locals and assert her claim on Rafa while she was at it.

"Okay, but you better spill, girlfriend—every little detail." She gave me the Babette special, a stare that could instantly pulverize lesser mortals. I bit back a retort and remained strong.

Instead of caving, I loaded up a pushcart with leads and collars, and shoved it her way. "You bet."

Ella helped stack more products, including my custom belts and engraving tools. With the combined sweat of two and a half dogged workers, we were able to stock my little stall in no time. I kept an eagle eye on Ella as she scampered gleefully around the aisles with Guinnie in tow, making friends everywhere she went.

Floor space in the Better Living Center was already at a premium. A profusion of dog crates, grooming tables, and custom camp chairs littered the outer perimeter of the arena. Savvy show veterans staked their claim to real estate before the start of the competition to ensure that they and their canine charges were comfortably settled. To do otherwise was to risk getting stuck with an uncomfortable berth or none at all.

Babette called time after an hour and led us back to Steady Eddie. "Come on, ladies. We need to freshen up before the social." In Croy-land, "freshen up" was a euphemism for putting on the glam. It worked for her, but it was simply not my thing. Don't get me wrong. I'm not totally without vanity. While my friend pawed through her wardrobe, I unbraided my hair, my one point of vanity, changed into a new pair of jeans, and applied lipstick. My jewelry was simple, but meaningful at least to me. It consisted of a small pair of ruby studs that Pip had given me, and a beautiful diamond key, courtesy of Wing Pruett. Ella had a child's version of that necklace, a fact that absolutely delighted her.

"Ms. Babette—look. Perri and I match." She pirouetted around the room.

"Well, aren't you two just something?" Babette said. "Two Tiffany models right before my eyes. You'll be the stars of the show."

Mrs. Croy was looking pretty snazzy herself, garbed in a sumptuous cashmere twinset and velvet slacks. In deference to her surroundings, she toned down the bling—no diamond over two carats anywhere on her person.

We settled the dogs in their crates and traipsed toward the center, where the opening cocktail party was in full swing. Already the wind had picked up, and a hint of snow was in the air. I feared that Pruett might have a tough time getting here from DC.

At first glimpse, the mostly female crowd was an unremarkable assemblage of handlers, vendors, judges, and members of the sponsoring dog clubs. There was a noticeable absence of scent in deference to the canine sensitivity to perfume, but that didn't deter most participants from gamely showing off their party duds. Rafa Ramos stood out for two reasons: the gaggle of groupies surrounding him and his bulging muscles. Lord, that man's forearms were veritable tree trunks! Sequoias. I bit my lip, mindful that Pruett would soon be there to quench any lingering lust of mine.

"Well, will you look at that?" Babette pointed toward Rafa. "I should have known that floozy psychic would make a run at him. The woman has no scruples." She bared her teeth in a grimace so savage that Ella recoiled. I squeezed her hand and ignored Babette's antics. To be fair, Bethany had a number of competitors vying for Rafa's affections. Presentable men were in short supply, and show veterans were well aware of the sexual shenanigans and alcohol-fueled brawls that marked the off hours. Tennyson's "nature, red in tooth and claw" described human antics as much as canine.

Babette had a fiery temper, but she was easily distracted. I nudged her toward the back corner of the room, where another interesting tableau was unfolding. Yael Lindsay huddled against the wall in deep conversation with Whit Wiley, a fellow pointer enthusiast and bitter rival. Word had it that Whit planned to unseat Yael by any means possible so that he might rule the pointer roost. I knew him slightly as a customer, and what I knew was unsavory. He bought my products but always tried to work a "deal"—his term for a sharp price reduction. Several times he also tried to return products that had obviously been used in the ring.

Babette stood on tiptoe, straining for a better view. Her refusal to wear glasses or contact lenses handicapped her snooping, but she bravely soldiered on. Beauty before function was her motto!

"Holy cow! Isn't that Whit cozying up to the chief heifer? He's up to something. Believe me. That guy always plays the angles." Babette gaped, forgetting for an instant about Rafael Ramos.

Arlene Kay

Whit Wiley's impeccable grooming and surface pleasantries masked the smarmy side of his personality. Although intelligent and well-spoken, his veneer of civility was only half an inch deep. Given a chance, he would sabotage competitors or friends indiscriminately. He'd done that to me more than once.

"Creep," I muttered. Ella was within earshot, so I restrained myself.

Babette shrugged. "He's not so bad. At least he supports agility and obedience competitions. Yael and her gang are such purists. With them it's conformation or nothing."

"What's conformation?" Ella asked.

I ruffled her hair. "Dog shows, honey. The kind of things Guinnie does." I pointed toward a long table laden with food. "Oh, look. They've got cake. Let's get some."

The three of us sped toward a yummy-looking cake with thick buttercream icing and, in the middle of the top, a marzipan figure of a pointer that resembled Guinnie. Fortunately, I have no weight problems, but Babette waged war against flab every day. Since she was a good sport as well as a sugar addict, we patiently waited our turn, then dug into the treat with gusto.

"Better watch it, ladies," said a familiar deep voice. "You're way too sweet already."

Ella squealed, and I nearly swooned as the strong arms of Pruett enveloped us.

* * * *

Wing Pruett, dubbed "Sexiest Man in DC" by *Washingtonian Magazine*, had earned that title ten times over in my opinion. If tall, lithe men with perfect features and mounds of luscious hair tickle your fancy, Pruett was your go-to guy. I was wary of him when we first met. Investigative journalist? Like most Americans, I had little use for the press, especially celebrity scribes. Perfect-looking men raised my hackles as well. Conceited and pompous—I labeled him immediately before even knowing him. Later, I learned how unfair that label was. True, he looked good and knew it, but any such man with a mirror would realize that. Unlike many superstars, however, Pruett never allowed physical perfection to rule his life. That—plus his genuine love for Ella and a host of beguiling ways too private to mention—had won my heart. Tonight, garbed in black jeans and leather jacket, he stole the show without even trying. I swear the temperature rose ten degrees the moment he set foot in that room. Female heads swiveled, and eyes fixed on the supple form of Ella's dad and my guy. Pruett accepted a kiss from Babette but kept his arms wound tight around me and Ella. I tried playing it cool but failed miserably. Besides, coolness was vastly overrated.

"I'm so glad you're here," I said. "Ella missed you."

Pruett flashed his saucy grin my way. "Just Ella? How about you, Persephone? Did you miss me too?" Only he and Babette ever used my formal name, and Pruett enunciated all four syllables, slowly and sensuously. I flushed but fought to maintain a shred of dignity.

"Oh, were you gone?" I kept my tone playful. "Funny. I didn't see your Jag in the parking lot."

Oddly enough, that flustered him. Pruett lowered his eyes and murmured. "I drove something else."

Babette had no inhibitions, and tact was never her strong suit. "Oh yeah?" she said. "You got something new?"

Automotive lust was harmless enough as addictions go, but for some reason, Pruett considered it a weakness. Knowing Babette would pester him for an answer, he tried a diversionary tactic. "I got an SUV. Ella's dog show gear didn't fit in a sedan."

"What'd you get?" Babette asked.

Ella piped up right away. "A macaroon, right, Daddy?"

Pruett hushed his daughter with a big hug. "Close. Actually, it's a Macan."

I knew very little about fancy vehicles since my aged Suburban fit both my needs and my pocketbook. High-end products were more suited to aficionados like Pruett and well-heeled matrons like Babette.

She nodded. "Cool. That's the new Porsche, right? What color?"

Pruett looked downright sheepish as he answered. "Deep red. Ella picked it out. I'll show it to you later on."

Above all, I was a realist. Wing Pruett was a gorgeous guy who fit perfectly in a Porsche and could afford to pay the freight. Maybe that described the vast cultural gulf between us—he was a sexy foreign import, I the sensible domestic product.

"So, you didn't miss me?" Pruett asked. My nether parts tingled, but I strove for indifference.

"We've been so busy," I said. "The show and all."

Pruett wasn't fooled one bit. "I wanted to surprise you about the car. You're always miles ahead of me on everything." He held out his arms to his daughter. "What are we ever going to do with her, Ella? She's incorrigible."

Ella knitted her brows. "What's incorrigible, Daddy?"

That gave Babette the opening she desired. "It means Ms. Perri is a brat, honey. There. I said it! All that mooning over this man, and she pretends she's an iceberg."

Before she continued analyzing my habits, fate in the person of Rafael Ramos intervened. He nodded to Babette and me, but his real target was Pruett. Rafa strode toward us with his arm extended.

"This is a distinct pleasure. Wing Pruett, am I correct? I am a big fan of your work, sir." The two men exchanged handshakes as Babette introduced her new friend.

"What brings you here?" Rafa asked. "Some big exposé in the show ring?"

Pruett laughed and shook his head. "Nothing so dramatic. I'm here strictly as an observer and chief cheering section for Lady Guinevere and my daughter." He glanced my way. "And to keep an eye on Perri too."

Rafa nodded. "That I can understand. A pair of champions—both of them. And who would ever think that this lovely lady was a leathersmith? In my country, that's a man's job."

I grinned. "Actually, I learned the trade from a man—an army buddy. He had a business making custom briefcases and luggage. I hung around until I learned how to do it myself." I spread my arms out wide. "The rest is history."

Babette burrowed her way into the conversation. "Perri's designs are fantastic. All my friends rave about them. And Ella, she's junior handler material for sure one day. She loves dogs."

I sensed a hesitation—fleeting and temporary—in Rafa's manner. "Follow me. I'll introduce you to Lee Holmes. He's the head honcho of the junior handlers. Any questions you have, he's the one with all the answers." Ella and Pruett followed him to the refreshment table, where a tall man with curly brown hair and matching mustache was holding court. Normally, Wing Pruett schmoozed with the best of them, but as he approached Lee Holmes, his body language said otherwise.

"Who is that?" I asked Babette. "He looks familiar, but I can't place him."

Babette giggled. Most women her age had stopped giggling years before, but it still worked for her. "Perri, you are in a daze. Lee looks like Tom Selleck. You know, the actor on the old TV show *Magnum PI*. Kind of a babe magnet if you're under thirty. Word is, he likes 'em young. Anyone under thirty." More giggling by Babette. "Of course, his wife passed thirty about three decades ago. Guess that power of the purse still counts."

I'm fairly sophisticated—worldly, but not jaded. My mouth dropped open, and I gaped at Babette as if I were the village idiot. I focused on canines, not human foibles, and avoided tales of marriages gone awry.

"Oh, grow up, Perri," Babette snorted. "You were in the army, for crying out loud. Besides, Lee mostly just leers at anything female. Probably afraid to touch the merchandise. His wife keeps him on a short leash with a choke collar."

"His *wife*? You keep mentioning her. Have I met her?"

My pal enjoyed the drama. "You knucklehead! Of course you have. Lee's wife is Yael Lindsay, the princess of pointers."

That gave me a jolt. No wonder Yael was so prickly. She looked at least a decade older than her randy spouse. Who could blame her if his wandering eye made her suspicious? I knew her casually through her occasional purchases at my shop, but I had never socialized with the couple. Now the contretemps between Yael and Bethany made some sense. Yael's lineage was well known at least in society circles. Her family was charter members of the Daughters of the American Revolution and maintained a venerable brick town house on Beacon Street in Boston. I didn't know the Boston dog crowd very well, but Babette was plugged in to every upper-echelon social network on the East Coast. Unlike me, she had both the cash and connections to penetrate any tightly knit and very exclusive community of privilege.

Babette stabbed my shoulder with her fingernail. "Don't just stand there like a ninny. We need to join the crowd. Shake a leg, Perri. Those women will mob Pruett if you're not careful." She bustled toward the knot of admirers surrounding Pruett while I trailed behind. I refused to loom over him just to assert my ownership. After all, we weren't married or even engaged. From experience, I knew that he was catnip to any sentient female within ten miles and exerted some type of gravitational pull on the fair sex. Mutual trust and respect united us, not the proverbial ball and chain of a marriage certificate. That was the shield I used to ward off doubt and insecurity. If I yearned for more, I resisted even thinking about it. The consequences of loss were simply too profound.

"Perri," Babette hissed, "get a load of that one slithering around him like a serpent."

I focused on a nubile brunette wearing a diaphanous caftan that left little to the imagination. "Oh. That's the pet psychic again. She's harmless. Fun to talk to."

"Huh!" Babette folded her arms and snorted. "You just tell yourself that, missy. I know a woman on the make when I see one. Plus, she has claws. Watch your step."

I shrugged and scanned the crowd, looking for Ella. It was easy enough to find her since Pruett, the doting dad, kept his eyes glued to his child. Ella hovered on the fringe of a group of handlers, drinking in their every word. One in particular, a precocious blonde with waist-length hair and plenty of curves, appeared to be their leader. She sidled up to Lee Holmes and whispered something in his ear. Judging by his reaction, her words must have packed a punch. He flushed, muttered something to her, and turned aside. That's when the fireworks started.

"Quite a crowd," a mocking voice said. Whit Wiley beamed a suspiciously innocent smile my way. "No wonder Lee takes his duties so seriously." He nodded toward the blonde. "In case you're wondering, that's Kiki Vesco, one of the up-and-coming handlers." He leered like a villain from a cheap melodrama, then lost his train of thought. A commotion that threatened to become a brawl stopped him in his tracks.

Chapter 3

A swarthy man with a compact frame and receding hairline leapt between Kiki and Lee Holmes, seizing him by the collar.

"Leave her alone," he growled. "Touch her again, and I swear I'll kill you."

"Oops," Whit said, "that's Kiki's ex-husband, Roy. Still crazy about her, they say. Guess he needs to stand in line."

Holmes struggled impotently, arms flailing. "Let me go," he squawked. Kiki burst into tears and beat on Roy's back, to little effect. The situation worsened when Yael Lindsay ran to her husband's side, shrieking. "The police are on the way, you hooligan."

The hooligan in question maintained his hold. "Cops! Great idea. We got laws against your kind, buster."

I considered intervening and moved toward them. After all, as an army sergeant, I had grown rather skilled at diffusing conflict. "Brawls are us" was our motto in my old squad. I stopped short as actors on several fronts beat me to it. Pruett and Rafa, twin towers of muscle, lunged toward the combatants and pried them apart.

Pruett grabbed the swarthy man by the collar and hauled him away from Lee Holmes. Instead of being grateful, Holmes turned surly. He dusted himself off and snarled.

"Just what we need, a super snoop from the big city. I could have handled that guy without your help. Next time, stay out of it and out of my business too. You have your own problems." He nodded toward me and sneered. "Better watch out for that leather lady, my friend. Looks like she could use a man's touch."

Pruett whispered something to Holmes that I could not hear. Whatever he said was incendiary. Lee Holmes turned tomato red and lunged for my guy's throat. Pruett deflected the blow and deftly stepped aside. Initially, Rafa held back and kept watch over the other combatant. Suddenly, Lee changed tactics, leapt up and sucker punched Roy Vesco. Pruett moved swiftly to end the brawl, displaying the wushu moves at which he excelled. Holmes collapsed in his wife's arms like a punctured balloon, robbed of dignity and aggression.

Babette, never a fan of fisticuffs, cowered behind me as Whit Wiley beamed his poisonous smile my way.

"Goodness gracious," he said, "looks like you have quite a fan club, Perri. Better watch out for Yael. The lady doesn't tolerate interlopers."

I considered several responses, one of which was a punch to Wiley's midsection. Fortunately, good sense prevailed, and I shrugged instead. "I'm safe. Truthfully, I don't even know that Lee Holmes guy. Could be he bought some of my products, but I have so many customers at these shows, he just didn't stand out."

Wiley curled his lip in a faux grin. "Well, my dear, he obviously knows your sweetie and doesn't like him much. Seems to appreciate your wares, such as they are. Wing Pruett must be on to something with that gentleman. I'll leave it to your imagination."

I turned away from Wiley and his vile suggestions. It was much more fun to study Pruett in warrior mode. All that testosterone fueled my own desires.

Rafa turned toward his fellow handlers and shook his head. "Relax everyone. Chill. Show's over." He grinned. "Not the big show, of course. That's what we're here for, after all. Dogs!"

He diffused a tense situation with a combination of charm and muscle that earned him admiring glances from the mostly female audience. Babette had the glazed look that presaged a bout of love sickness.

Pruett moved swiftly to Ella's side and put his arm around the little girl. I watched her, all big-eyed, clinging tightly to her dad. Who could blame her? Unfortunately, it was a disquieting and inauspicious introduction to the junior handler program for a nervous parent like Pruett. His doubts about the program were probably magnified threefold by such a dustup.

Yael Lindsay brushed off her husband's polo shirt, trying to contain her embarrassment and regain control. Control seemed very important to that redoubtable lady. Several of the other officials pitched in and herded the junior handlers to the side of the room. One woman in particular caught my eye. I recognized her from the German shepherd brigade, although her name escaped me at that moment. Whit Wiley came in handy once more.

"Oops," he said. "There's trouble."

Despite my misgivings, I bent down and whispered. "Who is that woman?"

"Jess Pendrake. German shepherd handler and man hater. Sees sexism behind every crate." He rolled his eyes and grinned. "I doubt it's from personal experience, though."

"I remember her," Babette piped up. "Says she has PTSD." She gave Jess the once-over. "Personally, I think if she fixed that hair and dressed better, she might actually find a man." She patted her own coiffeur. "That would settle her down."

I ignored Babette's comments. True, Jess could use some sprucing up, but for most women, that was a personal and very sensitive subject. My pal stocked more cosmetics than Sephora and made it her life's mission to transform every woman who crossed her path. I could personally testify on that subject. Nothing could dissuade Babette from the makeup crusade, even the risk of alienating members of her own gender.

Pruett locked eyes with me and nodded toward the exit. "Boy, am I thirsty. Where can a guy get a drink around here? I booked a hotel room at the Sheraton downtown just in case that snowstorm hits early."

For once in her life, Babette took the hint. She invited everyone to convene in Steady Eddie for adult beverages and snacks. Rafa promised to join us later, but Pruett squeezed my hand and wordlessly followed the procession. I had hoped for some alone time with him, but it was not to be.

Babette opened several bottles of wine and produced a tray of tasty treats for the adults. Ella settled willingly for hot chocolate and a sandwich. She was more concerned with Guinnie's welfare than assuaging her own hunger.

"She's been cooped up so long," Ella said, hugging the pointer. "Can't we take her for a run? Daddy, please?"

Pruett tried to tough it out, but one look at his pleading child ended that charade. "I guess so. How about it, Perri? I have some things to attend to, but I'll catch up with you."

Babette quickly agreed to hold down the fort and wait for Rafa. The woman had stars in her eyes as she envisioned doing Lord knows what in her alone time with him. After Pruett left, I listened patiently to yet another recitation of Rafa's virtues and his macho takedown of Lee Holmes. No mention of Pruett's contributions to resolving the conflict, but that was par for the course when my pal was on the hunt. Babette's single-track mind was focused on only one man.

I nodded to the point of foolishness, agreeing that Rafa was indeed a superior specimen. After five more minutes of blather, I collected our pet gear, leashed the four dogs, stowed potty bags, and headed out. I reminded myself that exercise was a more healthy and wholesome pursuit than sipping wine and staring into those mesmerizing Pruett eyes. Small consolation!

Snowflakes dotted the landscape around the Big E, and the wind howled louder than our canine corps. Using the "better safe than sorry" mantra, we donned caps, scarves, and boots before venturing out.

Keats and Poe quickly took the lead, streaking effortlessly through the fields toward the equine arena. My boys are Schutzhund-trained and very adept at protection and tracking. Like me, they never forgot their military training. The Malinois had mad skills, and they knew how to use them. With them at our side, both Ella and I were well protected.

I kept Clara at a heel, while Ella brought up the rear with the ever-compliant Guinnie. Ella's childish chatter made me laugh and lulled me into a state of complacency. Most days, I was a realist and seldom allowed myself the luxury of dreaming, but that evening, just for a moment, I did so. Pruett, Ella and I as a family unit—it felt so right. We were a bonded trio already. If only... Daydreaming exacts its own price, and at first, I missed the signals coming from my dogs. They stood statue still, their hackles raised in warning.

"What's going on, Ms. Perri?" Ella asked, her voice quivering. "The dogs are acting funny."

I held out my arm to keep her back. "I'll handle this, if you can hold Clara and Guinnie. No need to feel scared."

The dogs get testy when they're in Schutzhund mode. Schutzhund was a serious discipline that my boys excelled at. That training had saved my life and those of many others during their military careers. I had and would trust those Malinois any time, any place.

I advanced slowly toward the edge of the field, calling softly to my dogs. Keats and Poe had taken sentry positions around something—I couldn't quite make out what it was. I drew closer and saw a human arm outstretched as if in supplication. A familiar figure bent over the body, checking its vital signs.

"Stand back, Perri." Pruett's voice deepened. "I was looking for you guys and stumbled on him."

I couldn't help wondering what Pruett was up to. Was the dog show world the subject of Pruett's latest exposé? Since Ella was there, I hoped to shield her from what might be a grisly scene as long as possible. The night had turned dark and impenetrable as I approached the body, shining my pocket flashlight on the area, walking cautiously to avoid compromising a potential crime scene.

Lee Holmes lay sprawled on the field, snowflakes dotting his hair and face. His mouth opened in the perpetual scream of the recently departed. He was gone, no doubt about that. I had seen enough corpses in combat to know that. There was also the matter of the pretty pink grooming shears protruding from the center of his chest.

Chapter 4

Under other circumstances, I might have appreciated the aesthetics of the scene. Pink titanium grooming shears added an artistic, almost feminine touch to an otherwise grisly event. The impact was at once strange and so familiar that I immediately went on autopilot, viewing things as dispassionately as possible. First, the murder weapon: I sold that same product to a select group that wanted quality and didn't mind shelling out almost two hundred bucks for ten inches of durable, German-made cobalt steel. Poodle owners swore by them. I bent over and checked Lee's body for the sake of form. He was long gone, not likely to object to an impersonal survey of his remains. Meanwhile, Pruett joined me and went into action. He shielded Ella from the view, restrained Clara and Guinnie, and dialed the authorities on his cell phone.

"I'll stay here while you take Ella back to the trailer," he said. I shrugged and managed a half smile. "With Keats and Poe around, no one will mess with me. Maybe you should take Ella." His eyes met mine, and he nodded. "Be right back. The dispatcher said a cruiser is on the way." His voice was calm and reassuring as he spoke to his child and explained the situation.

"But Perri will be alone," Ella said, her voice quivering. "She might get scared in the dark." Once he mentioned Poe and Keats, the little girl relaxed. In her world, two dogs were all the company anybody needed to feel safe. Pruett held Ella's hand and, with Clara and Guinnie in tow, jogged toward Steady Eddie. I switched my flashlight on high beam and shone it over the surrounding area. The barren field stretched endlessly toward the Equine Pavilion, yielding no place for anyone to lurk. The grass was not fully saturated with snow, although it would soon be. I was quite alone under a star-filled sky with two ex-military dogs and a corpse for company.

Keats and Poe remained vigilant, settling into a down stay while awaiting my next command. To while away the time, I paced back and forth, trying to reconstruct the scene at the cocktail party and the participants. Had it only been an hour ago? Somehow it felt like another lifetime. In a flash, Lee Holmes had provoked his wife, a jealous ex-husband, and an unbalanced dog handler. No telling how many others loathed him, including the other owners, handlers, and show officials. No telling why a certain journalist was first on the scene either. It was nothing sinister—I felt confident of that. Pruett had probably wandered that way looking for me and Ella. The incident with Lee Holmes was a minor blip, nothing serious enough to provoke a murder. Surely the authorities would see it that way.

It wasn't personal for me. I didn't know the victim or care much about him, no matter what kind of sleazy suggestions he made about me. But the act of murder was an affront to all civilized people. The use of those pretty pink sheers added a garish touch, as if the murderer was playing a macabre prank, a contemptuous tweak to the deceased and everyone else as well. It smacked of premeditation and braggadocio, as if the killer were taunting us. "Aren't I clever? Look what I did."

No harm in trying to assess the scene, I told myself. The authorities might appreciate help from an astute observer like me. That was hogwash, and I knew it, but it was a comforting fiction. In the real world, police detested interference from any outsider. Civilians like me were meddlers from their point of view. Meddlers spelled nothing but trouble.

I studied the pretty pink grooming shears. They were probably a weapon of convenience, used in the heat of battle. There was another possibility as well. Was the killer avenging some crime connected with the poodle community? Lee moved in many dog show circles, and his wife was even better connected.

The curved blades of the weapon were extremely sharp, making it a most efficient device, one that would penetrate flesh easily. In this instance, someone had thrust those blades directly into Lee's heart. From the amount of blood pooled around him, I guessed that the aorta had been punctured. Blood spatter would likely have drenched the culprit's shoes and clothing. Unfortunately, the cops would have their hands full searching for evidence in the caravans, cars, and trucks that filled the parking area. Most show professionals wore plastic capes to preserve their clothing when grooming their charges. Plastic capes protected from fluids quite handily—even blood. They could also be disposed of rather easily, with nobody the wiser.

I was not fanciful, especially when accompanied by Keats and Poe. From our first encounter in a war zone, they had stood by my side, protecting and loving me. Still, when a sudden breeze swept through the tall grass, I shivered.

What was that old saw: someone walking over my grave? Fortunately, in this instance, the grave belonged to Lee Holmes, not me. According to legend, Lee was a ladies' man, lothario, roué, and all-around cad with a string of conquests to his credit. In my experience, jealousy, especially sexual jealousy, was a potent motive for revenge, and anyone—man or woman—could have done the deed. For the sake of convenience, many dog people carried the tools of their trade with them in pockets, purses, or satchels. Fancy shears were expensive, and experienced hands kept a weather eye on them. No one would think twice if a colleague had them on his or her person.

I peered at the murder weapon in case someone had scratched initials or other identifying marks into the blades. No such luck. With over 1,200 canines entered in the show, the list of human suspects was vast. Owners, handlers, vendors, and show officials would all be prime suspects. According to Whit Wiley, the victim was infamous in show circles for his sexual shenanigans. If there was any truth at all to the scene at the cocktail party, the character of the deceased left much to be desired. I hoped that Roy Vesco had a gold-plated alibi. Pruett and Rafa weren't out of the woods either. Someone was certain to blab about that dustup to the police. Come to think of it, Babette might let it slip. She tended to babble uncontrollably during moments of stress.

Pruett was taking his own sweet time getting back. Probably calling his editor with the big scoop. It was in his blood, and he had the Pulitzers to prove it. I'd learned to live with it, not like it. Since he was Johnny on the spot, the authorities were sure to quiz him about his presence. I was rather curious about that myself.

I heard them before I saw them. Naturally, Keats and Poe were far ahead of me, straining toward the source of the sound, ears alert, svelte bodies readied for action. A posse composed of Pruett and two uniformed officers swinging large flashlights strode briskly toward us. Babette was probably hunkered down in Steady Eddie with Ella. Although she denied it, my pal dissolved when any type of physical confrontation involved blood. Total meltdown. She took to her bed with a case of the vapors when she got even a hangnail.

The Malinois growled a warning until I gave them the *Fuss* command— Schutzhund for "heel." Like clockwork, they immediately hugged my left side and sat at attention.

The police officers approached warily, watching my dogs for any movement, resting their hands on their gun holsters. I didn't blame them. They were young and probably unfamiliar with homicides. Pruett stayed right on their heels, pointing toward me, my dogs, and the victim.

"This is Persephone Morgan," he said. "She's a highly regarded leathersmith." Neither cop seemed impressed by this information. They cautiously approached Lee's body.

"Stand back," the older one said to me and Pruett. "Don't compromise the crime scene." It sounded unnatural, as if he were reciting a line of bad dialogue from a B movie. More than likely, it was a by-product of television overload, the much-vaunted *CSI* effect.

I nodded and zipped my lip. Young guys tended to place emphasis on respect from civilians and reacted badly if they felt challenged. No need to antagonize either one of them. The older one, a muscular twentysomething, sported a thick mustache and a receding hairline that promised major male-pattern baldness in the future. His swagger suggested an ego problem and need to be in charge. His partner was a gangly youth with pale skin that still held a trace of adolescent acne. He hung back, allowing his partner to dictate terms. Naturally, the first question zeroed in on Lee Holmes and my knowledge of him.

I explained my brief acquaintance with Lee and his wife, without mentioning the fracas at the party. Call me elitist, but I knew that detectives would soon arrive to handle the case. Why waste time on rookies?

"What about you?" The older cop kept his hand on his holster and stood toe to toe with Pruett.

"I just met him tonight." Pruett's face had a suspiciously innocent look that didn't fool me one bit. Something was definitely up.

"Detectives are on their way," the younger cop said. "Sergeant Jansen. He'll take your statement." He rolled his eyes and smirked. "Crime scene techs too."

"Any chance we could go back to our trailer until then," Pruett asked. "It's mighty cold out here. I'm worried about my daughter too. She's only seven, and the shock . . ." He spread his hands out wide, using his most ingratiating smile and humble act. It didn't fool me, but both police officers were satisfied.

The tall cop suddenly asserted himself, stepping directly in Pruett's path. "Hey, aren't you that newspaper guy? Wing somebody. You wrote about those murders in Virginia last year."

Pruett kept his composure, but both officers stiffened immediately at the thought of media involvement. Police and the press don't always mix well for very obvious reasons. A careless word or thoughtless deed within earshot of a newshound could end anyone's career.

Pruett launched a charm offensive. I could attest to the fact that his line of patter worked wonders on recalcitrant officials. It was even more effective on susceptible females.

"Just a bystander," he said. "Here with my daughter and Ms. Morgan. As I said, Mr. Holmes was a stranger to me. Never laid eyes on him until tonight."

They gave both of us the "cop stare," a hard-eyed look designed to ferret out guilt. Sad to say, they were preaching to the choir, and I knew chapter and verse of that sermon. A similar guidance came straight out of the army manual for sergeants. Tactics 101. I folded my arms and matched his glare with a fierce one of my own.

"We'll gladly cooperate, officers, but we really need to shed these wet clothes and comfort that child." I stayed respectful but firm.

They agreed, and Pruett and I did a quick pivot, called the dogs, and loped toward Steady Eddie before either cop could change his mind.

"How much does your editor know?" I asked Pruett once we were safely away. "Moreover, what were you doing there? Don't tell me Lee Holmes was one of your sources."

Pruett shrugged. "My editor just knows the basics. He jumped at the headline, though—'Death by Dog Show.' Pretty catchy, don't you think?"

When he caught the scent of a big story, Pruett lost all perspective. His approach was reminiscent of a hound on the trail—the lion dog, a sleek, male Rhodesian ridgeback, would fit the bill, all tawny muscles and energy. Oh my!

"Remember. I have to make a living here," I said. "Don't alienate the dog show crowd unnecessarily." Every now and then, Pruett needed a stern lecture on civilians and their right to privacy. Not to mention the economic viability of my business.

"I was hoping you'd help me," he said. "You know. Show me the ropes. Dog shows are foreign territory for me."

Pruett's look of wounded innocence was a transparent ploy. Fortunately for our relationship, we reached Steady Eddie just as Babette flung open the door.

"You're back! Perri! Oh, Lord. Tell me everything right now!" Babette always spoke in italics and all caps when she was excited or upset—which was often. Clara and Guinnie stood behind her, as did Ella. I noted that Rafael Ramos was nowhere to be found. No big deal. Judges huddled together at meetings and briefings before most shows. It meant nothing. Then I recalled that Rafa's breed of choice was the standard poodle, the same breed most often barbered with ten-inch titanium shears just like the murder weapon.

"Where's Rafa?" I asked.

Babette gulped. That told me all I needed to know. She was worried, and for good reason. We knew next to nothing about Rafa. His relationship with Lee Holmes might have been contentious. For all we knew, there might have been a follow-up to the party brawl that ended badly. Babette was the ultimate dreamer who believed she could sense the essence of a man. Her romantic misadventures suggested otherwise.

Pruett nodded toward his daughter. "Come on, honey. Bedtime. Say good night to the ladies. Guinnie has a big day tomorrow." He said the magic word and focused all of Ella's attention on her beloved Guinnie.

Babette immediately played matchmaker. "Ella can sleep with me tonight. You and Perri take the other bedroom. No sense in driving with the bad weather." When my pal played the coquette, she was unstoppable. I had learned through experience to go with the flow.

Pruett's eyes met mine, telegraphing an unmistakable message. "I'm bushed," he said, and then yawned. "We probably won't get much sleep, though. Those detectives will be here soon."

I staunched a yawn myself and ambled toward the bedroom. "Might as well do our best."

Fortunately, sleep was the last thing on either of our minds.

* * * *

Wing Pruett could shed his clothes faster than any man on the planet. By the time I had performed perfunctory ablutions, he was tucked into that comfy queen bed with his arms wide open.

"I missed you," he whispered, gently brushing his lips up and down my neck. "So much." My neck was one erogenous zone that I immediately yielded to. In deference to Ella, however, I subdued my moans.

Pruett felt good, all muscular abs, taut muscles, and other manly parts. Quite irresistible. Since I subscribed to the theory that life was short, and temptation inevitable, I succumbed immediately.

"Come closer, baby," Pruett whispered. "Let me feel that sweet, soft skin of yours."

Before I could oblige, we heard a sharp rap on the trailer door. I switched on the lights and heaved a gigantic sigh. No sense in fighting fate. Everything from moppets to murder conspired against romance tonight. Pruett threw on his clothes and joined in the merriment.

Our faces wore big smiles as we confronted the law.

Chapter 5

Detective Sergeant Roar Jansen confounded every stereotype of the pudgy, donut-loving cop. I sized him up as he flashed his badge and introduced himself and his sidekick, Sergeant Genna Watts. Based on his curly brown hair, tan skin, and ice-blue eyes, I suspected he was a felicitous mix of Norwegian and African genes. Sergeant Watts, a sturdy no-nonsense woman in her forties with thin, neatly pinned gray hair and a cosmetic-free face, grunted a greeting and let her partner take the lead.

When Babette joined us, her reaction was both priceless and predictable. She widened her eyes, gaped at Roar Jansen, and immediately gushed a welcome.

"Can I get you some refreshments?" she asked, batting those thick eyelashes of hers. "Coffee, or something sweet?" Knowing Babette as I did, there were other unnamed menu items at the ready. Fortunately, both police officers refused and immediately got down to business. Sergeant Jansen's voice was deep and pleasing, rather like crashing waves. So was his partner's, minus the pleasing part.

"Roar? That's Scandinavian, isn't it?" Babette chirped. "So evocative."

Roar shared a special smile with her. Sergeant Watts glared. He asked the questions, while his partner observed us and took notes. They made an effective team that way. Since Pruett and I had discovered the corpse at almost the same time, they interviewed us simultaneously. I failed to mention that he had preceded me to the murder scene. They didn't ask, and I didn't volunteer. Every army alumna knew that old saw. Babette was allowed to remain strictly as a spectator and would-be hostess.

"How well did you know the victim, ah, Mr. Holmes?" Roar looked straight at me. It was not an unpleasant experience.

I explained that Lee Holmes was a veritable stranger to me, but that I knew his wife slightly.

Babette interrupted immediately. "I've known Yael for years. Same social set. Cocktail parties, fund-raisers. Yael comes from big Boston money."

Roar nodded as if encouraging a bright pupil. "And her husband?"

Nothing could stop the Croy express once that train left the station, especially when the audience included a gorgeous man. "She married Lee last year. Boy toy, you know. Happens to the best of us."

Sergeant Watts narrowed her eyes but remained silent. Her opinion of rich, randy matrons seemed clear.

"Any trouble between them?" Roar asked. He used that sultry smile again. "Tensions in the marriage?"

Even Babette knew when to stop. If only she had done so from the beginning, things might have gone better. She clamped her jaws shut and bowed her head. "Not really," she muttered. "Unless you count that dustup tonight. But Yael wasn't part of that."

Naturally, Roar Jansen pounced like the sleek, jungle cat he so closely resembled. "Let us be the judge. Tell me about this dustup."

After Babette described the evening's fracas, Roar turned to Pruett. "What's your take on it, Mr. Pruett. You are Wing Pruett, the journalist, I presume. I've enjoyed reading your pieces over the years. Were you a friend of the victim?"

Pruett gave the cop a quick, piercing glance and sketched out the incident between Holmes and Roy Vesco. He left nothing out, but neither did he embellish his account.

Roar kept a bland expression on his face that was difficult to decipher. His partner was far easier to read.

"You sure you didn't know Lee Holmes?" she asked Pruett. "We heard you were asking around about him. Poking into his personal life and such."

Pruett gave her his nice guy grin. "Occupational hazard, I'm afraid. Journalists have an insatiable curiosity about almost everyone."

Babette joined right in. "They're nosy, and that's a fact. Wing Pruett is no different than any other reporter. Besides, everyone except Perri knew the scoop on Lee Holmes. Major sleaze."

"That how you saw it, Ms. Morgan? You must have some opinion." I'd forgotten that Genna Watts was even in the room. Her sharp tone reminded me that she was very much part of the team. I waited a bit before answering to collect my thoughts. I'd learned that a witness's immediate response tended to be unguarded and often unwise.

"My first reaction was surprise," I said. "Everything happened quite suddenly. Also, I'd never heard any gossip about Lee before. Nothing troubling, that is."

Babette interjected again, by chortling a response. "That's our Perri. All business. Doesn't approve of rumors." She shared a smirk with Roar Jansen.

"Your friends left you alone when they went walking," Roar said to Babette.

In her zeal to please the dishy detective, Babette fell headlong into his trap. "Oh. I wanted to stay. I was waiting for Rafa to join us."

"Rafa?"

"Rafael Ramos, Roar. His name was on our list." Genna flashed a Cheshire cat grin our way.

"Did Mr. Ramos ever join you?" Roar asked.

Babette clamped her hand over her mouth. She quickly recovered and gave an enigmatic smile. "Nope. Stood me up."

His partner turned away to hide a smile, but Roar jumped right in. "I find that hard to believe," he said. Frankly, I thought his act was shopworn, but Babette's face glowed with the attention. She squared her shoulders, thrust out her chest, and spouted still more information.

"He's an important judge, you know. Came all the way from Spain. Very well known in poodle circles."

My mind flashed back to those pretty pink shears. Poodle groomers loved them. I refused to share that little factoid with the detectives, however. No sense maligning someone who probably had no involvement in the murder. For Babette's sake, I hoped that was true.

"Very interesting," Roar said, making a note. "We looked for him, but he wasn't around. Is that his trailer next door?"

Babette nodded. I hoped she had finally realized that silence was indeed golden when dealing with the authorities.

Pruett exchanged nods with Roar Jansen, the kind of guy-to-guy thing that bespoke camaraderie and male bonding. I observed that the two men were similar physical types—tall, fit, and packed with testosterone. An embarrassment of riches for any female observer.

"Mr. Ramos clashed with the victim tonight." Genna Watts didn't ask; she stated it as a fact and dared us to contradict. "You too, Mr. Pruett. According to his wife, you instigated things."

Fortunately, Babette buttoned her lip and avoided throwing gasoline on the fire. Pruett and I stayed silent, awaiting further questions from the sergeant.

"What about that, Ms. Morgan?" Roar leveled a self-deprecatory smile at me, the kind that had probably melted a hundred female hearts.

"I wouldn't say they clashed." I closed my eyes and visualized the fracas. "Mr. Pruett intervened in the brawl, but he certainly didn't cause it. Neither did Mr. Ramos."

"That your recollection too, Mr. Pruett?" More nice guy vibes from Roar. His act was polished, professional, and almost genuine.

Pruett nodded but volunteered nothing. As a journalist, he had used the same sneaky tricks to worm information from unsuspecting members of the public. Silence was indeed platinum.

Roar lowered his voice to a conspiratorial whisper. "Ever hear rumors about this Lee Holmes? I understand he was quite a stud." He stared directly at Babette and watched her melt.

"Stud?" she said. "In his own mind maybe. No grown woman ever took him seriously unless she was desperate."

The police pair exchanged glances and frowns. "Might have stirred up some boyfriends or husbands just the same," Roar said. He glanced down at his tablet. "Ah yes. Mr. Roy Vesco. Worried about his ex-wife, Kiki."

Pruett smiled. "You know how it is when you care for someone. A man gets protective."

Genna Watts snorted. "We've seen that woman. Kiki. Plenty to worry about there."

"Quite the temptress," Roar agreed. "Can't locate her ex, though. Seems like Mr. Roy Vesco has disappeared."

* * * *

The two cops left us soon after dropping that bombshell. It was obvious that Roy Vesco, avenging lover with a fiery temper, was suspect number one in their book. Couldn't say that I blamed them. If I were handling the case, he would have been high on my list too. The prissy pink murder weapon didn't fit his rough-hewn image, but that could be explained easily enough. Anyone—Vesco included—could have snatched the shears from a grooming cart. For all I knew, those shears may have belonged to Holmes himself. Forensic evidence would narrow down the possibilities. Or not.

Babette slid over to the granite counter and poured herself a slug of cognac. She downed it immediately and went for a refill without offering us a taste. That lapse in good manners was a violation of hospitality that would have scandalized her proper southern mama. It told me that my pal knew more than she told the cops, and whatever it was probably involved Rafa Ramos.

I walked to her side and put my arm around her. "Okay. Let's have it. You're among friends here."

Babette widened her baby blues and pointed toward Pruett. "What about you, Wing? No leaks to your editor this time." In our first encounter with Pruett, he had published some information that was both damning and humiliating. Babette had never quite forgiven him for it.

Pruett held up his palm. "Scout's honor. Strictly off the record."

After pouring each of us some cognac, she slouched into a chair, closed her eyes, and told her tale. Apparently, Rafa owned a pair of shears almost identical to the murder weapon. He was booked to demonstrate poodle grooming at the next day's show and had shown them to Babette. She had no idea if they were missing.

"He was real excited about it," she said. "Just went on and on about proper grooming techniques and stuff and the tools he used." She gave a wry smile. "Those weren't exactly the tools I was interested in seeing, if you catch my drift. That's why I waited for him while you guys walked the pups."

Somehow both Pruett and I kept our composure and focused on the issues.

"Did Rafa know Lee Holmes?" Pruett asked. "Seemed like it to me. In fact, Holmes made some kind of disparaging comment to him." No one mentioned Lee's puzzling remarks about me, but I hadn't forgotten them. The man knew nothing about me or my life. More likely he was targeting Pruett, hoping to score off him.

Babette shook her head. "Rafa didn't mention it, but I'll bet that creepy Whit Wiley would know. That guy collects dirt like a magnet. Probably cozying up to the cops as we speak."

I thought of the scene between Yael and Bethany that I had witnessed earlier. Could be that Lee had several irons in the romantic fire. Anyone—man or woman—might have plunged those shears into him in a fit of passion, including his long-suffering wife.

Pruett reached for his jacket. "Maybe I'll mosey over to the arena and see what's going on. Feel up to it, Perri?"

I had no reason to involve myself. On the other hand, I was curious about Pruett's role in this caper, and any time with him was time well spent.

"Sure. I'll check my stall while we're over there. You don't mind, do you, Babette?"

She risked a mini-frown but quickly recovered. "Y'all go ahead. I'll just hunker down with Ella and the pups." She reached into her backpack and thrust a set of keys my way. Naturally it was no ordinary backpack. Heaven forbid! In true Babette fashion, she sported an exquisite Alexander McQueen butterfly small chain backpack that cost the earth. Initially I lusted after it.

One glance at the price tag cooled my ardor. Any hunk of leather north of $3,000 settles me down right away.

My pal was oblivious to it all. "Here. Use these when you get back. I plan to lock up good and tight." She paused and flashed those dimples. "Unless Rafa needs some consolation, that is. Send him my way."

Chapter 6

"What's your take on this?" Pruett asked as we walked toward the Better Living Center.

I hesitated for a moment. "Right now, those cops are gathering information, evaluating facts and suspects. At least that's what I would do in their shoes." My first impression of Sergeant Roar and his flinty partner was that both were experienced and cautious. Until they fully assessed the situation, everyone was a suspect.

"Is there anything you want to tell me about the murder?" I asked. "Or about Lee Holmes? I'm afraid the cops might try to pin this thing on you, if they can. Did you study the look on Sergeant Watts's face? She didn't believe a thing you said. Roar Jansen seemed more balanced, but who can say?" I stopped walking and faced Pruett. "You know you can trust me. I'm on your side, no matter what."

Pruett pulled me to him and hugged me tight. "So suspicious. Might as well tell you now. I'm following some leads about money laundering using venues like dog shows. You know, innocent family-friendly events. Think of it. With all the traveling that goes on, the handlers and vendors are itinerants. Plenty of opportunity for bad actors."

I searched his face for signs of duplicity. When pursuing a story, Pruett could lie, mislead, and embellish with the best of them. "So, was Lee one of those leads?"

He gave me an enigmatic smile and said nothing.

Fortunately, we reached the Better Living Center just then. Despite the late hour, the building was awash with people and vehicles. Several police cars, an SUV with forensic tags, and a somber medical examiner's van ringed the area adjoining the field where the victim's body had been found. The proximity of such tragedy to festive canine capers was disquieting. Although a tent had been erected to shield the scene from the elements, the cops were fighting a losing batter with Mother Nature.

A uniformed officer stood guard at the front entry door to the building, but Pruett and I easily slipped in one of the many unlocked side entrances. Score one for the civilians. Our strategy was simple—divide and conquer. I headed toward my shop while Pruett sauntered toward the denuded refreshment table, where a mostly female crowd huddled. The women ringing the area immediately parted as if he were Moses dividing the Red Sea. Yael Lindsay was absent, but psychic Bethany Zahn was front and center. She stepped close, surrounding Pruett and edging out any other competitors for his attention. Since he was accustomed to doting females, Pruett appeared unfazed. Before long, he was chatting with the ladies as if they were fast friends or something even more intimate.

My quarry was far less glamorous. I spotted Jess Pendrake pacing back and forth in front of my shop, wearing a mega-frown that would quell the Furies. The woman obviously needed a friend, and at least temporarily, I was her designated pal du jour.

"Hi, Jess," I said. "Want something for the show?"

She scowled further, a most off-putting expression. "I guess."

I unlocked the door and beckoned to her. "Come on in. Let's see what we have."

Jess lacked social graces, and her physical attributes were certainly limited. I chided myself for being superficial, but damn, Babette had a point about makeup. Even a smidge of lip gloss would have worked wonders, and shampoo was certainly accessible enough. For a moment, it seemed that she could read my mind. Jess brushed back a lanky strand of hair and grunted, "I need shears." She lowered her head and managed to avoid looking at me.

Keep your cool, Perri. "Okay. What kind. German shepherds are your breed, right?"

I pasted a smile on my face and kept it there. Even dog show novices knew that shears and shepherds didn't mix.

"Not for my dogs," Jess sneered. "A friend needs 'em."

I nodded pleasantly and showed her my stock. "See anything here that works?"

She grunted something I couldn't quite hear and pointed to the ten-inch shears, the same kind that had skewered Lee Holmes. Fortunately, their lethal-looking blades were encased in plastic. Even so, I remained on alert. Erratic people such as Jess were tough to gauge. I had learned that the hard way during my army days.

Her eyes widened when I rang up the sale, but she pulled a roll of somewhat grubby bills from her pocket and willingly paid all two hundred dollars.

It was now or never, do-or-die time. I might never get another chance to chat with Jess, whose reclusive ways were legendary in the show world.

"Too bad about Lee," I said. "His poor wife."

Jess narrowed her eyes and grunted again. "He was a creep. Good riddance."

I nodded. "I saw that dustup tonight. Surprising."

Suddenly, she abandoned her monosyllabic act and launched into a virtual rant. "Adulterers don't deserve to live. They're vermin."

Control yourself, Perri. "Did Lee do that?" I managed to keep my voice level. "I heard rumors, but no specifics."

"Huh," she snorted. "Shows what you know. No self-respecting woman was safe around that man. I told them, but no one believed me."

I tried a new gambit. "Gee. Whit Wiley said he was okay."

Her reaction was immediate and explosive. "Whit Wiley? That piece of crap! He and Lee Holmes were thick as thieves. Why do you think that wife of his wins every pointer competition, huh?"

Jess clenched her fists as if she intended to use them. She wasn't an imposing woman, but her frame was wiry. Handling large dogs required major muscles, and Jess had plenty of them. I stepped back, preparing to defend myself, if necessary, and thanking my stars that those shears were encased in plastic.

Fortune favored me. Before tensions escalated further, Bethany Zahn slipped into my store, accompanied by her beloved Cavalier King Charles spaniel, Prudence. Like most of her breed, Prudence was all wiggles, wags, and good cheer. Even her little face lit up with doggy glee as she offered canine kisses to all. Bethany was another case entirely. She billed herself as a pet psychic, but perhaps her sixth sense extended to human needs as well. Either way, considering my situation, her arrival was most welcome.

Bethany's long black hair fell in waves that framed a pretty face with a sprinkling of freckles. Her garb—a spangled caftan awash with stars and canine images—was unusual for the dog set but consistent with the otherworldly image she projected. Despite her fits of whimsy, Bethany was a respected breeder-owner-handler, the trifecta in dog show circles.

"Sorry to interrupt," she said in a soft voice with a touch of southern sugar, "but I really need your help with a show lead. Want me to come back later?"

I willed my voice to remain calm, but it wasn't easy. "Not at all. We're finished here. Right, Jess?"

Jess Pendrake glowered, but in what I considered a major victory, she retreated without attacking either my customer or me. After she exited, I locked the door and sighed.

"Boy. That was one close call."

Bethany shook her head and laughed. "Wow! Looks like our Jess went off the rails again."

"What's her problem?" I asked, genuinely curious. "The woman acts seriously disturbed."

Maybe it was all the peace, tolerance, and love she preached that made Bethany dismiss her zany colleague without another thought. "We don't really know all her issues," she said. "Jess has always been peculiar, especially around men. Some people say it's PTSD."

I sensed that Bethany knew more than she was willing to say. Perhaps a bit of prodding would loosen her tongue.

"She really didn't like Lee Holmes. Called him a serial philanderer."

Bethany showed absolutely no reaction. Her pale, perfectly smooth complexion stayed as blank as granite. Babette swore that injectables were responsible for that serenity, and she had plenty of expertise in that particular area. Maybe Bethany was incapable of expressing emotion due to overuse of the needle. When silence turned awkward, she finally expressed an opinion.

"Lee Holmes was quite a man—creepy, charming, and a wizard around dogs. Naturally, his wife was insanely jealous."

"With reason?" I asked.

Bethany shrugged. "Who knows? That Kiki Vesco stuck to him like gum. No wonder her husband was concerned. I know they divorced, but Roy never did get over Kiki. A one-woman man, I guess." She fingered a show lead and immediately changed the subject. "Give me your advice. I want Prudence to stand out in the ring. Is this too flashy?"

After we spent a few minutes discussing the merits of various show gear, Bethany made her purchase and sashayed toward the door. She saved one parting shot for me, however.

"I promised Wing I'd do a reading for his daughter and her pointer. Such a lovely child, and he is the perfect parent." She winked. "The pointer's not bad either."

She had me there. What could I do but agree?

* * * *

Later I found that Pruett had had far better luck dishing the dirt than I had. Somehow, I was not surprised. People, particularly women, found him easy to confide in and even easier on the eyes.

The peripatetic Bethany, for instance, defended Lee's character and swore that rumors about him were malicious gossip spread by spurned admirers.

Several of Pruett's new pals hinted that Rafa and Lee were foes of long standing and that they had clashed before. I hoped for Babette's sake that Sergeant Roar hadn't heard the same thing.

"Why the animosity?" I asked. "Rafa seemed pretty easygoing to me."

Pruett's foxy smile was among his most endearing traits. Coyness served him well with his host of female groupies over the years, but that was one game I simply refused to play. Instead of begging for scraps, I ignored him. He lasted all of two minutes.

"Oh, come on, Perri. Give me a break. Here's the story. Apparently, Lee and Rafa co-owned a dog several years ago and had some dispute over training or some such thing."

You could tell that despite his many attributes, my guy Pruett was not a dog man and certainly was a novice in confirmation circles. Co-owning a big-time show dog required a major investment of time, ego, and money. Disputes frequently got hot and heavy and had led to many a fractured friendship. In his worldview, it seemed trivial, so Pruett had shrugged off the tiff without getting the particulars. Big mistake! A festering feud could spark all kinds of mischief—even murder. I felt confident that in the close-knit, gossipy dog world, any number of people could fill in the blanks. Most would never volunteer that information to the police, despite the charms of Roar Jansen, but they might feel safe tattling to me.

Pruett wasn't the only one with poor marks for today's efforts. I hadn't exactly covered myself with glory either. Time for plan B. I'd struck out with Bethany Zahn, but fortunately there was another player on our team who had just the right skills. This delicate operation sounded like the perfect task for Babette. If anyone could wheedle information from friend or foe, my BFF was the gal for the job. I would gladly delegate those tasks to her.

* * * *

I awakened the next morning with a smile on my face. Perhaps the sun streaming through the window of Steady Eddie had warmed my soul. More likely it was the sensation of Wing Pruett's arms wrapped around me good and tight. Occam's razor at work—sometimes the simplest explanation was the best.

In my first moments of consciousness, I planned the day ahead. Promoting and selling my leather wares was number one on the list, although a discreet spot of detecting was close behind. True, I had no need to involve myself in solving a stranger's murder. By all accounts, Lee Holmes was no loss to humanity, and Roar Jansen and his redoubtable partner were probably quite competent. I stopped there while I still retained even a shred of integrity and examined my conscience.

Finding his corpse had thrust me into the Holmes case in the most graphic way possible, but Pruett's mysterious behavior worried me. Suppose the cops pinned the murder on him? That was foolish thinking, but Pruett had used his martial arts skills on the deceased. He hadn't murdered him, of course, but it might look suspicious to Sergeant Roar. Every time my eyes closed, I visualized those pretty pink shears, blood-stained and protruding from the victim's chest. Even the word "victim" was value-laden. No one—well, very few—should be murdered, but some people deliberately tempt fate. Lee Holmes may well have been one of them. A chorus of otherwise sane voices argued that vengeance could sometimes be justified. I know the names that pop up every time that argument surfaces: Hitler, Stalin, and Theodore Bundy. The list goes on. My reaction was different. I focused instead on murder itself, the act that violated every tenant of civilized behavior and cried out for punishment. Pruett and I often debated the law versus justice argument, and I knew the two were not always aligned. But training and experience had taught me how vital those concepts were. I upbraided Pruett about the thin line between law and anarchy, and the need to adhere to a standard. Neither one of us would yield, and we always ended by calling a truce. I sighed as I considered Wing Pruett's very creative methods of conflict resolution. That man deserved the Nobel Peace Prize at least!

"Penny for your thoughts, Ms. Morgan," he said. "Or has the price risen with inflation?" He moved closer and massaged my back until I purred like a kitten. "Bet you're still thinking about that murder," he said.

I pled guilty. "Crazy Jess said that Lee was a predator. True or not, being called that could make someone react."

He responded immediately and without hesitation. "Only natural to defend those you love. I know a dozen ways of dealing with his kind that would never even be noticed."

"I'll keep that in mind in case any more corpses appear. Dangerous men turn me on, so watch your step." I snuggled closer, considering Pruett's words.

His reaction didn't surprise me. It was normal and also quite understandable. Kiki's performance in front of Lee and her former husband was certainly provocative, especially when a volatile man like Roy was involved. Perhaps a conversation with the coquette in question would be helpful.

I switched on the bedside lamp and glanced at Pruett. Never mind that mascara probably ringed my eyes and my hair was askew. Wing Pruett was perfect—utterly perfect. It wasn't fair, but there it was. The guy transformed rumpled hair and beard growth into an art form. Like many men, he slept nude, something I could never bring myself to do. Made me feel way too vulnerable, even though I knew that the watchful eyes and ears of my dogs would keep me safe. There was also the question of physical perfection. Like most women, I had my share of inhibitions. Body shaming or not, it was a fact of life. Pruett had not one iota of self-doubt about his appearance or almost any other aspect of life. No wonder. I had seen sculptures in fine European museums, and all six feet something of Pruett surpassed any hunk of marble on display. I could attest to that in the most personal of ways.

"Something wrong?" he asked. "Man, I need caffeine in the worst way. I'm dying here." He leapt up, grabbed his robe, and headed out the bedroom door.

"Babette brought her espresso machine," I said. "Knock yourself out while I get dressed." I scuttled toward the shower and immersed myself in lavender-scented suds. For a moment, I forgot the grisly murder and its probable aftermath and reveled in the sense of renewal that the waves of water brought. I emerged, fragrant, fresh, and ready for battle.

A cozy, domestic scene featuring Ella, Pruett, and Babette confronted me. My pal, wrapped in a Williams-Sonoma apron, poured freshly squeezed juice and carefully arranged matching linen napkins at each place. Betty Crocker never had it so good.

I blinked twice. Babette and aprons simply did not compute. She was a woman of many parts, none of which spelled earth mother.

"Sit down, Perri," she said. "You need protein. Big day ahead." She beamed at Ella. "Guinnie goes into the ring today, sweetie. Perri promised she'd make her win!"

That was a total fabrication, typical of Babette, who lived in a fantasy world of her own making. No one could guarantee anything at a dog show. I'd urged Pruett to find a professional handler for Guinnie, but he had dropped the ball. Now the onus was on me to avoid disappointing the child I loved.

"Don't worry, honey," I said. "Guinnie is a winner no matter what happens."

Babette beamed at both of us and added her special touch. "No problem about your store, Perri. I'll hold down the fort. You know how I connect with customers."

Salesmanship was not within her skill set, but I had other plans for Babette. Plans that involved deception and snooping—two of her strong suits.

"Come into the other room," I said. "I want to show you something." Fortunately, Babette abandoned her happy homemaker pose and complied. Pruett distracted Ella by asking about her favorite topic, dogs.

"What's up?" Babette asked. "You're acting kinda squirrelly."

I quickly outlined the problem and her assignment for the day.

"Why get involved?" she asked. It was a reasonable enough question, one that I had wrestled with last night. I targeted Babette's prime area of vulnerability—romance.

"Pruett could be in trouble," I said, "or maybe even Rafa. Rafa was MIA last night, and Pruett was at the scene of the crime. That Sergeant Watts acts like she has an axe to grind, and I don't want it to fall on anyone we care about. Besides, you might find out something Roar can't."

I knew she was hooked, but she played hard to get for a bit. "Maybe. I'll mingle with the hard-core show types and see what they say." She shrugged. "Couldn't hurt, I suppose."

After feeding and exercising the dogs, we grabbed our gear and headed toward the Better Living Center with some degree of optimism. Pruett was pursuing a story, while I sought the truth. Who knew how closely aligned those objectives were?

Chapter 7

Saturday was boom time in the show world. Handlers, owners, and the general public stormed into the Better Living Center, determined to enjoy their day, sell their wares, or go for glory. The beautiful creatures prancing around the rings were often oblivious to the hubbub. Show dogs—even the hyper-active breeds—tended to accept both canine and human hordes with equanimity. Bad temperament was a fatal flaw for canine competitors and was closely monitored by judges. Humans not so much. A number of them would never make the cut in any category where nipping, growling, or backbiting was strictly forbidden.

Pruett played the role of doting daddy to perfection. He trotted after Ella and Lady Guinevere, trading greetings with anyone he met as they did a wide circle of the complex. From the number of admiring glances he drew, I was quite certain that Pruett could claim platinum Grand Champion, Best of Breed, and Best in Show without any real competition.

Babette and I split up in a divide-and-conquer move. I scoped out Ring Nine, where the pointer competition would convene. Babette fluttered over to the main station and started chattering with club officials.

I was astounded—no, shocked—to see Yael Lindsay standing in the line in front of me. Nary a hair escaped from that impeccable French twist, and her jewelry was discreet but perfect. In an apparent concession to tragedy, Yael wore low-heeled black shoes and a severe navy knit suit with minimal gold braid. Her face was pale but composed—not exactly the picture of a bereaved spouse. On the other hand, I knew that people processed grief very differently. Some women would be prostrate; others worked through their misery and put on a brave face. My own sad experience illustrated that. The day after Pip passed was the start of one of my most productive periods. Hard work counteracted the crushing numbness I felt and masked the pain of his loss. I sailed along until two weeks later, when a cheery Christmas card arrived addressed to both of us. That leveled me, hitting with the force of a nuclear blast. Babette found me dissolved in a sobbing heap and gently nursed me back to reality. I would never forget her kindness. Perhaps Yael was in the same place and needed a friendly shoulder for comfort.

I didn't know her that well, but after retrieving my armband, I approached her and expressed my condolences. Her reaction left me speechless.

"I suppose you were one of them," she hissed. Her voice was low, audible only to me.

"Excuse me?"

"Don't think I had any illusions about my husband." Her voice was brittle, steeped in bitterness. "Lee chased women like hounds do rabbits." She looked me up and down in a distinctly unflattering way. "All kinds."

Grief buys one only so much leeway. "I didn't know your husband, Mrs. Holmes. I found his body." I kept my words clipped and impersonal, harkening back to my prior training. "That's my only connection to his death."

Something must have penetrated Yael's defenses. She raised a hand to her mouth and swayed back and forth. "Forgive me. Lee wasn't perfect, but he was a big part of my life."

"Can I get you some coffee or tea?"

She shook her head but allowed me to guide her toward one of the benches facing the ring. I sat beside her in total silence as she collected herself. Yael Lindsay was a proud woman, unwilling to parade her feelings in public. I could identify with that.

"The police questioned me," she said. "As if I knew who killed him. Lee was tempestuous. Blood feuds were his stock in trade. He lived for conflict. You probably saw that nonsense with that Vesco woman. Slut! She should be eliminated from the show ring. And that husband of hers . . ." Yael's lips pursed in disgust.

I nodded, trying to seem sympathetic without appearing intrusive. "Lots of shenanigans going on in the show world." Before I could safely broach Rafa's name, we were rudely interrupted by Whit Wiley. He hunkered down, put his arms around Yael, and gave her a hug. "My dear Yael. So brave in the face of tragedy."

His fawning manner was therapeutic, just the tonic the widow needed to revive her spirit. She stiffened, shrugged off his grasp, and spoke crisply. "Thank you for your concern, Whitney. Lee often spoke of you."

After a moment of frigid silence, Whit patted her shoulder and slowly slunk away. Yael narrowed her eyes as he retreated. "Odious little man. Lee detested him, and so do I."

Once again, silence served me well. I stared at the terriers trotting around the ring, silently admiring their sprightly gait and "true terrier temperament." Nada. Not a word from either one of us. After the open dog class concluded, Yael turned to me.

"I understand you were once an army officer."

"Sergeant," I said. "Three years in Afghanistan."

She nodded. "We got off to a bad start, but I now have a favor to ask."

I turned to face her, expecting the worst. For all I knew, this entitled Brahmin might order me off the premises or hurl more insults.

"Help me," Yael Lindsay asked.

"What are you thinking of?" I asked. "Roar Jansen seems quite competent."

Yael leveled me with the same type of look her ancestors probably used with indentured servants. "Nonsense. No one will tell him anything. Everyone has something to hide. I need someone who is part of this world."

I shook my head. "I don't think . . ."

"Of course, I'll pay you." She dismissed my objections as she would any tradesman. In her world, everything was apparently a matter of money.

My sympathy for the bereaved widow quickly evaporated. With a Gorgon-like Yael at home, small wonder that her husband had trolled the arena for female company. I summoned every shred of dignity I possessed.

"I neither need nor want your money, Mrs. Lindsay. Any information I get will be promptly shared with the police." I stood and faced her directly. "Excuse me. I have a dog to show."

* * * *

While Ella Pruett danced around my little store on tiptoes, Lady Guinevere was far more reserved. The pointer was everything a top show dog should be, plus a bit more. Pointers were the original emblem of the Westminster Kennel Club Dog Show and still commanded a loyal following. She calmly floated around the ring, commanding the eye of judges, spectators, and competitors alike. Handling her was a dream, even among a host of top-flight contenders. In the past, Guinnie had bested Yael Lindsay and Whit Wiley's entrants, a fact that galled both of them. Pruett had already promised Ella that if Guinnie continued her winning ways, he would sponsor her for the biggest prize in dogdom—the Westminster show in Manhattan. Fine and dandy, but first he had to retain a top-class handler. I did a passable job in the ring, but there was no substitute for a competent professional. Dogs knew it, and so did judges. Bless her heart, Lady Guinevere was astounding. Under the tutelage of the right handler, she would be extraordinary and have a real shot at Westminster. Maybe even Crufts, the big international show.

To my delight, Guinnie won the Best of Breed and four Grand Champion points to boot. I kept my eyes downcast to avoid Yael's grim visage and the shot of pure venom radiating my way from Whit Wiley. Ella and Pruett were delighted. The little girl danced around me and gave Guinnie a huge hug. Her dashing daddy put his arm around me and whispered something quite naughty in my ear. Unfortunately, we had to defer addressing that suggestion until Guinnie competed in the group ring.

"How about getting a bite of lunch?" Pruett said. "I saw your favorite on the way over here. Popeye's."

The man knew almost all of my secret vices and wasn't shy about using them against me. Popeye's! Just thinking of that spicy chicken, beans, and rice made me salivate.

"Can we, Daddy? Oh, boy!" Ella pirouetted with Guinnie as her partner.

A man with a body like Pruett's can eat just about anything with impunity. I knew for a fact, however, that Ella's mom banned any kind of fried food from her child's diet.

"I have to check my store," I said. "Tell you what. Take Ms. Babette and my dogs with you and bring me back a big batch of Popeye's!"

Pruett shrugged but accepted the inevitable. "Okay, spoilsport. Let's round up Babette and get this show on the road."

We sped toward the entrance of my stall, where Babette awaited us. After the lunch bunch headed out the door, I checked the cash register, rearranged stock, and did a quick grooming of Guinnie. Veteran that she was, the pointer jumped up on the steel table and waited patiently as I assembled the tools for sprucing her up. I was daydreaming, but her ears pricked up at a sound I hadn't even heard. Not surprising, since canine hearing was at least four times more acute than humans'. I quickly whirled around and saw the smiling face of Rafael Ramos.

"You startled me," I said, giving him a tight smile. "Babette's not here, if you're looking for her."

Rafa shook his head. He was taller than I had realized, over six feet and well-muscled. I knew how to defend myself, but somehow, I saw no need to panic. I took a step back behind the grooming table, keeping Guinnie between us. Better safe than sorry—a trite but true saying. Even with Keats and Poe watching over me, I erred on the side of caution.

"It's you I came to see," Rafa said.

I kept the conversation nice and easy. "Okay. What can I do for you?"

He leaned against the counter, locking both hands in front of him. "The police suspect me. I know they do."

"Have you spoken to them?" I hadn't seen Roar or his redoubtable partner since last evening.

Rafa grimaced. "Once. They knew we didn't get along. Then there's the problem of those damned shears. Poodle shears. My breed."

"Lots of shears in this place. Why connect them to you?"

He took two steps toward me. "Because they *were* mine. They went missing last night. I had them in my bag and lost sight of them when that brawl started."

Not good. In fact, it was close to catastrophic. The murder weapon probably harbored all sorts of fingerprints, most of them from Rafa himself.

"Have you found an attorney?" I asked. "Sounds like you might need one."

He shook his head. "That's like hanging a big guilty sign around my neck." My expression must have telegraphed my thoughts, because Rafa held up his arms in surrender. "Okay. I get it. If the cops start making moves, I'll hire someone. Wing gave me some names already. But I remain optimistic. Between the two of you, I know you can find the killer."

Trust Pruett to worm his way into the investigation without telling me. I took a deep breath and counted way past ten. "Whoa. Wait just a minute. What did you have in mind?"

Rafa bared a set of perfect teeth, sharing a winning grin with me. It had probably earned him plenty of fans over the years, but this time he was out of luck. I was not in the market for whatever he was selling. Besides, Pruett was in a class all his own; no other man even came close. Poor Babette. She was already putty in Rafa's hands. No telling what stunts she would pull to help him out.

"I repeat. What do you suggest?" I folded my arms to show I meant business.

"Talk to people. See if you can find any clues. No one will tell the police anything, but you and Wing are different."

Funny thing. Rafa was playing the same tune as Yael, albeit in a different key. I made a snap decision, one that I would later regret. After all, people confided in me and told me I had an honest face. Maybe I could inveigle some of them to share information. As for Pruett—that boy could get milk from granite. It was the secret to his success and the flaw that often imperiled him.

"Listen, Rafa, you've got to come clean with me. What business arrangements did you have with Lee? Pruett mentioned that you co-owned a dog at one time."

Rafael Ramos knew how to handle victory. Instead of gloating, he cracked his knuckles and leaned forward. Keats and Poe moved toward me, emitting a low growl as they did so. Rafa knew dogs as well as he knew women. He immediately backed against the wall and spoke to them in a soft, soothing voice.

"Platz," I said. That was the Schutzhund command for "lie down but remain alert." Both dogs immediately did so.

"It's a long story," Rafa said. "Might take some time, and you have a group showing soon."

I checked my watch. "Yikes! Guinnie's up in ten minutes. Let's meet at Babette's trailer after the show. That way Pruett can hear everything too."

Rafa nodded in agreement. "Sounds good. Meanwhile, I have a group of class poodles to judge. You know how jumpy owners get when they're trying to finish that championship. One more thing to consider, Perri. Pruett mixed it up with Lee too. I understand he was on the scene when the cops came. I'm not the only suspect." He strolled out the door and melted into the crowd before I could say anything more. For some reason, I didn't really trust Rafa. Wasn't even sure I liked him. The man was a magician who would likely pull a vanishing act when Babette needed him most. For now, I would withhold judgment, but like my dogs, I would remain vigilant.

Chapter 8

Guinnie's next challenge was a big one. If she prevailed in the Sporting Group competition, she would receive a one-way ticket to Best in Show, and that meant the big time! Competition was intense, but I had no doubt that she was the superior dog. Every handler in the Sporting Group harbored the same feelings about his entry.

Ella, Babette, and Pruett met me ringside. Their faces, rife with high-carb satisfaction, told me that Popeye's had once again hit the mark. I banished thoughts of Cajun chicken and focused on Guinnie. There were at least two contenders in the Sporting Group that might give her trouble. One, a sweet-natured Brittany spaniel, had already reached Grand Champion status. I also kept my eye on a sprightly English springer spaniel, whose lineage included two Westminster winners. Both dogs were presented by well-regarded handlers who acted mighty friendly with the judge. I bit my tongue and told myself not to invent excuses. Losers did that. Winners kept their eye on the prize. I spied Pruett snapping video with his iPhone as we trotted around the ring, while Ella and Babette cheered lustily for Guinnie. My hopes soared when the judge made her first cut, leaving us in the running with the springer, the Brittany, and a curly-coated retriever. As we stacked our dogs for a final inspection, the judge lined us up, decreed "once more around the ring," and then pointed to the Brittany, with Guinnie coming in second.

I was philosophical about it, but Ella sobbed inconsolably. "Poor Guinnie. Look, she's crying." The little girl threw her arms around the pointer and held on tight.

"Hey," I said. "Look at the bright side. Guinnie beat out six other dogs and still got three points toward her Bronze Grand Championship. That's impressive."

Pruett ruffled his daughter's hair and spoke softly to her. "Guinnie is a class act, Ella, and you have to behave the same way." He put his arm around me. "Come on. Ms. Perri must be really hungry."

I rubbed my tummy and nodded. "Popeye's, here I come. Hope you guys left me some."

"Oh yeah," Babette said. "Biscuits, red beans and rice, not to mention that chicken." She smacked her lips. "I might just have seconds on everything. How about it, Ella?" She took the little girl's hand and skipped toward the shop I had set up with the name Creature Comforts.

As we walked behind them, I told Pruett about my encounters with Rafa and Yael. "It's weird. Two different people with conflicting goals want us snooping around a murder scene."

Pruett's face wore a look of undeserved innocence. "Go figure. Maybe Rafa can clear things up tonight."

We both knew that if Roar Jansen found us interfering in his investigation, he would not be a happy camper. His partner's reaction would be even worse.

"You weren't the only one who was busy today," Pruett said. "I had coffee with Bethany Zahn. Whew! What a talker."

I rolled my eyes, picturing the scene between the two. Bethany had probably wound her shapely self around Pruett like a reptile. "So. What happened?"

He immediately went into crack reporter mode, pulling out his iPad and checking his notes. "Okay. She hinted that Lee was interested in her too. Naturally, she denied any involvement."

"Huh! I heard her with Yael."

"According to Bethany, she was only messing with Yael. Can't stand her and thinks she's an interfering busybody." He stopped at the door to my shop and kissed my cheek. "Look. I want to check out some things. See you tonight."

"Hold on one minute, buster." I wagged my finger at him. "The last time you said that, you ended up babysitting a corpse. Plus, you have other responsibilities too. Unless you want your little girl to cry her eyes out again, find a professional handler for Guinnie. It makes a difference."

Pruett looked down at me with a heat-seeking gaze that curled my toes. "You know the dog world better than I do. Pick someone, and I'll pay the freight. Please. For Ella." He winked and blew me a kiss. And with that, my handsome prince disappeared into never, never land intent on doing Lord knows what in pursuit of his story.

* * * *

Business was brisk that afternoon. Chicken satiated my hunger, but cash in hand soothed my soul. I was a self-supporting, small business entrepreneur. Out of necessity, I kept a sharp eye on my balance sheet and economized wherever possible. Detective work had its charms, but it really didn't pay the bills. Ask any foster child and you'll get a similar story: Appreciate good fortune, but never count on anything you didn't earn through hard work.

I was knee-deep in customers when Roar Jansen and Genna Watts stepped inside. Guilt, or something very much like it, made me quickly shoo out stragglers, summon my great big Brownie smile, and greet the detectives.

"Things are really jumping around here," Roar said. The impact of his smile hit me yet again. The powder-blue sweater he wore was merely icing on a very tasty cake. The guy was a babe, and he obviously knew it. Fortunately, I was impervious to his charms, but not oblivious. Sergeant Watts, a woman with little charm to spare, narrowed her eyes and grunted. She forswore social niceties and immediately got down to business.

"You didn't mention the other murders," she said, pulling out a tattered pad.
"Excuse me?"
"Virginia. Last year. You and Mr. Pruett jumped right in. Oh yeah. Mrs. Croy too."

Genna turned brusqueness into an art form, and it annoyed the hell out of me.

I straightened up to my full sixty-nine inches and stared her down. Two can play the intimidation game. In fact, I was rather good at it.

"Did I hear my name?" Babette asked. She and Ella bounded into the shop with Clara and Guinnie in tow.

The sergeant had a scowl that could tame a rampaging lion. It even temporarily subdued the ebullient Babette. "Maybe we should go downtown and discuss this," Genna growled, knowing full well what that would do to my day's profits.

Fortunately, Roar interceded, applying a liberal dose of soft soap. "No need. We just wanted to touch base with you." He walked slowly toward the grooming tools on display. "Hmm. Looks just like the murder weapon, doesn't it, Genna? No pink ones, though." He turned toward me with that disarming grin. "Big sellers, I bet."

I matched his grin with one of my own. A number of men had called it "fetching," although I couldn't swear as to its impact. "Grooming goes with the territory, Sergeant. Ask anyone."

Roar nodded. "Oh, I have. Funny thing, though. Ms. Lindsay told us just today that you and Wing Pruett were investigating things for her."

Denial was pointless in these situations. I chose the high road. "Poor woman. She's so distraught. Almost delusional."

Things might have calmed down had Babette not put her considerable oar into the water. "You'd be darn lucky if we joined in. Just ask the cops in Great Marsh."

That set Sergeant Watts off big-time. "Oh, we did. They had some choice words for all three of you. Especially Ms. Morgan."

Sometimes dignified silence was the better part of valor. In this instance, it drove Genna to distraction. Fortunately, Roar was far more nonchalant. He just shrugged and ambled toward the door. "Guess we'll be seeing you around, Perri. Watch yourself."

His partner had the last word. "And stay out of our way."

* * * *

Ella peaked out from behind a stack of boxes. "That lady doesn't like you, Ms. Perri. She's mean."

Trust a child to recognize a shrew when she saw one. In the interests of good parenting, however, I took the high road. "Don't mind her, honey. She's got a tough job to do."

Under her breath, Babette mumbled. "And that bitch is no lady either."

I poked my head out the door and checked my watch. "Things are winding down anyway. Let's head over to Steady Eddie and relax."

"Amen," said Babette, who hadn't had a particularly tiring day. She gave a huge yawn and said, "I am pooped."

I got a sudden brainstorm and decided to act on it right away. "You two go on back. Leave Keats and Poe here with me. I need to talk with some handlers first. Be right with you." At first, Babette protested—until I mentioned that Rafa would soon be there. That activated the beauty machine and all its attendant rituals. Babette pulled out a mirror and patted her hair. "Guess I should shower and change clothes." She held out her hand to Ella. "Come on, honey. Grab Guinnie, and let's make tracks." Accompanied by two trusty canines, the humans virtually skipped out the side door of the Big E.

They had vanished before I turned out the lights.

* * * *

I was a woman on a mission. With a little luck and persistence, I just might find the right handler for Lady Guinevere before her next show date. I also had an ulterior motive. By mingling with the professionals, I might glean more information about Lee Holmes, Rafa, and any other interested parties. It was certainly worth a try.

My first stop was the enclave where the poodle fanciers congregated. Most dog shows have distinct areas, segregated by breed, where dogs, owners, and handlers set up camp. It was strictly an informal arrangement, but in my experience, anyone with open ears and a friendly smile could burrow in and learn a lot.

With Keats and Poe at my side, I sauntered through the area, admiring the dogs on display. Despite the frivolity of the mandatory "show cut," standard poodles were tough, wickedly smart dogs that were frequently one step ahead of their owners. After ensuring that Rafa was nowhere around, I approached an area where several exquisitely manicured pups lounged on their grooming tables as if poised for a photo shoot. Their handlers, easily identified by protective capes, tools, and blow-dryers, were bunched in a knot, chatting and snacking. Most were strangers to me, but I spied at least one familiar face, a breeder-owner-handler from Maryland. I sidled over to her and settled into the personalized chair with POODLE POWER KENNELS stenciled on it. Most show veterans brought their own sturdy fold-up chairs emblazoned with the name of their kennels or show dogs on them. She was no exception.

"Punky," I said, smiling at the wisp of a woman clad in black, "I need some advice."

Patricia "Punky" West put her hands on her hips and grinned at me, "Sugar, you came to the right spot. I'm full of advice, and some of it is even good."

"Yeah, Punky, you sure are full of it." A blowsy blonde, sporting two inches of dark roots, hooted. She had once bought poodle shears from me, but her name eluded me.

Punky was barely five feet tall, but she was a silver pocket rocket, packed with energy and good humor. Her kennel was renowned in poodle circles for producing solid champion dogs and companion animals. Like most reputable breeders, she scrutinized prospective adopters with an eagle eye and welcomed back any of her "babies" needing a new home.

I explained my quest for a professional handler and a bit about Guinnie. The blonde, who introduced herself as Shirley Renaud, immediately volunteered a name. "What about Alf Walsh?" she asked. "Understand he's got some availability. Great guy too. Firm but gentle with the big breeds. I have his card somewhere." She rooted in a knapsack and extracted a rumpled, coffee-stained card with Walsh's name and cell number. "He was campaigning a big white male, but the poor dog got sick and left the show circuit. Broke his leg or something. I can't quite recall. Anyway, Alf was frantic."

"Campaigning" a dog was a time-intensive, costly endeavor that only serious owners with deep pockets even considered. It entailed virtually surrendering your dog to his handler for cross-country show appearances. Rewards were never guaranteed, although successful competitors amassed points toward national rankings. Campaigning was not for the faint-hearted or impoverished. Even pooches that reached the pinnacle of dogdom rarely enriched their owners' coffers. Conformation was a world unto its own, with risks and rewards that only a few could grasp.

"I'll look him up," I said. "Frankly, I'm not skilled enough to give Guinnie the push she deserves. Her owner is a darling child, and Wing Pruett would do anything to please her."

The din of female voices suddenly stopped as Punky, Shirley, and several of their cohort gaped at me.

"Did you say Wing Pruett?" Shirley asked. "The hot magazine guy? Perfect body, gorgeous hair, plenty of attitude?"

I nodded.

"Lordy, Lordy, that man is fine." Shirley rhapsodized. "Lead me to him. Hell, I'll show the dog for free if he's part of the deal." Her compatriots chuckled in agreement.

I kept my composure and managed a weak smile. After all, Pruett's magnetism was nothing new. Half the women in DC either lusted after him or had already dated him. Celebrities took such adoration in their stride, but I was no celebrity. That disparity between me and Pruett emphasized anew how unlikely our relationship was. I was strictly a one-man kind of gal, wary of trusting most men and certainly no babe magnet. He was a superstar.

Punky patted her pal on the shoulder and looked my way. "I think he's spoken for, right, Perri?"

"More or less. Nothing formal." I spread my hands in a hapless gesture and changed the subject. "So. Any other suggestions? I met Rafael Ramos recently, but he's a judge, so he's not available." That name changed the trajectory of the conversation immediately. Shirley lowered her voice and glanced over her shoulder. "You know about the murder, I guess."

I shrugged. "Unfortunately. I found the body. Gruesome."

"Rafa didn't do it," Punky whispered. "He couldn't have." She balled her hands up into tight fists.

"He's a great guy," Shirley chimed in. "That's more than I could say for Lee Holmes. Such a creep!"

I played my innocence card. "I didn't really know Lee. His wife competes in pointers, so she's an acquaintance. Poor thing."

Punky leapt up and began combing the black poodle nearest her. "Poor thing, my foot. She's well rid of him. Let me tell you. Yael Lindsay got nothing but heartbreak from that man."

Shirley nodded in agreement. "Besides, I figure Roy Vesco got him alone and evened up the score. You probably heard about the fracas last night."

"Hard to judge," I said, "when love is involved."

"Love! That's a hoot. Kiki's a born troublemaker. Always rubbing up against men, even that Whit Wiley, if you can believe it." Shirley curled her lip in disgust. "Talk about desperate. I'm never sure which team that guy even plays for. Probably both."

Punky halted the grooming and pointed a finger at her friend. "Come on, Shirl. Knock it off. Kiki is young, not even thirty." She hugged the poodle and spritzed him with water. "Take my word, Lee had plenty of other enemies. Always cheating people in business deals and lying about it. Leads to trouble, mark my words."

Time for me to interject something into the conversation. "He and Rafa co-owned dogs, didn't they? They must have been close at one time to do that."

Both women nodded in unison.

"You said it. Rafa did all the work, while Lee preened. Ask anyone who knew him. That Lee was one lazy sucker. Dumb too." Shirley snickered. "Guess the good Lord was giving out looks, not brains, the day Lee turned up."

I sighed and tried one last gambit. "The police grilled us big-time. I almost felt guilty myself after facing them."

Shirley rolled her eyes. "Speaking of hotties. The lead detective could grill me any time. Once over easy. Even his name is sexy—Roar. I might confess to the murder just to spend some up close and personal time with that boy."

Neither woman even mentioned Sergeant Watts, but in view of the conversation, that was hardly surprising. After a few more comments, I thanked them and ambled toward the exit door. Before I left, Bethany Zahn blocked my path. Today's outfit was a striking gold-mesh number that contrasted nicely with her tawny eyes. Her makeup and sculpted hair lent just the right touch to the persona of a pet psychic. Most dog show regulars saved the glam for their canine charges, but there were exceptions like Bethany.

"Perri, we need to talk," she said. "You won't believe what I found out today."

"Okay. Right now, I'm kind of pressed for time, though."

Bethany showed her dimples in a big grin. "This won't take long. I heard you're playing detective."

Despite my denials, she persisted. "Look. I'll stop by your store tonight around eight. Trust me, you'll be glad I did."

In every thriller I had ever read, this scenario spelled trouble. Typically, the informant ended up dead, and the hapless stooge—in this case me—was accused of the crime. I had no desire to play that role or subject myself to Sergeant Watts's gimlet eye. None at all. Genna had probably earned an advanced degree in torture from Torquemada U. and ached to practice her skills. Not on my watch.

"Look, Bethany. Come by our motor home instead. Have a drink, and let's chat."

She considered my offer and flashed a saucy smile my way. "Okay. I suppose Pruett will be there too. Don't worry. I don't mind sharing with him. In fact, he could get just about anything out of me. Okay then, Perri. See you at eight." She winked at me and sashayed toward the restroom area. Jealousy was counterproductive, a mean-spirited and worthless emotion that was unworthy of me. Nevertheless, I sprinted out the door straight toward Steady Eddie, having heard enough trash talk from horny women to last me all week.

Chapter 9

Bethany didn't die. Instead, she rapped on the door of Steady Eddie precisely at eight PM, sporting a fresh coat of makeup, warm winter gear, and a grin that would shame the Cheshire cat. By rights, I should have resented her, but despite the flashy persona, there was an air of vulnerability about the pet psychic that I found sympathetic. That didn't mean that I trusted her around Pruett. Far from it. For his part, Pruett seemed very much at ease, as he crossed his long legs and slowly sipped Babette's pricy bourbon.

"Come on in," Babette trilled. "Girl, you look like a snow angel. That stuff is really coming down, isn't it?"

Bethany shook herself like one of her spaniels, scattering the white stuff over the entryway. "They're talking about canceling Wednesday's show," she said. "Judges can't get in, airports and highways closed." She grinned at Pruett. "Real snuggling weather."

Pruett wisely chose to focus on his bourbon instead of boudoir talk. "This stuff is extraordinary," he sighed. "You, Mrs. Croy, are a woman of taste and distinction."

Babette never shied away from a compliment, especially one from a gorgeous male. She batted her lashes and positively glowed. "Why, thank you, kind sir. My late husband Wilbur taught me all about it. That man was a true connoisseur. In fact, he was sipping Buffalo Trace Bourbon when he passed away."

My pal knew all about whiskey and husbands. Wilbur, hubby number two, died at eighty-one with a smile on his face. He passed his considerable holdings on to the bride who had brightened his final years—Babette. One could only applaud her talent for unearthing wealthy men who doted on her and left this earth happy. Of her four husbands, only Carleton Croy, the youngest and most impoverished, had disappointed, but Babette was philosophical. As she observed, that's what prenuptial agreements were for. Carleton left with nothing more than he brought to their ill-fated union.

"I'll try some of that," Bethany drawled, making a dead set at Pruett. "By the way, where's that cute little girl of yours? Ella, right?"

Pruett beamed like the proud papa that he was and nodded toward the bedroom. Now it was his turn to glow. Ella held the key to his heart, and any praise for her was warmly received. "She's with Guinnie," he said. "It's past her bedtime. Ella's, not Guinnie's."

"When do you go to bed?" Bethany asked, looking him over. "You look well-rested enough."

Babette and Bethany giggled as if that were comic gold; however, I pushed the agenda forward. "Tell us, Bethany, we're dying to know. You mentioned some important information."

She tousled her curls and hunkered down at Pruett's feet. "Okay. But keep this between us. I have my career to think of."

Maybe it was my imagination, but the atmosphere in the room suddenly grew tense. Babette clenched her fists into tight knuckleballs, Pruett folded his arms and stayed impassive, and I took one deep, cleansing breath. Bethany certainly knew how to stage a show and engage her audience.

She jumped to her feet and immediately started pacing. "I found something out that you all should know. Remember that kooky chick who handles German shepherds?"

I nodded. "Jess Pendrake. Saw her just today."

Bethany's tawny eyes narrowed. "Well, she had one hell of a reason to hate Lee Holmes. See, he leased one of her shepherds, kept him for six months, then reneged on the deal. Can you believe it?"

Pruett wrinkled up his lip and said, "What? Leasing a dog!"

I sometimes forgot that this was very foreign territory for him. Until last year, Pruett had avoided all things canine whenever possible due to an unfortunate experience in childhood. Actually, dog leasing was not uncommon among serious breeders and handlers. At first, I too had reacted emotionally to the concept, since like most pet parents, I couldn't bear the thought of being separated from my dogs. When several breeders explained their rationale, I understood. Still didn't like it, though.

Bethany twirled a strand of hair around her fingers and beamed at Pruett. "Think of it this way, Wing. Most breeders have up to twenty dogs in their kennels and spend forty weeks a year crisscrossing the country. No way can they take every pup with them. If they have a hot show prospect, it makes sense to let someone from another part of the country keep him for a while."

Pruett shook his head. "So the breeder gets paid? Sounds kind of cold to me."

"Yeah," Babette said. "I couldn't bear it if Clara ever left my side."

This was strictly Bethany's show. I stayed silent as she continued the tutorial.

"Be practical," she said. "Selling puppies sounds cold too, but placing them in loving homes is different. Besides, there are safeguards in the leasing contracts. Breeders demand that the dog be shown to rack up championship points."

Pruett displayed his practical business side once again. "Doesn't sound like much of a deal for the lessee."

Bethany leaned over and pinched his cheek. Frankly, I could have done without that little gesture, but Pruett seemed to enjoy it. "Look," she said, "the lessee, as you call him, gets the right to breed the dog to his bitch without paying a stud fee. That's a big deal, so everyone makes out. Stud fees can easily climb into four figures for a high-value dog."

Babette and Pruett were unconvinced. In the midst of the debate, however, we overlooked the fact that a child with big eyes and open ears had wandered into the room. Ella clutched Guinnie in a death grip and said in a tremulous voice, "Daddy, don't send Guinnie away. Please."

Pruett leapt from his chair and embraced the little girl. "Don't worry, honey. We're just talking. No one will take Guinnie away. Promise."

"Time for the pups to take a potty break before you go to bed," I told Ella. "Come on."

Thoughts of walking the dogs banished all of Ella's immediate concerns. That was the wonderful thing about being seven years old. In the end, four adults and four canines and a kid saddled up and trekked through the snowy field for an evening romp. Bethany amused her audience by sharing anecdotes from the work-life of a pet psychic. While Babette rolled her eyes and jabbed me in the side, Pruett hung on to every syllable she uttered. I am a rationalist but not a confirmed skeptic, so I carefully evaluated Bethany's claims. Interspecies communication seemed plausible enough, and some humans showed a rare ability to bridge the gap. If Bethany were less toothsome, just a tiny bit homely, I might have really embraced her skills.

When we returned, Ella and Guinnie sped off to bed, while the adults sipped some more bourbon. Bethany had yet to share her big news with us, so I decided a subtle nudge was in order.

"You mentioned that you had some interesting news."

She opened those big green eyes and stared me down. Apparently, proximity to Pruett had robbed the woman of her senses. I immediately prompted her. "You know. About the murder."

Luckily, the light of reason dawned. Bethany lowered her voice to conspiratorial levels and said, "It has to do with that dog-leasing stuff. Jess

Pendrake had a leasing contract with Lee. You remember that shepherd of hers, Grand Champion before he was a year old? I can't for the life of me recall his name."

Talk about your pregnant pauses. I resisted the impulse to shake her like a terrier with a rat, substituting a friendly grin for the kick in the pants that she so richly deserved. Fortunately, Babette had no self-control at all. When she sought answers, she got them double quick.

"Who the hell cares what his name was, Bethany. Spill! We don't have all night."

For a moment, the psychic's temper flared, but after pasting a specious smile on her face, Bethany continued. "Jess leased her 'special' to Lee Holmes about two years ago without signing a contract."

Pruett frowned. He understood human nature too well to approve of forgoing contracts. Babette, on the other hand, was impulsive, but she had a litigious attorney who reined her in.

"So, what happened?" I asked. "Jess seems fairly cynical about men."

"That's just it! Lee put the big rush on her, and she totally bought it." Bethany smirked. "She doesn't get hit on by hot guys very often."

I held my tongue, but in truth, I doubted Jess had ever been courted by any guy, hot or not.

"Lee totally screwed her over," Bethany said. "He bred that dog five times and hardly ever showed him. Didn't get Jess's approval either. She threatened to sue him, and Yael finally intervened. It was a big mess."

Small wonder that Jess was bitter. My opinion of Lee Holmes sunk even lower.

"Does Sergeant Jansen know this?" I asked. "You really should contact him."

Bethany gave Pruett a big-eyed stare as phony as her hair color. "I don't know. What do you think, Wing?"

Babette curled her lip and muttered something rather rude. Fortunately, Bethany's psychic powers didn't extend to hearing, so a nasty scene was averted.

"That's something Roar should definitely hear," Pruett said.

"My experience with cops is mixed," Bethany said. "Could you go with me?"

He reached into his wallet and produced his business card. "Sure. Call me tomorrow when Roar talks with you. No problem."

"I guess I should probably leave," Bethany said. She peered out the side window. "It got awfully dark outside, didn't it? All that ice and snow."

She was fishing, using the oldest bait in the universe. Fortunately, Pruett, master of the dating game, wasn't easily hooked. He grabbed a flashlight and gestured toward the door. "Don't worry. Perri and I will walk you to your car." He flashed that prize-winning grin. "Guess I could use a little exercise."

* * * *

I could hardly wait to quiz Pruett on Bethany's revelations. Personally, although I distrust all varieties of psychics, her story rang true. Jess Pendrake was a simple soul who could easily be hurt by an attentive male. The dog show world was small enough for gossip to spread like a plague of mange. Jess's heartbreak would be magnified tenfold by the humiliation of knowing that her colleagues were tuned in to her troubles and snickering about them behind her back. Canine disputes were resolved openly, but humans preferred the lingering death by a thousand cuts. *Lingchi*, the ancient Chinese called it.

"Do you believe her?" I asked Pruett.

He sighed and immediately went into cynical investigative reporter mode. "Maybe. I suppose this dog-leasing business could escalate into violence."

"Count on it, especially with a volatile type like Jess. Dogs are her entire life and her livelihood. The betrayal would be enormous."

He squeezed my hand and loped toward Steady Eddie. "Seems easier to just sue the bastard. Murder is messy."

How like Pruett to reduce a complex emotional issue into a tabloid headline. Murder was indeed messy, but lawsuits took an emotional and financial toll.

"Jess is not rich, you know. One of the breeders just paid six thousand dollars in court costs to get back a neglected dog. Jess doesn't have that kind of cash."

He shook his head of raven hair and scoffed. "Wow! That's crazy."

Staring at Pruett temporarily distracted me. *Lord, that man was fine!* I collected my thoughts and got back to business. Discipline before ecstasy. "You're passionate about journalistic integrity, right? Well, for dog people, especially breeders, it's the same thing. That's why I sympathize with Jess, looney as she is."

Pruett nodded absently, as though he were evaluating the case. "Maybe I'll give Roar a call. Who knows if Bethany will chicken out? Homicides make even honest folks do weird things."

He was right about that. Average citizens cringed at the thought of facing the police. Believe it or not, even the normally audacious Babette Croy grew skittish when the cops arrived. Although Roar Jansen could easily charm information out of almost any woman, his partner was another matter indeed. Even the most intrepid soul would clam up if the long arm of Sergeant Watts reached in.

Pruett grabbed his cell phone and dialed Roar's number while I rejoined Babette. I could tell by the way her voice rose that she was jittery and itching to discuss the case.

"Well? What do you think?" she asked. "Do you believe that trollop or not?"

No use in cautioning my pal or pointing out that Bethany was not a hussy. Not really.

"Jess had no love for Lee Holmes. That's for sure. But to be fair, her motive was no stronger than Rafa's." I scanned the room. "Where is he, by the way?"

Babette feigned an interest in the TV guide. "Mark my words, missy. You better keep an eye on Ms. Bethany Zahn if you expect Pruett to keep it in his pants."

I folded my arms and said nothing. That technique always worked with a chatterbox like Babette. This time it took precisely forty seconds for her to crack.

"Okay," she said through gritted teeth. "Rafa took off this afternoon, and I haven't seen him since. Big deal. He doesn't owe me an explanation."

"What about his Airstream? Any signs of life in there?"

She shook her head dolefully. "I took a peek when you guys left, but nothing doing."

"When does he judge?" I grabbed the show program off the coffee table and leafed through it. "Looks like he's free until tomorrow morning. Nine o'clock sharp in Ring Two, unless they cancel the show." We exchanged glances. "Maybe we should join him there. Show him some support."

Babette nodded and linked arms with me. "The power of two. Can't beat it with a stick!"

Chapter 10

The next morning, Mother Nature held sway over all creatures, human and canine alike. Two feet of snow had a dampening effect on the entire Northeast and the show world in particular. After conferring with AKC officials, the sponsoring club officially canceled Wednesday's activities, citing the inability of judges to reach the Big E. That made sense, but with a murderer on the loose, it also added to the frustration. For the sake of propriety and propinquity, Pruett had returned to his hotel room in downtown Springfield the prior evening. I missed him but realized that the decision was sound. Despite Steady Eddie's expanse, three adults, a child, and four dogs were just too tight a squeeze. Besides, like the proverbial letter carrier, neither snow nor sleet would keep him from his appointed rounds. That superduper new Porsche was equipped with every possible amenity, including four-wheel drive and, for all I knew, wings. He had promised to join us for a strategy session before the police arrived, and if I knew my Pruett, nothing, including snow mounds, would deter him.

I bounded out of bed, took a quick shower, and spent a concentrated twenty minutes improving my appearance, or at least trying to. Cosmetics were more in Babette's wheelhouse than mine, but for pride's sake, I applied a dot of concealer, a dab of shadow, and a light coating of apricot lipstick. Fortunately, my one point of glory—my hair—cooperated nicely without too much fuss. I slipped on a pair of warm wool slacks and an emerald twinset, and surveyed the results. Vanity was not one of my failings, but I did offer a silent prayer of thanks for the long, slim legs bestowed upon me by the Creator and the DNA of some unknown ancestor. Babette constantly carped about how unfair clothing designers were to the vertically challenged, but that was one problem I didn't face. She altered every pair of slacks to suit her rather short legs and complained loudly about it.

"They're stumpy, Perri. Admit it. Squat." My pal loomed over me, clutching two steaming mugs of latte. Naturally, she could only loom when I was seated, since five inches in height separated us.

"What are you grumbling about?" I said, even though I had heard this song, with all its verses, many times before.

"My legs. Even though I exercise like a demon, they're still just stumps. Next to you I look dumpy."

No use arguing when the Croy pity party was in full whine. I inhaled that blessed caffeine and let her rant.

When she finally took a breath, I seized my chance. "Big whoop. I stand next to you and look flat-chested," I reminded my pal, acknowledging her bounteous bosom. "Face it. No woman is totally satisfied with her body. Be glad that you're alive and have two healthy legs. Not everyone is that lucky." I hugged her. "Besides, you are beautiful—inside and out—and you know it."

Babette brightened. "You know, I bet even Monique Allaire finds something wrong with herself, and that woman is damn close to perfect. Correction. She is perfect."

Nothing deflated my ego faster than comparisons to Pruett's ex-lover, Monique. In addition to her physical perfection, she was also a successful photojournalist who traveled the world and ran with the jet set. I ruefully acknowledged that brains and beauty were a formidable combination in any woman

Before Babette continued her list of superlatives, I hushed her by putting a finger to my lips. After all, Monique also happened to be Ella's mother. No need to upset the little girl with idle chatter about the woman who virtually ignored her.

That realization and the sudden appearance of Ella won a smile and shrug of resignation from Babette. We both focused on greeting the little girl and gearing up for a canine convenience stop. Boots, caps, gloves, and scarves were assembled, and dogs hitched to leads. "Wagons ho," Babette sang out. "Be careful not to slip on the steps." She couldn't resist taking a furtive peak at Rafa's Airstream, but it was buttoned up tight against the marauding elements.

Mounds of snow made our trek tedious and treacherous. Not for the dogs, of course. Human frailties were on full display, but my boys, Guinnie, and Clara delighted in bounding from drift to drift without the slightest difficulty. Ella tried valiantly to match them until she sank into a snow bank and vanished. Before we reached her, Wing Pruett, her personal superhero, swooped down from nowhere and extricated his child from the snow. When it came to Ella, his senses were always on high alert.

"There she is," her doting daddy said, wiping the snow from her face. His voice was calm, but I sensed incipient panic brewing. Ella hugged her dad and laughed. "Isn't it funny, Daddy? I'm covered in snow. Just like Guinnie."

Crisis averted, our entire tribe trudged back toward Steady Eddie and the promise of warmth and soothing sustenance. On the way, we ran smack into Roar Jansen and his trusty sidekick Genna, decked out in garb that equipped them for whatever the weather gods might decree.

"Join us for some espresso," said Babette ever the perfect hostess. "You'll freeze standing outside."

Roar gave her a dazzling smile, but before he responded, Genna jumped in. "Just had coffee. We're here to see the psychic." Her growl immediately dispelled any semblance of civility and cut straight to the business at hand. Roar shrugged it off by ignoring the entire matter.

"I sure could use some espresso," he said with a grin. "Station-house coffee can't compete with your brew, Mrs. Croy."

Babette tossed her curls and hurled a triumphant smile at Genna. "Coming right up," she chirped. She tugged open the door, and after stamping our boots on the mat, we clambered aboard Steady Eddie.

Roar sighed as he sipped the steaming beverage. When it came to social graces, his technique was world-class. "Perfect. Hits the spot." He seamlessly switched conversational gears and nodded to Pruett. "You were here when Bethany Zahn discussed this Jess Pendrake?"

Babette immediately interjected. "Here? That hussy Bethany practically sat in his lap. I don't know how Perri kept her cool."

Genna curled her lip as she turned my way, confirming my initial reaction that she was a most unpleasant person. Probably besotted with her partner too, although that was certainly understandable.

"Bethany isn't shy. She'll tell you that herself," Pruett said. "I suspect any number of people disliked Lee Holmes. Sounds like he had a talent for making enemies."

Roar's response heightened the tension in the room. "Sounds like maybe you were one of them, huh, Pruett? We really need to talk." He jumped to his feet and grabbed his snow gear. "Later, folks. Come on, Genna."

I bit my tongue to avoid gasping. Roar's words were more warning than casual aside. Without a solid motive, he couldn't really suspect Pruett of murder, but that didn't stop me from worrying. Pruett, on the other hand, seemed more blasé than normal.

"Perri! You in a trance, girl?" Tact wasn't always a strong point with Babette, as she so amply illustrated. "I asked what our next move was."

Guilt made the heat rise in my cheeks. "Sorry. Why don't you and Ella take the dogs over to the agility area? You know they'll be practicing, no matter what."

Babette frowned. "What about you?"

"I plan to actually work. Some customers texted me orders this morning, so it's tag and bag time for this working stiff."

Pruett narrowed his eyes as if he didn't quite buy my story. "I'll join you later, Perri. Who knows? Ella may want to build a snowman."

The little girl's peals of laughter echoed all the way over to the Better Living Center, proving yet again that happiness was a warm puppy and a happy child.

* * * *

Hustle and hard work helped to clear my mind. Lee Holmes had a ton of enemies, most of whom were capable of plunging those shears into his cheating heart. I did a quick mental count of the ones I knew of: Rafa Ramos, Jess Pendrake, Roy Vesco, Whit Wiley, and, of course, Yael Lindsay, the long-suffering spouse. They were probably the tip of a very deadly iceberg. Dog show folks tended to band together against outsiders, especially those wearing a badge. Hard to believe that the oleaginous Lee Holmes had sparked passion in a number of female breasts as well. Ugh! The man was the type who made my skin crawl. I recalled the fracas over him between Bethany and Yael. Roar must have gotten an earful about that already, and it was really none of my concern. Still, old habits die hard, and I had always been taught to do my civic duty. Since Babette was prowling around the agility enclosure, I texted her, mentioning Bethany and her connection to Lee Holmes. If I knew my Babette, she would be on that like a robin after a spring worm. Odds were, she might actually garner some useful information in the process.

Time to stretch my legs and give the pups some exercise. I signaled to Keats and Poe, grabbed my keys, and locked up my store. On the way out, I collided with one of my least favorite customers, Whit Wiley.

"Leaving so soon, Perri?" He flashed his specious smile while deftly avoiding the Malinois. Keats and Poe had never warmed up to Whit, a tribute to their innate sense of taste and his survival instincts.

"Just taking a break. Were you looking for anything special?" My smile was feigned, and he knew it.

Whit shrugged. "Nah. Let me walk out with you. Can't be too careful with a killer on the loose."

"Thanks, but I can take care of myself, and my dogs are great backup. Schutzhund-trained, you know."

He shuddered. "No joke. I was hoping you'd protect me from the killer. Fisticuffs aren't exactly my style, as you can plainly see." He steered me by the elbow as I secured my store and headed for the exit.

"They interviewed Vesco, you know. Read him his Miranda rights, just like on TV." Whit's piggy little eyes glinted with malice.

"Really? What happened?"

He curled his lip in a sneer. "Roy denied everything, of course, and lawyered up. That didn't bother the cops one bit, though. They just plowed right ahead. Even corralled that vixen Kiki. I heard she was yucking it up until that woman detective took her aside. Now that is one frightening female. And I don't mean Kiki."

I grinned. Couldn't help it, didn't try. Fearsome Genna had her uses, and striking fear of the law into a truculent temptress was just her style.

"Does Vesco show any dogs? I haven't seen him around the ring before."

My flesh crawled as Wiley squeezed my arm. "Darling. You always hibernate in that little store of yours, so, of course, you miss everything. Vesco is some kind of mechanic. No, maybe a truck driver. Anyhow, he appears with his big hulk of a dog whenever they have an Am Staff specialty. Won't admit that they're just Pit Bulls with a fancy name. Menacing, I call it. Roy and his dog too. Calls him Brutus, if you can believe it. I doubt that Roy is a Shakespeare aficionado, so you can guess where he got that name."

Although I would never admit it to Wiley, Roy did seem like the pit bull type. Even though handlers and breeders all swore that there was nothing inherently sinister about that or any other breed, I was unconvinced. A vigorous debate on the "nature versus nurture" issue typically ensued with neither side willing to cede ground to the other. Call me a bigot or a coward, but I gave American Staffordshire terriers and their mixes a wide berth whenever possible. Too many sad stories surrounded them.

My patience was wearing thin, so I tried one final maneuver. "Roy seems devoted to Kiki. Their divorce must have hit him hard."

Whit nodded. "Kiki never played the housewife, darling. That one has a yen for excitement, and she's not too choosy about her partners. You can imagine how Yael reacted when that news spread."

"Poor Yael," I said. "Bad enough to lose her husband, but all the unpleasantness too."

Whit stopped short, causing me to stumble into him. "Darling, Yael will be just fine. She planned to unload that parasite anyway. Didn't you know?"

I shook my head.

"Think of the money she would save. Lee ran up bills all over the show circuit. Failed businesses, theft of services—the works." He coughed, a suggestive, delicate sound. "Not to mention the hearts he broke."

That was my cue. Whit was the type who teased out one morsel of information at a time. Indifference was the best strategy to get him talking. I stared straight ahead and stayed silent.

"You really didn't know?" he asked. "I thought everybody on the show circuit kept a running score of Lee's conquests. Frankly, I'm surprised he didn't hit on you too, considering those remarks he made."

I summoned my most innocent smile. "Nope. Not my type."

Whit immediately turned coy. "Oh, I get it. Lee didn't stand a chance against Wing Pruett." He snickered. "Does our sexy psychic know that? I saw her hanging on him this morning. Or maybe she was just predicting his future. He seemed to be enjoying himself, though." I curled my lip, causing Whit to put his hand over his mouth. "Forget I said that, Perri. I'm sure he was just being polite."

I considered using a martial arts move to silence Wiley's malicious tongue forever. Fortunately, self-control is my superpower. Instead of venom, I radiated womanly charm or my best effort at it.

"Who could blame Bethany or any other woman for admiring Pruett? Men need their space, after all. Besides, I thought Bethany was interested in Rafa Ramos."

"Rafa!" Wiley hooted loudly. "Honey, that man could have his pick, but he's all business. Besides he's a family man. Has a brood somewhere in Spain, or so I heard."

My heart sank for poor Babette and another romantic disaster on the horizon. I swiftly changed the subject. "Someone told me that Jess Pendrake had a thing for Lee too." I gave the release signal to Keats and Poe and watched them streak gracefully into the snowy fields like silver bullets.

"Poor Jess," Whit said. "Such a pathetic creature. Even the dogs shy away from that one. Lee must have been desperate. No money or charm, and sex was out of the question. Whatever could he have been thinking?"

On impulse, I turned sharply toward Whit, causing him to slip on the snow. "You were Lee's business partner too, or so I heard."

The reaction was immediate and very instructive. Wiley's expression changed from snarky to wary as he dusted himself off. "You were misinformed, Perri. Better get your facts straight. I'm just helping Yael to tie up loose ends. Nothing more." He checked his watch. "In fact, I'm late for a meeting with her now. Take care of yourself."

He scuttled off toward the Better Living Center without further comment.

Chapter 11

One more surprise awaited me that day. As I sauntered toward the agility ring, Punky flagged me down and beckoned me closer. "I did you a favor today, Perri."

"Really?"

"Yep!" She flashed the impish grin that won her that nickname. "Still need a handler for your pointer?"

I nodded.

"Well, look no more. See that guy over there." She pointed several rows over, where a tall, bespectacled man was lovingly grooming a sizable briard. "That's Alf Walsh, the handler we told you about. Chanticleer, the briard, gave most handlers fits, but Alf has the patience of Job. I swear, the man talks dog better than almost anyone here. I already mentioned your pointer to him."

I put Keats and Poe in a sit/stay and ambled over to introduce myself. Alf was a slightly stooped middle-aged man with a wispy mustache and gentle blue eyes. He greeted me without interrupting his grooming routine.

"Ah, the pointer person," he said. "Lady Guinevere, am I right?"

I nodded, knowing that a true dog person focused on the canine rather than human element. After a brief discussion about Guinnie, Ella, and Pruett, we arranged to meet at Steady Eddie that evening. "It's important for everyone to connect," Alf said. "Otherwise, things can go south fast. Chanticleer here is an example. He's a dog who constantly tests you." Alf gently patted the briard as he spoke. "But the two of us understand each other, don't we, Chanty?"

The briard turned his head, and for a second, I swore that the dog rolled his eyes.

We humans had a far less complicated agenda. We sealed the deal and agreed to meet at eight PM.

* * * *

The moment I reached the trailer, I knew that something was up. Babette bustled about the kitchen, fairly bursting with news. She quickly arranged a spread of tasty edibles on the countertop and poured both of us a glass of wine. Ella settled for cookies dipped in a mug of foamy milk that she shared with Guinnie.

"I had quite the day," Babette said with a superior smirk. "First, Clara and I got a lot of agility practice in. She's a real winner, right, Ella?"

Between sips of milk, the little girl chirped agreement. "You should see her, Ms. Perri."

I downplayed my curiosity, knowing that Babette couldn't wait to spill the beans. "That's nice," I said. "I have news to report too. I think I found just the right handler for Guinnie. He's coming over tonight to meet you and your dad. Okay, Ella?"

Babette lowered her eyes, giving me what I termed her guilty look. "We ran into Pruett, and he said to tell you he'd be late tonight. Might not even make it."

"Okay. No problem." I gave myself a mental shake that dispelled all thoughts of Pruett and Bethany Zahn or any other potential threats. The man was a free agent, able to choose any companion he desired. Desire! Not a word I cared to dwell on when it came to Pruett. Better to focus on dogs and murder. I was on much firmer ground there.

Ella turned on the television and snuggled on the couch with Guinnie, watching Animal Planet. Babette beckoned me closer and lowered her voice. Her smug expression told me that she had gotten a big scoop.

"I really earned my gold detective shield today," she said. "Two words—Bethany Zahn."

"Okay," I dug into my pocket for liver treats and tossed them to the dogs.

My response or lack thereof deflated Babette. I could tell by the way she frowned and puckered her lips. A pouting Babette Croy was a fearsome prospect indeed.

"Cheer up," I said. "Frowning causes wrinkles. You know that."

She tossed artfully highlighted curls. "Pshaw. Honey, with the bucks I spend on Botox, there's no way I'll ever get frown lines. Trust me on that."

I bowed my head, acknowledging defeat. "Okay. Now what's your big scoop?"

Before speaking, Babette nodded toward Ella. "Go wash up before dinner, pumpkin."

As soon as the little girl left, the floodgates opened. "Ms. Z had plenty to say, but I was cagey about it. You know that way I have of getting even a clam to open up."

As difficult as it was to imagine a subtle Babette, I played along. "Nobody does it better. Come on. I'm dying from suspense. Put me out of my misery."

She finally took pity on me. "Chill, why don't you. I'll get there." She rubbed her hands together. "Okay. I really didn't even have to say a thing. The minute I got there, Bethany was all over me like a rash. Wanted every little detail of how you found him. Blood and all. Even the creepy stuff."

That puzzled me. From my limited exposure to Bethany, I pegged her as the sly type who would pick you clean without sharing anything. "Why was she so interested?"

Babette gave me her widest grin, dimples and all. "Exactly what I asked her. You know me. I played it coy."

Silence was often more platinum than golden. I buttoned my lip and nodded.

"Okay. Bethany was real interested in the murder weapon—those poodle shears. Asked everything, including the color and blade size."

I crossed my fingers and made a wish that for once in her well-intentioned life, Babette had not spilled the proverbial beans.

"What did you tell her?"

"That's just it. I told the truth. Naturally, I was willing to lie if necessary, but it wasn't. I said that you and Pruett found the corpse and were too traumatized to say much."

Something didn't register. Babette, major chatterbox, keeping quiet? It didn't compute. "She bought that?" I asked, skepticism radiating from my every pore. Bethany struck me as being one very tough cookie who didn't fool easily.

"Not at first." Another head toss. "But then I mentioned that awful woman cop, and she went ballistic. Seems Sergeant Watts gave her the third degree and really shook the psychic up. Practically accused her of murdering Lee."

"Well, did she?" Sexual jealousy had fueled murders throughout human history. Why not now? Dog show people were no better or worse than the rest of our unlovely species.

Babette's eyes narrowed into slits. "Are you nuts?" she snarled. "Like she would really blurt out a confession to me! I barely know the hussy."

When Babette got into a snit, tact and patience were the only things that worked. I pasted a sweet smile on my face and waited for her to cool down.

"Okay," Babette said, "as you know, Bethany has no love for Yael. She'd probably love to drop a dime on her. But she didn't. Her scoop concerned Rafa."

"Rafa!" Screeching was unbecoming. By an act of will, I kept my voice as monotone as possible. "What'd he do?"

"Apparently he was roaming around the building that night, practically foaming at the mouth. Probably explains why he stood me up." Babette skipped a beat. "He accused Lee of stealing his grooming shears. Said when he got his hands on the thief, those shears would come in handy."

Oops. Threats of mayhem were never a good idea, especially when the intended target ended up dead that same day. "I suppose Bethany shared that with Sergeant Watts?"

"Nope. Dog people band together. No one likes a snitch." She bit her lip, a sure sign that something else was coming up. Something bad.

"Anything else?"

Babette dithered until I seized her by the shoulders.

"Fess up. How bad can it be?"

"Bethany's a known liar, so don't take this seriously." She stifled a cough. "According to her, Pruett ran by at the same time, going toward the fields. The area where you found Lee."

We stared at each other, frozen by implications too hideous to consider. Pruett had left Steady Eddie at least fifteen minutes before I had. He was following leads, not committing murder. I knew that as surely as I knew my own name, but Roar—or, especially, Genna—might see things differently.

Fortunately, Ella and Guinnie bounded just then into the living area, ending that particular conversation. Better to defer action until I had a chance to mull everything over. Besides, in approximately five minutes, we would have a visitor. Knowing Babette, the presence of a male—any male—would keep her fully occupied. When I reminded her, she bustled off to make repairs; hair fluffing and a touch of lipstick were in order.

Alf Walsh was a big hit with all the females in attendance. I explained Pruett's absence and left the rest to the ladies. Guinnie immediately took to him, and Ella delighted in describing in excruciating detail the many attributes of her pet. Babette played hostess, plying our guest with wine and tasty snacks, and eliciting the most critical bit of information he possessed—his marital status.

"Afraid I'm not much of a catch," he said in a soft, southwestern drawl, probably Texas or Oklahoma. "Married and divorced before I finished my first champion."

That drew empathetic sighs from Babette. "Don't feel bad. I just got divorced myself." She tactfully omitted the three deceased spouses who had preceded Carleton Croy. Some men got nervous picturing a widow with a trail of dead husbands, even if those passings were of natural causes and the decedents quite elderly.

After discussing our handling needs, I relaxed, confident that Guinnie and Alf would be a perfect fit. His references included several reputable breeders of standard poodles as well as owners of a number of other Sporting breeds. Pruett would validate those bona fides since he thoroughly scrutinized any being in proximity to Ella. Babette was a much easier sell. She immediately concluded that Alf Walsh was someone of discernment and taste whose company was more than welcome. His appearance was average at best, but Alf possessed the traits she valued most: he was both available and male.

We spent a pleasant hour discussing the ups and downs of the professional handler's life. Alf was conversant with the dog show world and entertained us with carefully edited anecdotes about the canine and human foibles he had encountered. I gave him points for delicacy since he avoided the seamier side of competition. Ella dozed on the couch with Guinnie, but children tended to have exceptional hearing at the most inopportune times.

"You must know Rafa," Babette said. "That's his Airstream next to us."

Alf got a guarded look in his eyes. "Everyone in poodle circles knows Rafa, especially the ladies. Wish I had his way with females."

"I don't know," said I. "Seems like Guinnie and Ella are already on your side."

Alf chuckled. "Just my speed—dogs and kids. But seriously, Rafa is a good guy. Too bad about this trouble with Lee."

Babette leaned toward him and stage-whispered. "We think Rafa is innocent even though we just met him. Perri used to be in the army, and her instincts are right on target."

I hastened to downplay my stint with the military and stressed my strictly amateur status now. "Murder is very bad business for everyone concerned. I didn't know him, but Lee Holmes certainly incited a lot of drama. What was your take on him?"

Alf shook his head. "Not my kind of guy. Some fellows are fine to have a drink with or play cards. Stuff like that. Not Lee. He was either on the scent of some woman or cooking up a get-rich-quick business deal." He took a sip of his wine. "Course, anyone with a lick of sense steered clear of Lee and his schemes. That's where he and Rafa clashed. Lee was touting some high-end supplement guaranteed to make any dog a superstar. Pricey stuff but supposedly safe and effective."

I knew there was more to this story and that it probably had not ended well. Babette couldn't wait to hear the particulars. Her big blue eyes widened as she encouraged Alf.

"And? What happened?"

Alf shook his head and hesitated. "Maybe you should ask Rafa or check the Internet. Plenty of stories out there. I just felt bad for Yael. She's a real lady and didn't deserve that blowback."

I thought I detected a faint blush on Alf's cheeks when he mentioned Yael. Hmm. Seemed like he had a soft spot for the Widow Lindsay after all. I filed that tidbit away for further consideration.

Conversation lagged, and after leaving a contract for Pruett to review, Alf stood up and took his leave.

Babette could barely contain herself. As soon as the door closed, she stood, hands on hips, and pounced. "I liked him. Alf, I mean. Simple guy with no obvious agenda. Kind of attractive, too, in a down-home Texas kind of way. Comforting. Now what do you make of that story about Lee Holmes and Rafa?"

I shrugged. "Who knows? After we take the pups out for a final walk, I plan to hunker down and search the Internet. If Lee Holmes harmed someone's dog with his schemes, that would be more than enough motive for murder."

"It would for me," Babette raised a clenched fist. "If he hurt my Clara, I'd personally kill the bastard and enjoy every minute of it."

* * * *

Pruett went MIA that night. By exercising rigorous discipline, I focused on the task at hand and avoided checking my watch. In the three hours I spent hunched over my computer, I read innumerable harrowing and heartbreaking accounts of contaminated products that injured or killed dogs. More than I could endure. Those tales by bereaved owners tugged at my heartstrings and roused my anger; there were far too many examples of human greed and canine suffering to digest in one sitting. I put my head down on the counter, intent on taking just a quick break. That ended when my iPhone chimed the next morning at seven AM. I rubbed my bleary eyes, turned off the computer screen, and tried mightily to stretch the kinks out of my upper back. I had little to show for my efforts except a galloping case of eyestrain and a stiff neck. Nothing so far had linked Lee Holmes to the corporations involved. That would require even more research.

Babette buzzed in soon after that in full perky mode. I love Babette, but perky was something I found unendurable even when I was alert and at peak performance.

"My goodness, Perri," she chirped. "Just look at you. Rode hard and put away wet, as they say."

My tolerance evaporated quickly. "A gross expression that is unfair to horses. Who says that, anyway? Excuse me for spending the night trying to make some sense of Lee's murder while you snored your way into slumber."

Babette clucked sympathetically. "Touchy, touchy. Let me get you some espresso. That'll revive you." She struck a pose. "Besides, I do not snore."

I refused to be sidetracked. Sulkiness has its comforts, and I cherished them. "Forget it. I have to take the dogs out first."

Babette tugged at the belt on her ruby-red cashmere robe. It was a lovely shade and straight from the racks of Neiman Marcus. She looked like a million bucks, camera-ready and perfectly made-up and coiffed. In that instance, I came close to hating her.

"Better get your snow gear on. We got another six inches of that wet stuff last night, according to the local station." She flipped the kitchen blinds open. "Good thing those plows are up and at 'em already."

Naturally, it never occurred to her to lead the potty patrol. That was a task more suited to a grungy, unkempt menial like yours truly. I took a deep breath and counted to ten. Babette meant no harm, and I knew that. In her world, distasteful tasks were delegated to others, either employees or helpful pals like me.

"No Pruett, I see." She tilted her head like an inquisitive sparrow. I curled my lip in a semi-snarl but was spared from making a response by the appearance of Ella and Guinnie.

"Hi," the little girl said with her irresistible smile. "Don't worry. I can take the pups for their walk, Ms. Perri."

"Hey! Don't take my job away, little girl. We'll both go for a jaunt." Ella's sweet smile instantly raised my guilt level and erased my anger. "Come on. Boots, scarf, hat, and gloves. Then off we go."

Babette flashed a benign grin our way. "Perfect. I'll rustle up breakfast while you do that. How about pancakes and sausage, Ella?"

Even though I knew for a fact that those cakes were prepackaged by Babette's faithful personal chef, I chose not to spoil the illusion. That would be churlish and unworthy of me. Besides, no sense in denting my pal's good mood or spoiling her image. Babette Croy, the Martha Stewart of canine competition, beamed as she sent us on our way.

Our caravan of four dogs and one and one-half humans trudged slowly through the snow toward the field. Correction. The humans trudged, the canines floated over the icy terrain like butterflies, joining an increasing crowd of show-goers with the same agenda. While Ella frolicked with the pups, I tried to process the information I had gathered during my computer search. Such absorption came at a cost, however. When Roar Jansen tapped me on the shoulder, I jumped like a scalded cat.

"Sorry," he said with a sly smile. "You were deep in thought."

He annoyed me, but it was hard to stay angry when a gorgeous guy beamed down at you. I surveyed the terrain, expecting to see his partner the garden gnome glaring at me from the sidelines.

"On your own today?" I asked. "That's unusual."

Roar showed those perfect white teeth again, along with a pair of dimples. "True. Genna decided to do some research at the office." He planted his hands on his hips. "Why? Do I need protection?"

I shook my head. "Not from me, Sergeant. I'm harmless."

"Really? I don't believe that for one minute." Roar stripped off his mittens and reached into his backpack. "Actually, I was hoping to pick your brain. So much noise in the system about Lee Holmes just complicates everything."

"True." I found comfort in a monosyllabic response—saying less, absorbing more.

"Can we go someplace and talk?" Roar's dancing eyes made even that mild request sound salacious. "Today's Thursday. That means I've only got a few more days until this show finishes and all my suspects disperse. I could use some help."

He was right, of course. By Sunday afternoon, the Big E would be a ghost town until the livestock show, the next special event on the calendar, geared up.

"I'm desperate for caffeine," I said. "Let's head back to Steady Eddie and fill up. Right now, I can't string together a coherent sentence."

Roar rolled his eyes. "I was hoping for some privacy, but okay."

"Look. Let me get in gear, and we can go over to my store." I signaled to Ella, and we led the pack back toward espresso heaven. I could have predicted Babette's reaction to our unexpected visitor. She patted her hair and batted her long lashes at Roar as she invited him to breakfast.

"We have plenty," she said with a sly grin. "Pruett never showed last night. You can have his share."

Roar raised his sandy eyebrows but wisely said nothing. Fortunately, Ella was furtively sharing her breakfast with Guinnie and missed the entire exchange. I stayed steadfast and silent. Our only conversation concerned the day's show, prospective judges, and potential competitors. Babette forgot about matchmaking and scrutinized the brochure to verify the ring times for Clara and Guinnie. Thursday was the first official day of the show, and Ella was all atwitter. Babette agreed to reconnoiter with Alf Walsh and to chaperone the proceedings. The glint in her eyes made me think that she had transferred her affections from the elusive Rafa to Alf, at least temporarily.

After breakfast, Roar Jansen followed me and the Malinois into the arena as I unlocked my store and turned on the lights. "Officially we're still closed,"

I said. "Don't answer the door until we have our discussion, or we'll never have any privacy."

"Good. I don't want to share you today." His eyes sparkled with mischief. I ignored the implication and focused on the murder instead. Roar wasn't having it. "Forgive me in advance. This might sound impertinent, but I must ask. Are you and Pruett a couple?"

I shrugged. "I guess you could say that."

Persistence was the trademark of a skilled investigator, and Roar was very good at his job. "Engaged?" He touched my right hand. "Don't see a ring or anything."

I tried mightily to control the flush that stained my cheeks. "I thought you were interested in Lee's murder." For once, I yearned for the mood-killing presence of Sergeant Watts, the perfect antidote to romance.

"I am, Ms. Morgan, but that question was personal. Thought I'd get it out of the way before we started."

"Pruett and I care for each other. No engagement." I channeled the stiff upper lip of Brits everywhere. "There. Did that satisfy your curiosity?"

He flashed those dimples again. "Sure. Means there's still hope for me. You're not a suspect, so there's no conflict of interest. I think we have a lot in common."

I'm no femme fatale. I have few illusions about my charms. Roar Jansen probably made those moves on every reasonably attractive female he encountered. Trouble was, shopworn or not, those smooth lines worked. I stayed strong, resisting the impulse to smooth my hair, dab on lipstick, or stutter like a schoolgirl.

"Back to business, Sergeant. From what I've gathered, Lee Holmes was a thoroughly despicable character, what they used to call a cad. Cheated on his wife enraged his business partners, and disappointed just about everyone he had anything to do with. That leaves a field of suspects a mile wide."

"Popular with the ladies, though." Roar raised his eyebrows. "Regular Don Juan, so I hear."

It took one to know one, but I restrained myself. "Somehow I don't think this has anything to do with sex. Lots of people on the show circuit screw around. Too many lonely nights and enough alcohol to tempt a saint. Leads to bad judgment, sometimes a fistfight or two. But murder? Not likely."

Roar folded his arms. "Okay. Help me out. What made someone plunge those pretty pink shears into Lee's aorta? Killer made sure that boy was good and dead. Feels very personal to me."

"Any luck with Roy Vesco?"

He shook his head. "Nah. Said he had an alibi, so Genna checked it out. Not airtight but good enough for now."

The next question was delicate. That didn't stop me, but at least I recognized the danger. "And Kiki? Women can be dangerous too. All those hormones surging."

Roar ran his fingers through sun-kissed strands of hair. "Glad you said it, not me. Don't want to be accused of sexism. Department frowns on it, you know."

"Well?" I recognized evasion when I heard it.

"Kiki swore that Lee never touched her." Roar laughed and leaned back against the wall. "Seemed kind of put out about that too. Personally, I think that girl is all talk. Probably still saving it for Roy."

Having seen Kiki in action, I was confident that her untouched status was subject to change at any moment. I mentioned my research into dog deaths and faulty products. "Lee fronted for several businesses. Maybe one of them was involved. Check out the comments online. Heartbreaking."

His eyes turned flinty. "Guess we've gone full circle then. Lee's partner in one of those dirty little schemes was none other than your friend Rafa Ramos, and your boyfriend was tracking them down for his exposé. Mighty suspicious."

"True. But there were others involved, plus those who lost their pets. It's hard sometimes for people to realize how attached someone gets to a companion animal. They mean as much as human family members, or more."

For a moment, Roar lost focus. He gulped, stared into space, and said nothing. "Believe it or not, I get it. Dogs have always meant a lot to me." He reached into his pocket and retrieved a printout. "Here. Check this out. Le Chien Champ. Some very interesting names involved. You might even recognize a few."

He held my hand just a touch too long, prompting me to pull away. "You married, Roar?"

"Nope. Not anymore. Doesn't mean I'm not looking, though."

"Keep looking," I said. "Knock yourself out. Don't let me stop you. Meanwhile, I'll focus on this Le Chien business. You wouldn't mention it if it weren't important." I was confident that Roar had a definite plan in mind and was probably using me as a stalking horse. Most women would fall all over themselves to help this cop cutie. Too bad I wasn't one of them. My heart was bulletproof, diamond-hard, and out of reach. A super journalist named Pruett held the only key.

"Tell me. Does Sergeant Watts approve of this?" I asked. "Involving civilians in your business?"

Roar shrugged. "Does Wing Pruett?"

Touché. I thought of several snarky replies but refrained from playing Roar's game. "Any luck questioning Jess Pendrake?"

He laughed out loud. "Luckily, Genna took on that chore. I understand they had quite a tussle. Nothing physical, thank goodness."

I would have spent my last dime to witness that scene. Considering the opponents, it was impossible to predict the victor. Personally, my money was on the redoubtable Sergeant Watts.

"Well? What did she find out?" I watched Roar closely, waiting for a reaction.

Roar gave an ambiguous shrug that could have meant almost anything. "Ms. Pendrake has quite a temper. Seems once she got started, Genna could barely shut her up. She painted Lee Holmes as a cross between a hyena and a vulture. Very vivid."

I gave that some thought. Jess's hatred for Lee had been fueled by personal betrayal, but the abuse of her dog probably propelled her over the line into crazy land. I had seen her around animals and never questioned for one moment the bond she felt with them. It was real and enduring. Lee or anyone else who threatened it would do so at their own peril.

"I'll read this stuff and talk to some of the crowd," I told Roar. "Bad news spreads fast, and if Lee was involved in selling shady products, someone will know it. His amorous adventures were no secret either, even from his wife." Despite the trail of frustrated females Lee left in his wake, I had the very strong feeling that the murder had nothing to do with sex. Most exhibitors were philosophical about human frailties and saved their passion for the show ring.

"Just one more thing I forgot to mention. Someone told me Wing Pruett was in the area before you found Lee's body. Any truth to that?"

"Pruett? He only met Lee Holmes that night." I shook my head. "You're going to have to dig a lot harder for a suspect."

Roar winked and gathered up his outdoor gear. "Wonder why he was in Springfield two days ahead of you. Great city, but kind of an odd coincidence. I'm counting on you, Persephone. I'm a very persistent man when I want something. Remember that."

Very few people knew my formal name, and even fewer used it. That meant that Sergeant Roar Jansen had been checking up on me. Was it personal interest or just sound police work? Either way, I could live with it.

Chapter 12

"Open up, Perri. This is an emergency." That desperate plea sounded suspiciously like my pal and constant headache, Babette. When she hit panic mode, ignoring her was out of the question. It simply didn't work. Roar sighed as I bowed to the inevitable and unlatched the door. Babette, Clara, Ella, and Guinnie immediately bolted into Creature Comforts in a panic.

"Guinnie's show lead is missing," Ella sobbed. "She'll lose her chance."

If only all problems were that easy to correct. I led Ella to the selection of custom show leads, and after much discussion, she chose a vibrant red that contrasted nicely with Guinnie's coat.

Meanwhile, Babette had cornered Roar and was quizzing him on Lord knows what. I suspected—no, I feared—that she was asking him his intentions toward me. When Babette trotted out her heavy artillery, anything was possible. Fortunately, time was on my side. Guinnie's appearance in the ring was scheduled for ten AM, and Ella was anxious. The little girl jumped from one foot to another in a frenzied dance that Babette either ignored or didn't see. "Please, Ms. Babette," she pleaded. "We'll be late."

"Check your watch," I told my pal. "Guinnie's ring time is coming up, and you have to find Alf Walsh and get his arm band. Better shove off."

Babette groaned and finally gave up. Meanwhile, Roar took his cue and escaped while the coast was clear.

"Check back with you later," he told me. "Don't let me down."

"What's he talking about?" Babette asked. "Don't freeze me out of this. We're partners."

"Later," I said.

I sent her and Ella off while I attended to some anxious customers with cash in hand. One of them just happened to be that sultry psychic, Bethany Zahn.

Had she spent last night with Pruett? I refused to even consider the possibility. Better to focus on the task at hand: tracing Lee Holmes's business dealings.

Bethany looked especially toothsome in a bold yellow shift with strategically placed cutouts. In comparison, I felt dowdy and drab, a poor contender in the race for male affection. Her high spirits made mine plummet to the basement, but I refused to question her activities. After all, Pruett was a very big boy with his own agenda. I was neither strumpet nor sexpot. Any man worth his salt would know and appreciate that.

Bethany stretched in a feline gesture that spoke more eloquently than words. "Perri, I've got to hand it to you, girl. Keeping Wing Pruett in line must be a full-time job."

I busied myself by sorting the woven leather leads by size and color. If Bethany were really a psychic, there was no need for me to tell her my thoughts. None at all.

"Let me ask you something," I said. "Ever hear of an outfit called Le Chien Champ?"

Bethany got full marks for poise. She furrowed her brow as if she were really trying to help. I got the distinct impression, however, that Ms. Zahn knew something and wasn't inclined to spill the beans, at least not to me. She might react differently if Roar Jansen posed the question. Men seemed to activate her psychic powers more than mere females ever could. Sergeant Watts was another story entirely. She was fully capable of scaring information out of any recalcitrant subject. Come to think of it, she even made me shiver.

"Oh, yeah. I remember now." Bethany projected faux innocence and synthetic charm. "Somebody was hawking that Le Chien Champ stuff a while back. Expensive, though. Too rich for my blood." She edged toward the door, but I placed my hand on her shoulder.

"Hold on. Who promoted that product? It's important, Bethany. Think."

She pulled away but managed one parting shot. "I keep information to myself, Perri. A girl never knows when it could pay off for her. It just so happens that I hear stuff. I keep my eyes open."

I stepped in front of the door to bar her path. "Please listen. If you know anything, go to the police. Sergeant Jansen. He'll help you. It's too dangerous to screw around with a murderer."

Bethany didn't listen. In fact, she scoffed at me. "Listen here, Goody Two-shoes. People confide in me, especially men. They think I'm sympathetic." She grinned. "Most of them underestimate me too. Think I'm stupid or something. But that's their mistake." She reached around me and grasped the door handle. "Try it sometime, or maybe you should ask your boyfriend. He knows all about that and plenty of other things too."

I asked the question I most feared. "You've said that Pruett was hanging around the murder scene last night. Do you know something for sure, or are you just talking?"

She threw her head back and stretched like a particularly smug feline. "Makes you wonder, doesn't it?"

* * * *

The rest of my morning passed in a blur of eager customers with their eyes on the prize. Professional handlers were philosophical, but owners and pet parents could match the intensity of any Little League or stage parent. They showed their commitment by indiscriminately scarfing up dog treats, toys, collars, and leashes for their beloved charges. Not a bad thing at all. I welcomed all purchases, whether celebratory tributes or consolation prizes.

When Babette and Ella returned, I could read by their expression that all was well. Guinnie had won among champions of her breed and was headed for the Sporting Group competition. If she prevailed there, it was on to the Best in Show. Ella's sweet face was wreathed in smiles, but Babette's grin was even more ecstatic.

"Alf was terrific," she gushed. "Total professional. You were right, Perri. I know you tried hard, but Guinnie never looked so good. You'd think they'd been together since she was a pup."

"I assume she faced stiff competition," I said. "Yael and Whit Wiley were in the mix."

Babette dismissed them with a wave. "Eh! They weren't even close. Guinnie got five Grand Champion points today, didn't she, sugar?"

Ella hugged her pet and nodded. Flushed with victory, Babette agreed to staff my store while I did a spot of detecting. Although her sales skills were deficient, Babette had an uncanny ability to dredge up information from anyone who walked into the store. It wasn't guile—she was truly interested in them and their adventures. That suited me just fine because Rafa Ramos was assigned to judge poodles in Ring One, and I would be watching from the sidelines.

Ring One was on the other side of the pavilion. That meant I had to dodge dogs, carts, sightseers, and handlers in order to be on time and snag a good seat. Poodles were popular and always drew a sizable crowd of onlookers. Good seats were at a premium, and benches filled up fast. Show veterans usually brought their own chairs, but I was focused and fleet of foot. I zeroed in on an empty bench space and immediately claimed it.

Rafa stood at the judging table, carefully studying his notes. I'd never seen him wear a suit before, and I must admit that he looked as slick as the creatures he would soon judge. No wonder Babette was entranced by him—Rafa could easily pose for *GQ* or some other men's fashion magazine. His raven hair fell in soft curls past his collar, and those brawny arms were contained in a form-fitting navy suit with rep tie. Nothing to complain about there. Not one thing.

As the first entrants claimed the ring, Rafa gave each handler his undivided attention. The familiar ritual of circling the ring and standing for examination lulled me into a type of stupor. That ended abruptly when a pair of hands encircled my neck and Pruett whispered into my ear. "How goes it, Ms. Morgan? Missed you last night."

I patted the empty space next to me. "Have a seat. You must be tired. Word is you were a busy boy last night."

Pruett grinned. "Now, what little birdie told you that, I wonder?" He put his hands into his pockets and stretched out his long legs. "Journalism demands so much, Perri. It's a cruel master."

"Or mistress," I said with attitude. "No big deal. Word gets out in the dog world, especially when a superstar prowls around." I hunkered down, watching Rafa as he led the handlers through their paces. The guy knew what he was doing, and the competitors did as well. One of the handlers with an eye-catching apricot poodle was a lithe woman in her early twenties. Both she and her client moved seamlessly about the ring displaying rhythm and a good deal of leg. That duo was fine, but I would have chosen another entrant, a majestic chocolate poodle handled by an older woman. Would Rafa be swayed by appearance? To his credit, the honors went to the chocolate poodle.

"Can you imagine?" a voice snarled. "Giving that grotesque creature any kind of recognition—it's criminal. Rafa must be blind."

I knew immediately that Whit Wiley was on the scene. He wedged himself between Pruett and me and continued his diatribe. "Presentation is everything at a dog show, don't you know. After all, he's not judging hogs at the county fair."

For once, Pruett was speechless. I, however, was not. "Funny thing, Whit. I thought this was a dog show, not the Miss America pageant. The dog, not the handler, was the winner."

Wiley ignored my comment. "No wonder Rafa and Lee Holmes sparred all the time. Lee certainly sought out lookers—human and canine."

I heard opportunity knock and decided to answer. "Hey. What about this supplement business Lee had? Le Chien Champ, I think they called it. Pretty dicey, huh?"

Whit brushed aside my comment as if it were lint. "Yesterday's news, darling. Just another of Lee's pipe dreams. That man had a different get-rich scheme every day." Whit snickered. "The only one that worked was marrying a wealthy woman, and even that wouldn't have lasted much longer. Of course, I did hear there were some unhappy customers." He left the thought unfinished and smirked.

Pruett ended his silence by edging into the conversation. "He must have signed a prenuptial agreement. Pretty standard when big bucks are involved. Still, you can bet he'd come out of it with something worthwhile."

Whit, sultan of snide, happily spread his poison. "I suppose you'll insist on that when you get married, Mr. Pruett. Better beware, Perri."

Pruett tensed, but his reply was silky smooth as he squeezed my shoulder. "When you find the right woman, money doesn't matter much. It's fairly low on my list."

To my chagrin, I blushed—full-body action. Pruett and I had never once discussed marriage or even promised exclusivity. I'd pushed all thoughts of it from my mind, knowing how fragile my emotions were. Truth was, I cared for Pruett more than any woman should ever admit. After losing Pip to cancer, I had deliberately focused on work and avoided all romantic attachments, fearing that another calamity would break my heart. Enter Wing Pruett, babe magnet with a tender side. Add an endearing moppet named Ella and I was hooked. I vowed to treasure every day and let the chips fall. Couldn't predict the outcome and refused to try.

Despite the personal drama unfolding at our bench, Rafa continued the seamless rhythm of the dog show routine. Ribbons were awarded, handlers were commended, and the final cut among the all classes of poodles was made. My personal favorite—Ethan, the chocolate male—was awarded Best of Breed and advanced to the Non-sporting Group finals. Afterward, Rafa was mobbed by a group of mostly female admirers, chatting or asking advice. Pruett squeezed my hand and said, "Well, will you look at that. Rafa scores with all the ladies."

Considering that the Spaniard oozed virility from virtually every pore, that was hardly surprising. Dog show denizens were so accustomed to evaluating breeding stock that sex among all species was par for the course and no big deal. Based on physical prowess, beauty, and grace, Rafa Ramos made the grade as a top stud choice. Best in show, for sure.

"Well, looky there," Whit pointed toward the scrum. "The long claw of the law reaches out and finds a victim."

To my amazement, Genna Watts barreled her way into the crowd and singled Rafa out. One look at her face confirmed just how much she differed from others in the adoring throng. This was no fan girl—no, siree. Genna was clearly there on police business.

"Oops," Whit said. "Looks like Rafa may finally pay the piper. Wonder what that's all about." He rose and sidled over toward the show ring, getting as close as he dared to Rafa and Genna.

Whit Wiley was an affront to all vertebrates. I envisioned him slithering around the Garden of Eden, a serpent seeking gullible victims and causing the fall of humankind. In this instance, his plan was foiled by Genna's curled lip and gruff comment. Whit slunk off to the sidelines double quick, but Rafa kept his emotions in check. He finished his paperwork and calmly followed the sergeant out of the ring toward the exit.

"That Wiley is really something," Pruett said. "No surprise if he turns up with shears in his back." He squeezed my hand and looked toward the opposite side of the arena. "See you later. Gotta follow a lead." Pruett slid out of his seat and followed the party out the door. I made no attempt to join in or to question him on his whereabouts last evening. Instead, I corralled Punky West and her posse as they led their dogs from the show ring.

"Nice job today," I said. "Your dog must almost be finished. Another champion under your belt. Pretty sweet!"

Punky gave me her aw-shucks routine, but I knew how much success meant to her. Breeder-owner-handler was a tough proposition that yielded more pain than pleasure and deserved praise when it was warranted.

"You know, Perri, the moment that pup was whelped, I knew he'd be a star. Warms the heart, don't it?" Punky tossed her mop of curls and grinned.

I agreed and upped the ante. "Hey, you did me a solid by recommending Alf Walsh. Ella loves him, and Babette sings his praises. Nice guy."

"Lots of good handlers around," Punky said, "but not that many nice guys. You know, Alf sobbed like a child when that client of his died. The dog, not the owner."

I nodded and broached a more sensitive subject. "Listen, Punky, I need your help. What do you know about this Le Chien Champ business? The cops have been crawling all over asking about it."

Punky motioned toward the exit. "Come outside with me while I have a smoke." She wagged her finger my way before I said a word. "I know. Cigarettes will kill me some day. Heard it all before. Save the sermon."

I had enough of my own vices to sort out without lecturing others. Judge not; don't cast the first stone—a mantra to live by. Hectoring others was simply not my thing, but I didn't mind ribbing my pal. "I heard smoking gives you wrinkles, Punky. Better watch out, or you'll lose your edge with the guys."

She swatted my behind with her purse. "Honey. After four husbands, that's the least of my worries. Come over by that tree. The snow's so deep I can bury the cancer sticks afterward."

We trudged through the snow, avoiding the shoveled area where dogs and handlers congregated. Punky pulled out a wrinkled pack of Winstons, lit one, and inhaled deeply. "Lord, that tastes so good! Now, what about that Le Chien Champ stuff interests you? Pure garbage, if you ask me. Another of Lee's scams. I never got involved, even though he offered all sorts of perks. Wanted to recruit breeders. You know the drill."

Since Punky was a keen observer who could spot a phony a mile off, I opted for truth or a reasonable facsimile of it. "I read up on it, and the articles said some dogs died from whatever was in it. Sounds like a motive for murder, if you ask me."

She smoked silently for a bit before answering. "Are you on the case or something, Perri?"

"Not really. Roar Jansen asked for my help, and I agreed to try."

Punky puckered up her lips and gave me a wry smile. "You hit the daily double man-wise, didn't you, hon? The cop and the writer! I saw that dreamboat of yours a while ago on the scent too. You guys teaming up for good or what?"

I shook my head. "Who, Pruett?" I turned aside to avoid blushing. "Nothing new on that front."

Punky inhaled the last bit of nicotine and doused the butt in the snow. "Some people on the circuit tried that Le Chien stuff. Lee was giving away free samples at all the big shows. Bragging about it—well, you know, he was good at that. Not much else unless you count screwing."

I took a deep breath to avoid reacting. "Punky! You too?"

She snorted. "Damn straight. It gets lonely going from one cheap motel to another. Lee was a loser at most things, but damn, girl, he knew his way around women. Besides, not everyone hooks a stud like your Pruett."

"But Yael . . ."

"Phooey." Punky lit another Winston. "That woman gave up on him long ago. She mopped up after his business screwups and kept a brave face, but honestly, after five years with Lee, I don't think she gave a damn about him. Could you blame her?"

I was no expert on husbands, but infidelity still shocked me. "Why stay with him then?"

"Some women just want a warm body around," Punky shrugged. "Word was she planned to dump him anyway. Stick with dogs, I say. Much better companions. More loyal too."

Our chat was interrupted by a canine crisis. A handler leading a Newfoundland named Kirk slipped in the snow and went down for the count. Newfies are friendly souls geared to help others. This strapping fellow immediately plopped all two hundred pounds of himself on his handler and commenced licking her face. Punky and I rushed over to join several others in extricating the young woman from her furry friend. Fortunately, all was well with both the handler and her helpful charge. Kirk received plenty of praise and liver treats for his altruism, while his handler received pats on the back and pledges of help.

Until we had hauled the Newfie off her, I failed to recognize the lissome form of Kiki Vesco. Despite the winter cold and the problems of dog drool, she had opted for fashion first. She wore a micro-mini, fishnet hose, and thigh-high boots with a two-inch heel. Charity was a virtue that temporarily deserted me. No wonder the little chit fell—no sane person wears heels in the dog ring, let alone on icy terrain.

"Better get you some sensible shoes, Kiki." Punky summoned her most maternal tone. "You can't show dogs with a broken ankle."

Kiki curled her lip. "Thanks for the advice. I figured that out myself."

Punky ignored the snark, checked her watch, and sped back to the Better Living Center. I chose to seize the moment.

"You must be devastated, Kiki," I said. "I'm so sorry."

She raised her eyebrows. "Huh?"

"About Lee's death, I mean. You two were close; at least, I heard that you were." I kept my eyes downcast to hide my true motive.

Kiki hid her face by hugging Kirk's vast neck. "Listen here. I barely knew him. I already told the cops that. Bug off, lady, or I'll tell Roy."

This time, I stared unblinkingly at Kiki's sullen face. "And then what? Are you threatening me? I'm not afraid of you or your ex-husband."

She clenched her fists, tightening the lead until poor Kirk yelped. I stepped back, expecting a physical assault. Instead, Kiki Vesco morphed back into normalcy and stamped her foot.

"Leave me alone," she said. "Just leave me alone." She turned around and trotted, slipping and sliding, toward the entryway with Kirk lumbering at her side.

I followed, still ruminating over Punky's final comments. When I'd asked straight out who her candidate for the murderer was, Punky demurred. "Damned if I know," she said. "Plenty of candidates for murder *victim* around here. Jess, Bethany, and that creepy Whit Wiley—hell! I wouldn't mind knocking off any of them myself. But killers—I just don't know. Most of us take out our hostility in the ring."

She made a valid point. Handlers, owners, and breeders were a relatively close group thrown together in small-town venues nationwide. Left unchecked, the usual emotions of jealousy, passion, and hatred had plenty of time to marinate into a murderous stew. The hijinks of an unscrupulous man like Lee Holmes could easily stir the pot and make it boil over.

Chapter 13

Lunch was a feast that featured tasty comestibles for all palates. Pruett broke the bank with a vast selection suited to vegetarians and meat eaters alike.

"Wow," Babette said as she inhaled a sizable portion of dim sum. "Remind me to send you out again. You're a mealtime wonder."

Ella beamed proudly. "My dad does takeout better than anyone."

What an innocent child she was. Little did she know! Her dad did many things—some of them quite private—better than anyone. I smiled recalling the lines of a song that said just that about a certain British spy.

"Perri! Hello in there." As usual Babette saw right through me. "You do a lot of dreaming for a business owner. You'll never guess who came into your store."

I know the best weapon against Babette. I folded my arms and patiently waited in utter silence.

Pruett broke the stalemate. "I, for one, can't wait to hear, Babette."

It didn't take much encouragement for Babette to spill whatever she knew. One look at Pruett's handsome mug turned her into a pile of mush.

"I'm glad someone appreciates me," she said. "Thank you, Wing. The customer in question was none other than Roy Vesco." She smirked. "Got your attention, didn't I? Now you're really interested."

Pruett clapped his hands, giving Babette the applause she craved. "Tell us."

"Well...Roy needed some kind of collar—I don't know the type—but he did. Seems that ugly-lookin' pit bull of his chewed one up. Probably aiming for the show rep instead."

There was more to this story. I knew that with patience and fortitude it would all emerge.

"Anyhow, Roy and I started talking. He's really a pretty nice guy, you know. Misunderstood. Anyhow, he said the cops grilled him like a porterhouse steak."

"Genna, again?"

Babette shook her head. "Nope. This time gorgeous Roar let loose. Anyhow, Kiki and Roy had a rock-solid alibi for the night Lee Holmes bought it."

I leaned in. "Really?"

After much posturing and teasing, Babette finally relented. "Yep. They spent two hours with the cops taking anger management class. Seems someone reported that little dustup with Lee Holmes, and this was their way out. Roy was boiling mad, I can tell you."

I gave that some thought. Vesco hardly qualified as a mastermind. That didn't mean he wouldn't stick a pair of shears into somebody if provoked. In fact, it was precisely the type of impetuous action that fit a hothead like him to perfection.

Babette gave me the stink eye. "He's really a nice guy, Perri, even if he drags that pit bull around with him everywhere. He's got his own business and does quite well. Kiki is wife number two, by the way."

"What happened to his first wife?" Pruett asked.

"Dumped him for a computer nerd. Told Roy she was trying to improve her mind by taking night courses. Huh!"

I rewarded Babette by trading information about Rafa and his encounter with the redoubtable Sergeant Watts. Before she could interrogate me or share her opinions, a glut of customers transformed me from Nancy Drew into Susie Saleswoman. Pruett, Babette, and Ella quickly vanished, leaving me with my boon companions, the doggy duo of Keats and Poe. After the crowd dissipated, I leafed idly through the sheaf of circulars on my counter and got a surprise. At six PM that very evening, the show organizers planned a tribute and memorial service for Lee Holmes. All exhibitors and vendors were invited to attend, and refreshments would be provided. Talk about kismet.

As fate would have it, I attended Lee's memorial alone. Babette sent me a mysterious text urging me to go without her because she had plans. Meeting a friend—or so she said. The smug emoji accompanying it convinced me this *friend* was definitely male. Meanwhile, Pruett joined the text parade by notifying me that Ella, Guinnie, and he had gone for an extended hike and would probably catch dinner at Ella's other favorite spot, Applebee's. I didn't mind being abandoned; in fact, it was liberating. It freed me to join the throng at Lee Holmes's memorial event without constraints. Lacking Babette's well-intentioned interference, I felt more empowered than I had since leaving Great Marsh. Who knew? If Roar Jansen put in an appearance without his trusty watchdog, Genna, I might throw caution to the winds and flirt shamelessly with him.

I sped back to Steady Eddie, fed and crated my dogs, and sharpened my female wiles. Nothing too dramatic—just a touch of makeup, a spritz of perfume, and a thorough grooming of my hair. I chose somber clothing in deference to the occasion and because it suited my mood and pocketbook. Babette's wardrobe rivaled the holdings of a mid-size specialty store, but mine was far more limited. Happily, black was one color that made me feel feminine and a bit sultry in a modest leathersmithy way. That prompted a pep talk guaranteed to buoy my spirits. After all, I wasn't married, engaged, or even promised to Pruett. Men still gave me the eye on occasion. I studied my reflection in the mirror and told myself that, at thirty years old, Persephone Morgan was still a catch. Too bad I had the right bait but zero interest in catching anyone.

Self-pity was pathetic in and of itself and so unlike a bold former squad leader and leathersmith. I shed my insecurities like my dogs did excess water. The game was definitely afoot tonight, and I planned to take full advantage of it. I trooped into the Better Living Center, merging with a stream of fellow dog enthusiasts. There was a certain irony in the building's title, considering that, at least for the deceased, better living was no longer even a possibility. A modest crowd gathered in the main showroom to commemorate Lee Holmes or pretend to. Sorrow was kept to a minimum, and most guests seemed either impassive or nonchalant. Some hardly knew Lee but appreciated free booze, food, and temporary escape from the tedium of show life. Others probably attended out of respect for Yael. The third group, in which I included myself, had mixed motives.

I scrutinized those in attendance, noting Yael's tight-lipped smile, Whit Wiley's contemptuous grin, and Bethany Zahn's very noticeable cleavage. Jess Pendrake was nowhere to be seen, but to my surprise both Rafa and Alf Walsh were present, lurking around the fringes of the room and trying to look inconspicuous. Neither had been a fan of the deceased, but their somber expressions and subdued clothing allowed them to blend seamlessly into the crowd. Immediately before the official starting time, Babette waltzed in arm and arm with her "friends." A murmur spread through the crowd as Roy and Kiki Vesco took their place in the second row. I blinked at the duo, marveling at the transformation in the Vesco clan. Roy had traded his polyester gear for a handsome linen shirt and black denim jeans. True, he still clung to some of his old ways. Wearing a string tie was a debatable fashion choice, but in Roy's case it was forgivable and the least of several possible fashion faux pas. Most of my attention was focused on his companion. With her face scrubbed free of makeup and that perpetual pout, Kiki resembled an ingénue rather than a harlot. Even her tattoos had been removed or were hidden by the long-sleeved shirt and dark slacks she wore. Score one for Babette. Her talent for scene setting and staging was clearly on display, and it worked like a charm. Both Roy and Kiki vaulted up the social scale from oddball to normal.

Babette gave me the royal wave and busied herself by whispering something to Roy. Whatever she said had impact: the tips of his ears grew cherry red, and the poor fellow ducked his head. Kiki ignored the rest of us and studied the pair with undisguised interest. Looking innocent and being virtuous were two very different things.

Promptly at six PM, the AKC rep called us to attention. He listed all of Yael's many contributions to the dog world and briefly referenced Lee's enthusiasm, energy, and spirit. No mention of friends or good deeds. This crowd knew way too much for that. Frankly, as the man droned on, I zoned out. My mind was cluttered with the image of those pretty pink shears protruding from Lee Holmes's bloody back. Unlike other murder methods, stabbing was a full-contact sport that was oddly personal. I'd seen my share of gore during the war, and it wasn't pretty. If poison was a female thing, knife wounds skewed more to the male side. I stopped and gave myself a mental shake. How incredibly sexist of me to hew to the old social conventions! Plenty of women were strong and fit, fully capable of dispatching a man with those lethal shears. Jess Pendrake, for one. I'd felt her wiry strength when she grabbed my arm the other day. That chick had major muscles.

"Penny for your thoughts." A pleasant baritone rang in my ear.

I met the soulful gaze of Roar Jansen. "Penny doesn't get you much these days, you know. You have to up the ante, Sergeant."

He dazzled me with his pearly whites. "On a cop's salary, that's about all I can afford." In deference to the occasion, he also chose to wear black. The Jansen version was leather—from head to toe. It leant a rakish air to a man who needed very little adornment to up his sex appeal. In self-defense, I kept my eyes firmly fixed on his face to avoid even the hint of temptation.

I quickly scanned the arena for any sign of trouble. No sense incurring the wrath of Genna. "Here all alone, are you? No one to safeguard your virtue?"

Another grin from Roar. "I could ask you the same thing, Ms. Persephone."

I threw him my steely, stony stare and paraphrased Shakespeare. "I'm here to bury Lee Holmes, not to praise him. After all, he was a colleague of sorts."

Roar threw back his head and laughed. Actually, he guffawed. "You slay me, Leather Lady. Peddle that line of bull to someone else, why don't you? Now let's cut to the chase. Tell me everything you know or suspect. I'm a colleague of sorts too."

He had a point, even though I hated to admit it. I had no official standing whatsoever and no close connection to the victim. Truth be told, I didn't even like him. In my opinion, his wife was no prize package either. Yael was one of those entitled plutocrats who automatically assumed she had a right to anything her little heart desired. She viewed the rest of the earth as a vast wilderness populated by serfs, like me, born to service their betters. A harsh but fairly accurate assessment. Despite all that, I felt a strange surge of sympathy for the woman. Men were a tricky proposition at the best of times, but a cheating, conniving spouse like Lee Holmes was downright lethal. If Yael had dispatched her slimy spouse, a panel of jurors might just vindicate her—assuming they were female, of course.

"Guess I'm losing my touch," Roar said with a self-deprecating grin. That maneuver, accompanied by a show of fetching dimples, probably scored big-time with anyone even remotely female. Pruett had a few moves like that to unleash on his credulous fans, and they tended to work well. I let the nonsense sail right over my head, without moving a muscle, and beckoned to Roar, pointing to an empty bench near Ring Two. No sense in spilling my secrets to the entire show world. Besides, I really hadn't made much progress. Roar remained impassive as I listed the major points: the harmful Le Chien supplement and its effects, romantic entanglements, and the nefarious double-dealing that characterized Lee Holmes's life. There were motives aplenty but few suspects and even less evidence.

When I concluded, Roar flexed his hands and sighed. "Not much to go on, I'm afraid. You only confirmed what we already knew. Lee Holmes was a sleaze that nobody liked and some actively hated. Big deal. The same goes for half the politicians in this country and most of the news media." He showed those dimples again. "Sorry, Perri. I don't see where that helps us much. Naturally, Genna and I both appreciate your efforts."

He was right, of course, but that didn't mean I had to like it. My pride suffered an unexpected blow. Roar showed no respect at all for my investigative skills or instincts and regarded me as some sort of bumbling amateur. I vowed to prove him wrong.

"There might be another piece to the puzzle," I said. "Nothing definite."

Roar folded his arms. "Come on. Share. What are partners for? I don't suppose it concerns Pruett, does it? He's been nosing around this case since the get-go."

"Why in the world would a world-class journalist get involved with a small-timer like Lee Holmes? Where's your motive, Sergeant?"

"You tell me. You have the inside track on him."

Smug men push every one of my buttons. I decided to investigate further before spilling anything, despite the winsome ways of Sergeant Roar Jansen. Did he really suspect Pruett of the murder, or was it simply another ploy? As soon as I ridded myself of his company, I planned to follow up on Bethany's hints. The woman knew something, and I meant to extract that information from her by whatever means were necessary. I glanced over toward the center of the ring, keeping an eagle eye on the psychic in question. Despite the solemnity of the occasion, Bethany had no problem whispering, flirting, and flashing cleavage at anything remotely male that crossed her path. Small wonder that Pruett and a certain hot cop enjoyed her company. To my chagrin, instead of waiting for a decent interval, she flounced out the exit to the restroom area as soon as the speeches concluded and the liquor started flowing. That behavior was odd and completely atypical for the Bethany I knew. She could belly up to the bar with the best of them and usually did so, particularly when somebody else paid the freight.

Roar fiddled with his keys as he waited for my answer. The boy had patience, I'll give him that. Fortunately, my salvation came in the curvaceous form of Babette Croy. My pal, accompanied by Kiki and Roy, sidled up to me and poured out her heart or something very like it. Through extravagant hand gestures and head tosses, Babette distracted me and enabled Roar to escape. It was purely accidental—at least I thought it was. When Babette was involved, one never really knew.

After ten minutes of aimless palaver, I slipped away and checked out the restroom. For once, it was vacant—ominously so. Bethany must have used the side exit to make her escape. I dashed back to the auditorium to check things out, deflecting questions from handlers and one of Punky's pals. Nothing could deter me. I was a woman on a mission, determined to confront Bethany and find answers. She billed herself as a pet psychic without much evidence that I could see. If it were true—and I had my doubts—she must realize that hiding any knowledge about a murder was dangerous. Lordy. Didn't these people read crime novels or watch television? Were they too busy clipping, bathing, and brushing their canine charges to join the real world? I planned to confront Bethany and shake some sense into her. One way or another, she would confide in me.

Free-flowing alcohol had loosened up the gathering and unleashed occasional peals of laughter. Babette had cornered Rafa, to the displeasure of a number of ladies, but Bethany was nowhere to be found. I checked the central clock—9:45 on the dot. Just as I admitted defeat, a wisp of metallic fabric floated out the exit to Gate Nine. It was Bethany—had to be. No one else dared to wear such festive garb at a memorial service. I resolved to follow her and have a final showdown. Pruett had disappeared, and Babette was too far away to be of help. Time to play the Lone Ranger.

Snow was still piled in heaping mounds around the entryway, and ice shards lined the paths. I gingerly picked my way through the sodden mess, straining to get my bearings and avoid a nasty fall. Bethany far outpaced me. I could see the faint glow of her flashlight—at least I thought it was hers—gliding through the parking lot like a disembodied spirit. If only Keats and Poe were with me to buoy my confidence. Dogs have phenomenal hearing and night vision, traits that most humans sorely lack. My boys had saved many lives during our military service and several times since. They could sense danger before my training and instincts even began to kick in.

I reached into my bag and retrieved my trusty flashlight. It might alert Bethany, but at that point, I opted for safety over stealth. I hoped I wouldn't discover her in a clinch with some man, particularly a certain investigative scribe. A fleeting thought—which I banished immediately—featured Bethany wound around Pruett like a nubile serpent. Nope. Not likely. Surely Pruett had enough class to rent a hotel room for a rendezvous.

I followed the thread of light, trudging through the fields toward the Equine Pavilion. Was I following Bethany or some innocent stranger? More to the point, what in the world was she doing out in the elements? I suspected an assignation. Unless she was particularly hearty, any outdoor antics were highly unlikely. Bethany had been dressed for display rather than hiking, and she wore only a wool shawl to fend off the icy wind. She had to be freezing. I adore cold weather, but that frigid wind whipping through the trees was fierce enough to make me relish my winter hat and gloves.

The cavernous equine arena was abandoned during the winter months. Horses were too likely to slip on the snow and damage their delicate legs. Come spring, the area would awaken, and the pavilion would hum with glorious creatures, riders, and throngs of spectators. Suddenly, the light vanished, and I heard a faint thud. Had she injured herself? Hardly the best way to spark a romantic encounter or to further a career in the show ring. I strained to hear something—anything. Never did that old cliché "The silence was deafening" seem truer. Time for me to abandon stealth and act. "Bethany," I called in a voice that sounded suspiciously tinny even to me. "It's Perri. Are you okay? Where are you?"

At first, there was no response. I edged cautiously toward the pavilion, skirting the main area until I reached Horse Barn E. Time was not my friend as I searched in vain for an unlocked entrance. I glanced at my watch. At least fifteen minutes had elapsed since I last saw a hint of light. To quell the dread building up inside me, I tried humor. Maybe Bethany was the earthy type who preferred a literal roll in the hay to the comfort of clean sheets. Even now she and her paramour might be primed for action, emitting moans and groans of pleasure. I shuddered, imagining an abandoned barn as a passion pit. Straw was filled with all manner of noxious things. If Pruett were involved, that would serve the faithless wretch right. A bout of hay fever would almost be punishment enough.

The main building was locked up tight, but someone had wedged open the side barn door. I called out to Bethany again and heard a faint moan. *Stupid woman!* She'd probably wrenched her ankle in a hole and couldn't walk. Emboldened, I panned the area with my flashlight and felt an immediate jolt. Jess Pendrake, her eyes vacant and unseeing, crouched next to the crumpled body of Bethany Zahn. Blood gushed from a vicious wound in the psychic's throat as she tried unsuccessfully to speak. After one final gasp, her body went limp. No need to wonder which weapon had been used. A gore-soaked plough gauge, a tool often used by leathersmiths, lay beside her. It housed a blade that was sharp enough to eviscerate cowhide. Penetrating human flesh was no problem at all.

I fumbled in my bag, found my cell phone and dialed 911.

Chapter 14

Facing death was never easy. Confronting murder was unendurable. Death during wartime was inevitable, and one had to accept that. While serving in the army, I steeled myself to endure the attendant casualties. I had seen corpses many times before but never grew complacent about it. That was a good thing that kept me sane and reaffirmed my humanity. After all, the life of all God's creatures had value, a philosophy that initially drew Pip and me together. Homicide at innocuous venues like a dog show was particularly outrageous and unexpected. Dog shows were family events that celebrated the universal love of beauty and all canine creatures. That simplicity intensified the horror of this crime. I shivered, thankful for the warmth of my cashmere coat. I cherished the coat, a Christmas present from Pruett, more for the giver than the gift. Tonight, I also appreciated the practical side of the garment as it cocooned me in a warm embrace.

I shook myself back into reality. This was scarcely the time for daydreams and distractions. I crept up to Bethany's corpse, all the while keeping a close eye on Jess Pendrake and that lethal weapon. With its razor-sharp cutting blade, a plough gauge left little room for error. It sliced through a sheet of leather as if it were sweet cream butter. I had no desire to test the impact on human flesh, especially my human flesh.

"What happened here, Jess?" I summoned my official voice to avoid any misunderstandings and went on autopilot. Jess wasn't the type to crave sympathy or to respond to it. Her hands were stained with blood—presumably Bethany's—but her clothing was unblemished. Unlike the rest of us, Jess had made no concession to propriety or the rituals of Lee's memorial service. She was dressed in her usual peacoat, scuffed boots, and jeans.

"She's dead," said Jess, stating the obvious. Her voice was flat and devoid of expression.

"I noticed." I shifted into neutral to avoid the snarky retorts perched on the tip of my tongue. "Did you see who did it?"

She shook her head. "Nope. She wanted to meet me, but I was late."

From what I knew, Jess and Bethany were scarcely intimates. Jess barely spoke to anyone, and Bethany confided in men whenever possible. What connection could these two polar opposites possibly have?

The cavalry arrived before I asked anything else. Roar Jansen glided into the barn, with his hand conspicuously gripping his Glock. Oddly enough, he was accompanied by the dogged prince of the printed page, Wing Pruett.

"You okay, Perri?" Roar asked.

I nodded but stayed silent. Pruett's face was impassive as he stood to one side, taking everything in. Probably had his tape recorder or iPhone switched on too. Personal experience had taught me that when a big story intervened, Wing Pruett was a journalist first and foremost. Friendships and even romantic ties came in a very distant second. I'd learned that lesson the hard way.

"Care to tell us what happened, Ms. Pendrake?" Roar's voice stayed pleasant and neutral, as if they were two friends chatting about a sporting event. "Before you answer, let me read you your rights. Got to follow procedure, you know." He produced a card from the pocket of his leather jacket and rattled off the Miranda warning that every cop show devotee knew by heart. Jess's eyes had a glazed look that suggested she was close to collapse. Nevertheless, she balled up her fists and blurted out a response. "Like I already told her," she pointed to me, "Bethany asked to meet me, so I came. She was like that when I showed up." Jess looked down at her bloodstained hands. "I touched her. Tried to help her."

Roar scored big-time on interview technique. No bullying or sarcasm. He showed those dimples in a sympathetic smile. "I understand. What did she want? You two were close friends, I guess."

Jess shook her head emphatically. "Nope. I hated her. She was like all those other bitches—mean to me. We hardly said even hello."

His eyebrows raised in a quizzical expression. "Odd. She must have hinted something to make you come to a dump like this on such a cold night."

Jess swallowed hard. In a voice that was barely audible, she mumbled. "It was about Lee. She knew who killed him."

That confirmed what Bethany told me this afternoon. What I couldn't understand was why she would choose Jess as a confidant. Unless . . .

"She accused you?" Roar said. "Why?"

Jess's snort would have shamed a racehorse at the starting gate. "Not me. She was probably scared. Guess she thought I was safe." She tossed her head. "Don't matter now, though. Someone got to her before I showed up." Suddenly she pointed toward me. "Ask her about that knife thing. She knows all about it."

As Pruett stepped toward me, his eyes telegraphed a warning. "Even I know what that is, Roar. Some kind of craft tool. What do they call it, Perri?"

My voice was rock solid when I answered. "A plough gauge. Similar to what I use but slightly different. Designed to slice through leather."

Roar studied me for a moment. "Whatever the name, it sure did its job, alright. Not one of yours, is it, Perri?"

Pruett put his arms around me and gave me a gentle squeeze. "This place must have plenty of those things, don't you agree? After all, this is a horse barn, and they use all that leather stuff." He shuddered. "Not my field of expertise, obviously."

That diversion gave me time to regroup. I looked Roar straight in those baby blues and shrugged. "Can't say if it's mine. Probably not, though. I hardly ever use a plough gauge, and last time I checked my tools, nothing was missing. I assumed you didn't want the crime scene contaminated, so I haven't examined it."

Roar grimaced and turned back to Jess. She sat motionless, with her legs tucked under her in lotus position. A faint smile painted her lips. She was either smirking or approaching ecstasy.

"We'll need a complete statement from you, Ms. Pendrake. As soon as my partner arrives, she'll take you down to the station." He nodded my way. "You too, Perri."

Putting the fear of Genna Watts into us worked like a charm. Jess's contemplative air vanished immediately, and truth be told, my own adrenaline soared too. Talk about the perfect ending to an exhausting day. Pruett squeezed my shoulder again. "Can't this wait until tomorrow morning? You'll be busy here anyway, and Perri looks exhausted."

Roar motioned us off. "Go on. Just be at the station bright and early. Both of you." Those eyes of his took on a fiendish gleam. "You'd have access to that plough gauge too, Mr. Pruett. Makes a body think." He waved us off. "Don't be late now. I'd hate to send Genna chasing after you. Missing witnesses make her really cranky."

He shifted his focus, laser sharp, to Jess and the gore-encrusted weapon beside her. "Just take it easy, Ms. Pendrake. We'll get this sorted out as quickly as possible."

Pruett and I knew an exit line when we heard one. We fled the area, narrowly escaping just as the forensic team, accompanied by Genna Watts, stomped into view.

"Whew," I said. "That was close. I didn't feel up to confronting that she-devil right now." We marched silently over the snowy terrain, using my flashlight for safety. Pruett draped his arm around my waist, a gesture that comforted me more than I cared to admit. Before meeting Pip, independence had been my watchword. He taught me that sharing a burden with someone who loved you strengthened rather than weakened you. When Pip passed, those bonds of trust dissolved too, and I retreated into solitude. Now, despite everything, I tried not to rely on Pruett, in case he too vanished into the clouds. Considering the number of local beauties who pursued him, that scenario was a distinct possibility.

Tonight was different. I cast my insecurities aside and reveled in the solace he provided. After watching Bethany Zahn take her final breath, I needed comfort and strength in every possible way. Caution and hedging my bets flew out the window as I leaned on his shoulder.

"Don't worry about Ella," Pruett said. "She and Guinnie are tucked in that trailer with Babette, all safe and sound."

"Does Babette know what happened?" I asked. Staying on the sidelines was odd behavior for my pal, especially since she fancied herself my sleuthing partner—a Watson or, at the very least, Robin.

"Not everything." He rolled his eyes. "She may think we were having a private moment. Why spoil the illusion?"

That explained everything. Babette was the ultimate romantic, especially when it involved me. Her heart was in the right place, but her mind had its erratic moments. I pictured the scene at Lee's memorial. Rafa, Alf, Kiki, Whit—they were all there. Had one of them slipped out before I left the arena? My eyes were trained on Bethany, so anything was possible. I was uncertain of the route, so I had trudged slowly and cautiously through the snow. On the other hand, Bethany's killer knew exactly where to go and could have done so without ever using a flashlight.

"Any suspects come to mind?" Pruett asked. "I bet Roar and especially Genna think both murders are all wrapped up."

I saw the wheels turning in that big brain of his as he spoke. The "Death by Dog Show" piece was practically writing itself.

"I don't think she did it, Pruett. Jess was the perfect patsy. Too perfect."

He shrugged. "Here's how the cops probably see it. Jess hated Lee Holmes for deceiving her. When Bethany tried a spot of blackmail, Jess knocked her off." He rubbed his hands together gleefully. "Q.E.D. Case closed."

"You turn me on when you speak Latin, big fellow." I batted my eyelashes, trying unsuccessfully to play the vamp. "Look, I know cops usually pick the most likely solution, but Jess Pendrake just doesn't compute. She's a weirdo, true, but kind of innocent too."

"Whoever murdered those poor sods wasn't innocent. The gash on Bethany's throat was vicious, and those poodle shears—ugh. Maybe you should re-evaluate your suspects, Ms. Morgan."

I hated to break the spell, but honesty compelled me to. "Roar considers you a suspect too, you know. Says you've been in the area longer than I thought."

Pruett held out his hand. "Come on. That's just silly. I told you I was on assignment. Lee Holmes was a part of it but a very minor part. As for Bethany—whatever she knew or thought she knew died with her tonight." He pulled me to him and kissed the top of my head. "You need to get some rest. I'll just hold you 'til you fall asleep. Promise. No funny business."

I stood on tiptoe and ran my fingers through his hair. "I may need some help to make me sleep, so brush up on your routine. Funny business has an upside."

Pruett grinned. "Hmm. Since you put it that way...drugs are not the answer, but I know just what you need. Trust me."

In the end, we resolved the issue amicably, and both of us slept like babies.

* * * *

Bad news travels swiftly in a closed community. Promptly at seven the next morning, Babette burst into my bedroom, ready to rumble. She wore her idea of casual chic: a cashmere twinset and exquisitely tailored jeans. Her boots were Prada's answer to harsh-weather gear.

"What happened?" she gasped, ignoring our partially clothed bodies. "Rafa just left. Told me all about it." She gave an elaborate shiver. "Who's next? Maybe we should head out of here before some crazed killer strikes again."

First things first. "Where's Ella?" I asked. "We need to keep her close at all times."

Pruett poked his head out of the blankets then. "Ella?" His voice had an unaccustomed panicky quality to it.

No response was needed as Ella, Guinnie, and my Malinois bounded into the room and clambered onto the bed. Correction. Ella leapt into her father's arms. Keats, Poe, and Guinnie maintained a respectful presence at our bedside.

"We had fun already, Daddy," Ella said. "Ms. Babette took all of us on a hike."

Something was definitely amiss. The Babette that I knew and loved avoided hiking and all types of physical exertion unless mandated by her personal trainer in an air-conditioned gym. I glared at my pal until she bowed her head.

"Well, Rafa likes a morning jog, and you know how committed I am to fitness."

"Rafa briefed you on the excitement last night?"

She nodded. "That psycho cop grabbed him while he was taking a stroll. Gave him the third degree too."

Oh Lord! Sergeant Watts at work. I needed to make myself presentable before she collared me as well. "How about some breakfast?" I asked. "Sure could use some espresso."

"Good idea," Pruett said, peeking out of the window. "Looks like the snow finally stopped. How about chowing down in a restaurant for a change? I'll drive."

Babette clapped her hands. "Terrific. Mind if I invite Rafa? He needs sustenance after facing that woman."

Since I was unwilling to grace the next cover of the police gazette, I begged off. I was quite confident that Pruett would milk Rafa for any relevant information about the murder, without any help from me. Pruett dashed for the shower while I inhaled a mug of espresso, courtesy of my charming hostess. He returned, bright-eyed and barbered, before I finished my second serving. Men, especially specimens like Pruett, have a tactical advantage that way. I promised to explain his absence to Roar, but I couldn't count on Genna's acquiescence. After collecting Rafa from his Airstream, the three adults, accompanied by Ella, whisked gaily off in Pruett's Porsche in search of a cholesterol-laden repast. I bit my lip just thinking of blueberry pancakes dripping with maple syrup. Who needed the calories? Virtue would triumph over gluttony. Even I didn't believe those tired clichés.

Just as I finished my own morning rituals, a sharp rap on the door announced the arrival of the law. Sergeant Watts, unaccompanied by Roar, wore a full-throttle sneer, a no-nonsense parka, and a rigid body posture. She sat primly on the edge of one of the club chairs and refused my offer of refreshment.

"Finding bodies a habit with you, Ms. Morgan?" Her opening salvo did not bode well for our interview. "Let's hear your side of the story."

I took a deep breath and counted way past ten. Control was everything in these situations. I responded with a smile rather than a scowl. "There really is no side, Sergeant, just the truth. I followed the victim from the main arena, got lost, and ultimately found her with Jess Pendrake."

Genna's eyes narrowed. "Why follow her in the first place? You said yourself that Lee Holmes was practically a stranger to you. Kind of odd, wouldn't you say?"

I flashed that beatific grin her way once more and got just what I'd hoped for. Genna's reaction was volcanic and immediate, a charging bull intent on vanquishing the matador. She didn't paw the ground, but she came damn close.

"Bethany knew who the murderer was," I said, "or thought she did. She told me that yesterday morning."

Genna folded her arms in front of her in a derisive gesture. "Why keep it to yourself, Ms. Morgan? That's what the police are for."

Score one for Genna. I had no logical reason to hoard information in a homicide investigation. None at all, unless you counted my fears that Pruett was somehow involved. Had my penchant for secrecy cost the pet psychic her life or allowed a killer to escape? I examined my conscience and realized that my reasoning was sound. I wanted to be absolutely certain before involving the police or anyone else in the matter. Bethany could easily have been teasing me, trying to make me look foolish in Pruett's eyes. Pruett. How did he factor into my actions if at all?

"Still with me?" Genna grunted. "How does Wing Pruett fit into this? Bet you were helping him get a scoop. A big story to make him appreciate you." She leaned forward. "Or maybe you were covering up for him."

My cheeks burned with humiliation. Was I that transparent? "Mr. Pruett does his own investigative work without any help from me. He's a serious journalist. Check out the awards he's won over the years."

That earned me a malevolent grin from the sergeant. "Oh, I have, Ms. Morgan. Let's see. Wing Pruett, the sexiest man in the nation's capital, according to the *Washingtonian.* Most impressive. That passes for serious journalism in DC these days, I suppose."

In this war of attrition, Genna was head and shoulders above me. I vowed to change the odds and fight back. As they say, a good offense beats a spirited defense any day.

"Back to Bethany," I said. "She was dying when I found her."

"What did she say?"

I shrugged. "Nothing. She just gasped and took a final breath. Unless she told Jess something, of course. I wouldn't know about that."

"We're still questioning Ms. Pendrake."

"She didn't do it." Something stubborn arose inside me, forcing me to oppose anything this irascible cop said. It made no sense. Genna and I had common backgrounds and goals and should have been allies, not adversaries. Sadly, sisterhood was out of the question. An alliance was simply not in the cards.

"That's not up to you," Genna growled. "For all we know, you might have skewered Ms. Zahn in a fit of passion. She got awfully cozy with your lover, I hear. He's a prime suspect as far as I'm concerned."

My mouth was Sahara-dry. I swallowed several times before responding and once again summoned a saccharine smile. "You know how people gossip in these places, Sergeant. Wing Pruett's a free agent who can do whatever he pleases." I ignored the sour taste that those words conferred, and the reminder that Pruett had disappeared two nights ago without explanation. Despite an enormous act of will, Bethany's coy smile hovered around the recesses of my mind and refused to vanish.

"You didn't like her much, did you?" Genna asked.

"Bethany enjoyed snooping," I said. "If she heard something incriminating, she wouldn't shrink from a spot of blackmail. Not that most dog show folks have deep pockets."

Genna's sharp eyes blinked. I think she actually took me seriously for a change. "Blackmail, huh? Dangerous game to play with a murderer." She shook her head. "Doesn't end well, by and large."

For once, we were in complete accord. The name that immediately popped into my mind was Yael Lindsay, the wealthy, not so bereaved widow. There were other possibilities, of course. Whit Whitley wasn't hurting for cash, and who knew the full story about Rafa?

"Your friend Mrs. Croy has plenty," Genna said, "and Wing Pruett certainly does too."

I abandoned my vow of silence and jumped down her throat. "Don't be absurd. Babette didn't really know Lee Holmes. Believe me, she had bigger fish to fry. As for Pruett, you're on the wrong track."

Genna's supercilious smirk could try the patience of a saint. Since I renounced the celestial crown long ago, I considered the penalties for assaulting a police officer. Genna was undeterred and plowed ahead with her vile spiel.

"Some folks say Mrs. Croy's man-crazy. After anything in pants. Lee Holmes attracted that type, I hear, and he always wore pants."

"Some folks need to button their lip." I rose and drew myself up to my full height. "Word of advice, Sergeant. If you mess with Mrs. Croy, be prepared for a legal tussle. That woman has a battery of attorneys on speed dial."

To her credit, Genna didn't back down. "What about you? Circumstantial evidence is enough for an arrest warrant, you know. Opportunity, means—you were on the scene and comfortable with those weapons. Tools of your trade they call them, so I hear." Genna's chuckle had more venom than humor in it. "Once I pin down that motive, I may come calling again."

I shrugged. "Go ahead. Knock yourself out. In case you didn't know, Wing Pruett serves as my legal adviser."

A loud, totally unprofessional cackle spewed from her lips. "I'll just bet. Seems like that pretty boy has a lot of uses. He just might need a lawyer of his own." And with that, Sergeant Genna Watts stalked out of Steady Eddie without saying another word.

Chapter 15

For the first time ever, the dog show world lost its luster. Even the smiling, furry faces surrounding me lost their power to enthrall, temporarily at least, and the antics of humans scurrying around the Better Living Center provoked me into near madness. How could they focus on championship points, Best of Show, and other minutia when two lives had been brutally snuffed out? I was weary of everything and everyone. Weather, competition, and even the customers who kept me in business were now sources of annoyance instead of joy. Word of Bethany's murder spread quickly through our closed community, and the air was rife with speculation. I kept my head down and limited any discussion of events or my role in them. It was a Band-Aid tactic, not a permanent fix, that worked for a while but not long enough. Soon after I reopened Creature Comforts, my pal Punky bounced in on the pretext of buying a show collar. Punky was a straight shooter who wasted no time on preliminaries. As soon as the coast was clear, she cornered me and started the inquisition.

"Tell me everything," she said. "I never pegged ole Jess Pendrake for a killer, let alone a double murderer, but she had potential. Hated everything that wasn't canine." Punky took a deep breath. "Still, it's not natural. Woman must have gone loony."

"Is that what everyone thinks?" I asked. "Even the cops haven't made any arrests, you know. Jess is still hanging in there"

Punky fixed me with a death stare. "Tell the truth. You found her, right, Perri?"

I nodded.

"It's simple then. Jess hated Lee Holmes like poison and Bethany just as much." Punky laughed, a raspy, smoker's sound. "Come to think of it, who didn't hate Bethany? Woman was a pure waste of time. Had no respect for anybody or anything. Just a greedy, grasping creature. A good breeder would put down any pup in a litter with those traits."

I kept my expression as stone-faced as Mount Rushmore. Meanwhile, Punky rambled on, oblivious to me or anyone else in the area. She seemed genuinely puzzled by the grisly events of the past two days. "You've got to wonder, though, why Bethany picked Jess to blab to. Those two never had a civil word to share, far as I could tell."

"Maybe the murderer tricked Jess into showing up." The more I considered that idea, the better I liked it. Jess was a natural victim, the kind of woman with few friends who would be typecast for the part of villain. Too bad Roar Jansen had her buttoned up in some holding pen. Despite my prior experience, I had accepted Jess's statement at face value without probing further. That was probably a mistake. Perhaps someone sent a note or e-mail arranging the meeting. I'd kept a close watch on Bethany during the memorial service as she flirted shamelessly with the few males in the crowd. Rafa, Alf, and even Whit Wiley had exchanged words with Bethany, but Jess had skipped the entire event. Babette had shadowed Roy and Kiki the entire time, so it was unlikely that either of them escaped her eagle eye. If only Pruett were available. His insights and analysis were usually right on target about most subjects, especially designing females such as Bethany. I gulped, recalling that Pruett had problems of his own.

I cornered Punky before she could change the subject. "You know, I questioned Bethany about that pet supplement business, but she got pretty cagey. Evasive as hell, if you want the truth. I think she was hiding something."

Punky gave a muddled response that straddled the fence between a cough and a chortle. As she emitted a lung-wrenching bellow, I slapped her on the back until she finally settled down.

"That nasty habit will ruin you, my friend. Try the nicotine patch for a change."

I didn't expect her to acquiesce, and Punky didn't disappoint. "My lungs and my nasty habits are my own business, lady. Only my mother could tell me that, and she's long passed. But as for Bethany, you nailed it. She could bob and weave with the best of them, especially when it suited her pocketbook."

I gaped at my friend as if I were the village idiot. "Huh?"

Another guffaw from Punky. "Girl, grow up. Thought you were supposed to be a superduper sophisticate, not a rookie. You didn't know Jack about Bethany or Lee Holmes, did you? Bet ya Babette knows the score. Ask her."

Her grin was so disarming that I forgave the impudence. After all, truth will out. I had been so captivated by my own concerns that my usually keen instincts had gone on strike. Time to activate Persephone Morgan, woman of the world.

"Stop stalling," I told Punky. "What scam did Bethany have going?"

Punky took her sweet time. She batted her lashes and executed several dance steps before finally spilling her guts. "Blackmail, baby. Blackmail. Bethany used that pet psychic dodge to ingratiate herself with the show people and learn their business. When she got a juicy tidbit, she put the bite on them, so to speak."

Suddenly, things began to make sense. If Bethany knew or saw something about Lee Holmes's murder, she wouldn't hesitate one minute to capitalize upon it. Knowledge was money, a negotiable currency in any world, and murder would fetch a pretty price indeed. Unfortunately for her, a killer's idea of foreplay often had deadly consequences. There was no discernible difference in the penalty for two murders versus one. Massachusetts had no death penalty, and life without parole was a calculated risk that some criminals were more than willing to take.

"Kind of makes you wonder, don't it?" Punky said. "Who had the stones to skewer Lee and then do Bethany for dessert? Sweet!"

I was preoccupied with another question. Who had the most to gain from eliminating both Lee and Bethany? Admittedly, Lee was a despicable creature who drew enemies the way dogs do fleas. Even at his memorial service, I had sensed more relief than grief from the assembled crowd. That extended to his betrayed bride, Yael Lindsay, his professional rivals, and the dozens of women who appreciated his physical charms. The names bubbled up to the surface like molten lava. Babette vouched for Roy Vesco and Kiki, but my wonderful pal lacked judgment where men were concerned. Her marital track record affirmed that. The perfidious Whit Wiley was capable of almost anything, but murder—I wasn't so sure. His strong suit was more character assassination than the real deed. In my view, the little twerp couldn't face a veteran brawler like Lee Holmes without running for cover. Our double murderer was both decisive and fearless, two traits that Whit had never before displayed. Rafa, Roy Vesco, and even Alf Walsh were far better possibilities than Whit. Come to think of it, several female candidates sprang to mind as well. Jess was the one most physically suited to the task, but Yael Lindsay had a steely side to her, buttressed by family fortune and bedrock pilgrim stock. Like many in her income bracket, she had no need to sully her manicured fingers in brawls if she chose not to. Yael was more likely to write a check to have the deal done.

I whirled around to ask Punky her opinion, but she was long gone. Instead, I spied Pruett's lithe figure gliding toward my store. Damn! That man had the moves of a panther or some other jungle cat. I powered down and pretended to be unaffected by his arrival. Fat chance.

"Miss me, Perri?" he asked, putting his arms around me and nuzzling my neck. The faint scent of his cologne and the warmth of his arms mesmerized me as I leaned in. I silently cursed the weakness of the flesh and my pesky carnal thoughts. Blast it all, the man was bone and sinew, just like the rest of us, not some deity. The perfect alignment of his parts was merely a happy accident.

I yawned. "Were you gone?" My bid for nonchalance was a dismal failure, and we both knew it.

"Look," Pruett said, "you should know that I've decided to move Ella somewhere safe. With a murderer around, I can't take any chances."

"Good idea," I said. "We'll take care of Guinnie for her."

Pruett hesitated. "Actually, her mother was in town doing a shoot, and I asked her to pitch in." He looked away as he always did when the name of Monique Allaire arose. I loathed the heifer, but she was Ella's mother, and I respected that, if not the woman with the title. Monique treated me with the barely concealed contempt a monarch feels for her inferiors. She dismissed my lack of physical charms as if I were an errant peasant toiling in the fields. Since I had access to several mirrors, it didn't surprise me. I was attractive enough, but certainly not superstar material. On the other hand, Ella loved me, and at times I believed that her daddy did too. Apparently, Monique Allaire fumed at the very thought of my alliance with Pruett. I gave myself a mental pat on the head and smiled.

"Good move," I told Pruett. "Makes sense." I pasted a sympathetic smile on my lips, thinking all the while that Pruett's unexplained absences now also made sense. I didn't know and never asked if they maintained any physical relationship. Frankly, I couldn't bear to know the answer.

"Anything new on the case?" he asked. "I spoke with Roar, and it's driving him nuts. Genna is chomping at the bit for an arrest. Things don't look good for Jess, I'm afraid."

"Jess a double murderer? I don't buy that for a moment. Someone set her up."

Pruett folded his arms and stared me down. "And you know this how? ESP or facts?" Luckily for him, Pruett didn't say women's intuition. That sexist nonsense would have opened a major fissure in our relationship.

"Okay. I admit it may be supposition, but look at the facts. Both murders were cold and efficiently executed. Hallmarks of premeditation. That suggests a calm, calculated killer, maybe even a professional who had done it before. Jess might attack in a fit of passion, but she'd probably leave a trail a mile long." I made a mock bow. "There. I rest my case."

"Maybe. I suppose you already figured out the motive?" He was taunting me, using his many wiles to distract me and doing a pretty fair job of it. Pruett's eyes were a particularly yummy shade of brown, something that suggested molten chocolate with flecks of gold. I tried to avoid sweet treats, but there were times when I shamelessly craved them. Now was one of those times.

"Unlike you, I don't have an agenda," I reminded him. "I'm not writing the next best seller or trying to extricate myself from a murder rap." My motives were pure, but I had little to buttress my beliefs. Petty grievances abounded in the show world, but nothing that would prompt a double murder. Love, deceit, larceny—there were motives aplenty, but in retrospect they seemed trivial.

"Seems like a man's crime," Pruett declared loftily. "Women tend to shy away from violent actions. Poison is their preferred method in all the detective novels I've read."

Now it was my turn to scoff. "And we all know that fiction mimics real life. Get a grip, Pruett, or you'll be writing for *True Detective* instead of the *New Yorker*."

We were officially at an impasse, or at least our investigative efforts were. At times like that, I favored meditation. Pruett voted for the "liquor is quicker" solution. Compromise was in order, so I signaled to Keats and Poe, and the four of us repaired to Steady Eddie for some serious thought. Call me weak, but I secretly hoped that Babette and her collection of misfits were somewhere else, preferably far away. The sexual tension between me and Pruett was toxic to my thought processes. A little relief would go a long way.

Unfortunately, Babette was very much in evidence, ensconced on the sofa with the faithful Clara and a box of tissues in hand. She gave us a winsome smile punctuated by a pronounced series of sniffles. An attack of the vapors was nothing new to my pal and usually involved man troubles. Been there, done that. The only solution was to divert her attention from her woes.

"Where's Rafa?" I asked, dreading the answer.

Babette waved her arms and immediately began to hiccup. "Don't mind me," she said. "You two go have fun. I'm not in the mood for company."

Pruett leapt into the breach. "Nonsense. I have it on good authority that the dog people are convening in O'Doul's, that Irish pub across the street. Live music and plenty of booze. What more could you ask for?"

I could have named several things offhand, but I played along. "Ah, come on. No need to brood. We'll all feel better for it."

After several minutes of wheedling and coaxing, Babette agreed to the plan. Naturally, she demanded time to freshen up while we exercised the pups, but that was a small price to pay for harmony. Pruett and I harnessed Guinnie, Clara, and the Malinois boys and headed for the open fields. Fortunately, a full moon shed its shimmery light over the snowy fields, illuminating the entire area. No dark crevices or shadowy bushes this time. My nerves could ill afford to find another corpse, especially with Genna on the prowl for suspects.

Pruett took my hand and gently squeezed it. "We haven't spent any time alone for a while. Miss you."

I ignored the surge of warmth that suffused my being. Instead, I nodded and kept my own counsel. If snuggling with his former lover and baby mama satisfied him, what could I possibly say or do? "Me too," I whispered. "Let's hope this thing ends soon."

"What do you know about Alfred Walsh?" Pruett asked. "Ella adores him, but she loves anyone who likes Guinnie."

I thought before replying. "Not that much. Punky recommended him, and he's an AKC-certified handler. Naturally, Babette raves about him, but she's not alone. The other breeders and handlers like him too."

Pruett donned his alpha-male persona. "I'll check out his history on the Internet. Some of those search engines are really scary the way they get down to the nitty-gritty. You can't always go on a person's reputation, you know. Remember what happened last time."

Déjà vu. I had badly misjudged someone who ended up being a murderer, and Pruett never let me forget it. Fortunately, my bodyguards Keats and Poe had keener instincts than their loving mama and came to my rescue. I threw Pruett off the scent by agreeing with him. "You're so right. These days, every little thing ends up on the Internet." Apparently, he had missed Page Six, the snarky gossip section of the *New York Post*. This morning's edition featured a candid shot of Monique Allaire draped over the hot bod of a certain journalist. Unfortunately, both Pruett and Monique looked camera-ready and very pleased with themselves. Some might even mistake them for lovers.

"What's our plan for this shindig tonight?" I asked Pruett. "Divide and conquer might be a sound strategy."

He nodded. "Caution flies out the window when people get lubricated. Naturally, I'll stick to sparkling water."

We hoofed it back to Steady Eddie in time to freshen up and admire the refurbished Babette Croy. By fluffing her hair and adjusting her makeup, she managed to eliminate all traces of wear and traded tears for a becoming shade of rose blush.

"Very nice," I told her. "Just the right touch."

Babette mugged for an imaginary camera and pirouetted. "That shade of blush would work for you too, Perri. They call it 'Orgasm.'"

Pruett's laugh was more of a guffaw—deep, hearty, and very masculine. "Sign her up. Anything to get Perri in the mood."

Babette immediately plunged into a detailed discussion of scent, nail polish, and foundation. When I reached capacity, I held out my palm and cried, "Stop." Pruett looked chastened, but Babette was in her glory.

I used my official voice. "Hey, time's a-wasting. Let me change so we can get moving." With a bit of help from the cosmetic gods and the addition of a black silk shirt, I prepared to face my critics. My friends' reaction buoyed my spirits: Pruett whistled, and Babette cheered. We crated the pups and surfed a wave of optimism all the way to O'Doul's.

●

Chapter 16

I'm not crazy about crowds. Too much alcohol fuels all manner of feuds, fisticuffs, and romantic encounters, most of which lead to trouble. In my prior life, I'd been forced to sort out lots of these shindigs. Mediating nasty scenes was simply not my thing anymore. Despite those misgivings, I tried to be a good sport. I agreed to Pruett's divide-and-conquer strategy and vowed to do my part. Babette, on the other hand, was thrilled to participate in what she gleefully termed a "sting operation."

"Sounds more like a pincer movement," I observed.

Pruett drew me close and kissed my forehead. "Bet you learned that in the army, show-off. That's okay. I love brainy broads."

Not to be outdone, Babette paraded her knowledge too. "It means attacking both enemy flanks simultaneously," she said proudly licking her lips. "Remember: hubby number one was an ex-general. Omar loved talking dirty with those military terms. Really turned him on. Enjoyed everything except the Battle of the Bulge." She chortled. "That's one fight the poor baby lost."

Since none of us could top that, we got down to business. Pruett was typecast. His assignment was to ingratiate himself with the ladies, particularly the younger handlers like Punky and her crew. Babette agreed to shadow Yael Lindsay. Since they moved in similar social circles, Yael might well confide in her instead of a peasant like me. My assignment involved quizzing Rafa, Alf Wash, and, Lord help me, Whit Wiley. As the designated corpse collector, I attracted the curious among the group, who would gobble up any tidbits on offer. Information was power in the dog world, just like everywhere else.

Most Irish pubs have a similar vibe, scent, and structure. Donnie O'Doul's was certainly no different. The posters boasted generous portions of food, craft beers, and live music provided by a contingent of locals with big dreams and middling talent. By the time we arrived, the vinyl booths were packed, and every bar stool was taken. We quickly split up and went about our assigned tasks with at least the appearance of good cheer. Pruett had no trouble at all insinuating himself into a group of female handlers, most of whom were already past the legal drinking limit. Unlike their canine charges, these ladies didn't pant or drool when they saw him, but they came too damn close for my taste. When last seen or heard from, he had lent his surprisingly pleasant baritone to a spirited rendition of "Me and Bobby McGee" and was being pressed for an encore. Funny thing. I had never before heard Wing Pruett sing. How many facets of this man were still hidden from me?

Babette, her face a mask of solicitude, made a beeline for the corner booth housing the not-so-grieving widow, Yael Lindsay. Fortunately, Whit Wiley, the constant suitor, was at the bar ordering drinks. That gave Babette the very opening that she sought. By the time Whit returned, Yael was too deep into conversation with Mrs. Croy to even acknowledge his existence. She dismissed him with a peremptory wave of her hand.

I sauntered toward a corner booth, where a trio of show hands was gathered. Alf, Rafa, and Roy Vesco hunched over their beers as they swapped secrets and boasts. Joining their group was a piece of cake since most of my working life had been spent bonding with guys just like them. It took only a measure of courage and a pinch of guile to worm my way into their inner circle.

"Mind if I join you?" I asked. "Just promise not to talk about murder. That's off the menu. Anything else is fine."

They hooted at that as if it were comic gold. Everyone in O'Doul's was jawing about the murders and little else. One could hardly blame them. Dog shows have a lot of down time, and the pros who staff them welcome any diversion. Double murder qualified as the ultimate diversion.

Rafa hoisted his beer, sipped, and poured a glass for me. I loathe beer, but in the spirit of fellowship I bravely downed a swallow.

"Hmm," he said licking his lips. "Sure tastes good. For a while, I thought I'd had my last one of these."

"What?" Roy Vesco wasn't the sharpest knife in the drawer. That didn't mean he wasn't the murderer, of course. Didn't take a genius to stab a drunk or an unsuspecting woman, but cunning was obviously absent from Roy's repertoire.

"He's talking jail, Roy. No beers in the hoosegow. Keep up, boy." Alf patted his buddy on the back. His touch was gentle and his manner kind. Hard not to like this guy, I thought.

Rafa turned to me. "Any hot rumors, Perri? You're pretty tight with that sergeant."

"That ugly broad?" Roy yelped. "She's a menace. Always prowling around the place even before the trouble. Doesn't like dogs, if you can believe it."

Alf laughed so hard he almost slid off the patched vinyl seat. "You slay me, Roy boy. Perri has pull with the pretty guy. Roar, that's his name, isn't it, Perri? He did some private security work at the Big E last year too. Seemed like a pretty nice guy."

I nodded. "He doesn't confide in me, of course, but at least he's civil. Unlike his partner."

Rafa curled his lip. "Just because I'm a Spaniard, they think I'm guilty."

"It probably had more to do with those shears," I said. "After all, they were yours."

Rafa shrugged, but Alf immediately joined the fray. "Anyone could have pinched those shears. We all leave our stuff out during the day, Perri. You know that. Besides, Lee Holmes was a crumb who deserved to die." No more Mr. Nice Guy. Alf Walsh was on the warpath, ready to rumble. He brushed back a strand of thinning brown hair and grimaced.

"You can say that again," Vesco said. "Didn't trust him one bit around my wife."

No one dared to follow up on that comment. My own view was that little Kiki could take care of herself without any help. When conversation lagged, I decided to prime the pump.

"Bethany, though—that was a real puzzler. She said she knew who the killer was, you know." I scanned the faces around the table.

Rafa jumped right in. "You weren't the only one she told. Bethany spread the word."

"Yeah," Roy said, "that girl was flapping her jaw to everyone. Didn't have a lick of sense. She even told Kiki, for gosh sakes, and that's like tellin' the whole show world."

That answered one of my questions and expanded the pool of suspects to anyone within earshot. Poor, deluded Bethany. She thought she was just a tad smarter than everyone else, but the murderer proved her wrong.

I lowered my voice to a conspiratorial level. "Someone told me blackmail was involved. Might explain everything."

Rafa refilled each of our mugs and signaled for another pitcher of beer. "Seems to me you're too curious for your own good with a murderer around. You took a big chance following her. Better watch your back, Ms. Perri, or you might be next." His tone was grim, and I couldn't determine if he was trying to protect or warn me. "I kind of liked Ms. Bethany. Beautiful women are hard to ignore, and she was foxy."

"Didn't put out none," Roy sniffed. "Least ways, not to me."

"Don't feel bad, buddy. She had some other fish on the line. Whit told me all about it." Alf shook his head in disbelief.

"Whit Wiley? Surely not." A swallow of brew got stuck in my throat and nearly choked me. Bethany involved with that truly dreadful man? Death or abstinence was preferable to that.

Alf reached over and wacked my back. "You okay, Perri? Whit told me about it, but it wasn't him. Some outsider, he said." Alf's smile transformed his rather plain face into something almost handsome. "Here we are, gossiping like old washerwomen, with the best-looking gal in the room sitting beside us. Don't blame us, honey. Rafa got a good going over from that cop, and it shook him up. Roy had those other cops to deal with. We're all worried that the AKC might clamp down on us."

If that were true, my friend's very livelihood was at stake. Reputation was everything in the show world, and gossip ranked as high as a five-point major. Might make a man—or woman—jumpy enough to commit murder.

Alf closed his eyes as if he were meditating. "You know, Bethany wasn't really one of us, not a real dog person. Oh, she bred a few dogs and showed them some. Had a pug she finished once. Grand Champion. Got all the way up to bronze. Nice dog, not that she ever did much with him. Bethany just sort of hung around on the fringes, scooping up what business she could. Mostly she drew in the civilians and sold them nonsense about their pets. Harmless enough, though."

Not in someone's eyes. Bethany gambled on her instincts, and for once, they had let her down. I calculated the pocketbooks of the most likely suspects and came up empty. What could Bethany gain from extorting anyone except Yael? I knew on good authority that Yael had a solid alibi for both murders. Roar had confirmed that, and the redoubtable Genna nodded her agreement. The others had mostly pocket change to offer and plenty to lose.

"I hear Ella's left the show," Alf said. "Too bad. I sure liked that little lady."

"Don't worry. It's just until this unpleasantness is cleared up. Pruett left her with her mom. We still have Guinnie, though, so your services are desperately needed."

Rafa gave me a thumbs-up and sipped his beer. "Just four more days and this show is history. Can't come soon enough for me."

That was an opportunity I couldn't pass up. "Are you going back to Spain to see your family?" I asked. Duplicity comes naturally to me but carries with it a scintilla of guilt. Still, I owed it to Babette to learn the truth.

Rafa cocked his head and gave me a look that was far from friendly. "Family? My dogs are the only family I have in Spain, other than my brother. We raise standard poodles, as you probably know."

Not everyone can hold his liquor, and Roy Vesco was squarely in the sloppy drunk camp. As he slid toward total inebriation, his speech became slightly slurred and his eyes blurry. With any luck, impaired judgment would soon follow, along with a free flow of information. "Too bad Lee screwed you around about that property. Would have made a perfect kennel. Right here near the Big E. Couldn't get much better than that."

Rafa's jaw was locked tighter than a vault, and Alf shifted in his seat. Obviously, Roy had hit a very sore subject. I knew better than to say anything. Watchful waiting was in order.

After an awkward pause, Rafa spoke. "It's no big secret around here. Lee made a damn fool out of me. Cost me a bundle too. Should have known better than to trust that *malparido* anyway."

"That's Spanish for bastard, Perri," Roy offered helpfully. "Rafa taught me."

Roy's absolute cluelessness dissipated the tension, as the rest of us dissolved into laughter. He looked quizzically at us, as though puzzled. Once again, Alf rode to the rescue.

"Things never get dull with Roy around," he laughed. "Count on it."

Rafa put down his drink and sighed. "Guess that makes me suspect number one in your book, eh, Perri?" His eyes were watchful as he spoke, as if expecting an accusation.

In all honesty, Rafa placed near the top of my suspect list—except for one thing. I could easily picture him plunging those shears into Lee Holmes, but not stalking and slaying a woman, even a perfidious one like Bethany Zahn. Passion, yes. Premeditation, no.

"I won't run to the police with this," I said. "That's their job, not mine. Just as long as I don't trip over any more bodies. Sergeant Watts practically accused me of murdering them to impress Pruett! She suspects him too."

That caused an explosion of grunts and guffaws from the guys and allayed their distrust of me. Apparently, Genna made quite a vivid impression everywhere she went. I should have defended my gender, but she made it impossible to do so.

Roy stifled a belch and weighed in once again. "No one wanted her here, but that mean cop has been sniffing around here a lot. Only one she ever talked to was Yael. Something about 'waste management'—that's what she called it."

I suspected that Genna, ever vigilant, had caught Yael disposing of waste in the wrong location. A big no-no in dog show circles. No doubt, Yael ignored her or brushed off warnings like lint.

Alf pointed across the room, where Pruett was holding court. "Looks like your boy has his hands full with those ladies. Better watch out or you could lose him."

Several of the handlers draped themselves over Pruett, and Punky edged closer and closer to his lap. That didn't worry me, although he obviously believed in method acting—Stanislavsky lived on in Wing Pruett. Meanwhile, Babette and Yael Lindsay stayed in their corner, gossiping like old friends. As the saying goes, blood and money are thicker than water.

I excused myself and wandered toward the restroom, all the while keeping a weather eye out for Whit Whitly. It was a distasteful task, but I had agreed to quiz that loathsome creature about Bethany. A sudden tap on my shoulder startled me. There stood a vision of male pulchritude in the person of Sergeant Roar Jansen, out of uniform but more in step than ever. Tonight, he was wearing a pricey-looking baby-blue cable-knit sweater and form-fitting gray flannels. His ringlets formed a heavenly nimbus around his head. Fortunately, my store of self-control kicked in just in time to tether me to earth.

"Surprised to see you here, Perri," he said. "Slumming with the natives or hunting for clues?" His message was serious, but his eyes twinkled a bit.

I shrugged. "Just kicking back."

Roar's grin was a thing of beauty. "Why do I not believe you? Listen. This stuff—fooling around with a double murderer—is serious. Cut it out before you get hurt."

Like an obedient child, I nodded. Luckily, Roar didn't see that my fingers were crossed. "Any progress to report?"

He stepped in close enough to touch my hand. "Sorry. That's police business. No civilians allowed."

"Persistence" was my middle name, with "plucky" a close second. Some have suggested that "pesky" was an even better fit. Either way, I had to somehow penetrate the thin blue line between cop and civilian. I tried a throw-away comment. "Bethany was blackmailing someone. I think she saw Lee's killer."

Genna Watts would have slapped me in cuffs. Roar exhaled instead. "Do tell." There was that insouciant grin again. I stifled the impulse to slap it off his handsome face.

"I suppose you already knew that."

"Yep." He was either vying for a John Wayne role or deliberately baiting me. I chose door number two.

"I thought you wanted my help. You know, the insider perspective."

Roar put his hands on my shoulders and gave me the thousand-yard cop stare. "Genna set me straight on that. Besides we know this arena pretty well anyway. You probably noticed there's an onsite police station at the Big E Coliseum."

Sometimes I plow ahead, despite hints to the contrary. This was one of those times. "I've been wracking my brain, trying to figure things out. Lee

Holmes would have been an easy kill, but Bethany—that level of brutality was exceptional. Not many men or women would have the stomach for it. Especially amateurs."

That got his attention. Roar studied me before going to the next level. "Argues for a professional, is that what you're suggesting? Believe it or not, Genna and I are pros too. We checked all our sources, but no one heard anything about a contract or hit man."

"Lots of ex-military in the Springfield area. Could be one of them."

Roar's expression told me that he was fed up with my meddling. Gone was his cherubic, slightly naughty persona. In rushed stern Sergeant Jansen. "Let me put it this way, Ms. Morgan. You're ex-military yourself. My partner's already sizing up Pruett for the collar, and this will only encourage her. She might make a double play and nab you too. Tread carefully."

He moved closer. Close enough for me to finger the soft fabric of his sweater—cashmere, unless I missed my guess. "You have good taste," I said. "Expensive too."

"You know how it is. Only the best. On a cop's salary, I have to get lucky. Find a great bargain."

He was teasing me. That sweater was definitely a gift from an admirer of the female persuasion. Roar Jansen would attract plenty of them, and the horsewomen and dog enthusiasts who populated the Big E had ready cash to spare.

Why not capitalize on his change of mood, I thought. "Made any arrests yet?"

"Why? Got anyone special in mind?" He moved closer, close enough to stroke my hair. "A woman's crowning glory—isn't that what they call hair? Yours is lovely."

Vanity may be a sin, but on occasion even I plead guilty to it. Hair was my one remarkable feature in an otherwise average appearance. Pruett spent time brushing it when he got a chance, and the experience was sensual beyond belief.

"We were discussing suspects." I edged back several steps, enough to discourage further contact but not enough to offend.

"Were we?" Flirtatious Roar disappeared; stern Sergeant Jansen took his place. "Ask away."

"Have you arrested Jess Pendrake? She's not guilty, you know."

Roar folded his arms and glowered at me. This time it was no act. He was very seriously displeased. "As yet we haven't made any arrests." His words were stiff and unyielding, like his posture. "When we do, Ms. Morgan, the charge will stick, no matter who it is."

Afterward, I envisioned several cutting remarks and witty asides that would have flattened him. At the time, however, I buttoned my lips and kept my mouth shut. The tension between us was thicker than London fog until Wing Pruett, my unlikely savior, intervened.

"Hey, you two," he said. "Not trying to steal my gal, are you, Roar?"

I eyed those monuments to male pulchritude with interest. Blond and brunette, brawny and tall, they were most women's concept of one very pleasant dream team. The boys seemed to be enjoying themselves too. Was this a bromance in the making or a carefully crafted charade?

"Still writing that article?" Roar asked. "Hope you make me the star. Genna will go ape-shit."

Pruett chuckled. "You know, that's not a bad idea. What about it, Perri?"

"Leave me out of it. That's your department." I spied Whit Wiley slithering toward the buffet and left the Hardy Boys to their own devices. At least Jess was still free. I wondered where in the world she was keeping herself?

Meanwhile, I cornered my prey at the bar as he gulped down scotch at an alarming rate. Something had obviously gone wrong in his carefully constructed world, and I meant to capitalize on it.

"Hey, Whit. What's going on?" I resurrected my friendly girl-next-door persona from the refuse pile. The routine was a bit rusty but still serviceable. "Boy, this place is packed."

The look he gave me was anything but friendly. Still, I persisted.

"One man isn't enough for you, I see." He hissed like the viper that he was.

"Who, me? Nah. I was concerned about Jess Pendrake and asked Sergeant Jansen what the score was." I shrugged. "He didn't tell me much."

Whit swiveled his bar stool my way and stared. "Why do you care? You barely know these people. All you want is glory for your boyfriend and a few new customers. Unless, of course, you're trying to protect someone."

"Whew! That's pretty harsh, my friend. Aren't you interested in finding the murderer, for Yael's sake, if nothing else?"

The venomous look he gave me made Whit Wiley look even more unpleasant than usual. Funny. I hadn't thought that was possible.

"Leave Yael out of this," he snarled. "She's suffered enough."

One of my superpowers was selective hearing. It enabled me to rise above petty insults from twerps like Whit. I invoked it and allowed his snarky comments to sail right over my head. "Losing Lee was bad enough, but now with Bethany gone . . ." I shook my head mournfully. "I'm afraid that Sergeant Jansen will connect the dots."

Whit pushed forward. It was an aggressive move designed to intimidate me. "So?"

I towered over the little shit by at least two inches, and that gave me a strategic advantage. "Well, Whit," I said, keeping my voice just above sneer level, "those dots lead straight to you and Yael. Could get nasty."

As he processed my words, his face grew ashen. "Wait! I had nothing against Bethany. She was annoying. A pest. But that's all."

"She saw Lee's murderer," I said sotto voce.

Whit went from pale to pasty. "I never touched that woman. Besides, Jess killed both of them. Ask anyone."

Most people describe me as a nice person. There are times, however, when a mean streak a mile wide suffuses my being. This was one of those times.

"Looks like you're out of the loop, Whit." My voice was all sugary sweetness. "The cops haven't charged Jess. Roar Jansen just confirmed that. Weird, isn't it? Seems like they're looking elsewhere. Could mean trouble." I shook my head mournfully.

He gulped down the dregs of his drink and leapt off the stool. "You don't fool me one bit, Perri Morgan. You're not as smart as you think. Back off."

His macho act was truly pitiful. Whit Wiley was better suited to innuendo and snark than overt actions. My assessment hadn't changed one bit. In my experience, murderers were a cold-hearted, resolute lot who took their chances and did the deed. Whit simply didn't measure up. He might plan a crime, but he would have to leave the execution to others.

I faced him without moving an inch or blinking. Apparently, Whit was accustomed to more pliant females, and I unnerved him. He pivoted and stormed toward the exit without even saying good-bye. I really loathe sore losers. Impolite ones are even worse.

Chapter 17

Our crackerjack trio reconvened at the entrance ten minutes later. Babette was flushed with excitement, but Pruett and I were less enthused. Despite our efforts, the pincer movement had yielded few tangible results.

"Come on, you two," Babette trilled. "Spill." Hearing a wealthy suburban matron use noir terms worthy of Mickey Spillane and Dashiell Hammett was almost worth a night of cringe-inducing failures. I clapped my pal on the shoulder and hugged her.

"Not here," Pruett said. "Back to your place, Babette, and keep smiling."

We planted foolish grins on our faces and took our leave without arousing suspicion. Most of the dog show crowd was either cackling with alcohol-induced hilarity or glued together, enjoying the minuscule dance floor and catchy tunes. Roar had his baby blues fixed on Punky; Rafa held Yael Lindsay in a tight embrace. Slow, soulful songs brought out emotion in almost everyone. If only our dogs could have added a howl or two to complete the effect. Not everyone joined in the festivities, however. Alf and Roy Vesco stood on the fringes, arms folded, like frozen sentries guarding the terrain. Whit Wiley had vanished.

"We missed our chance to slow dance," Pruett said. "Too bad."

"Go on back," Babette said. Her voice trailed off, and the exuberance of only a moment ago left with it.

Pruett gently brushed his finger over my lips. "No problem. We'll have plenty of time later on. Right, Perri?"

I swallowed several times before answering. Damn. That man did more with a simple touch than most guys could in an all-night session. No wonder he'd been dubbed DC's Sexiest Man. I could attest.

Fortunately, Babette was oblivious to our antics. "I don't know about you all, but I'm famished. What say I whip up an omelet when we get there?"

We crunched through the snow and piled into Pruett's Porsche. I'm no car person, but who can resist glove-soft leather, mahogany paneling, and the sweet, sweet sound of John Coltrane wafting from ten loudspeakers connected to the Burmester stereo? Babette was immediately hooked.

"This is some ride, Pruett," she said, discarding the blues. "Makes a gal forget her cares and woes. What do you call the color, anyway? I love it."

Pruett mumbled a response. Once again, he seemed abashed, not proud, of his glorious vehicle. "Carmine red. Ella loves red too. She picked it."

"Well, it's one hot car for a very hot guy. Lets the ladies know you're in town."

I wisely kept my own counsel and banished the vivid mental images of Pruett and the following he attracted. Jealousy was not among my flaws, and I intended to keep it that way. So what if the list of Pruett's conquests was long and legendary? Why anguish over the past or doom the future?

When we arrived at Steady Eddie, another surprise awaited us. Huddled at the door was the shivering, shaking form of Jess Pendrake.

* * * *

While Pruett parked the Porsche, I hustled toward Jess. "You must be frozen stiff," I said. "Are you okay?"

Her teeth were chattering, but she managed a stiff nod. Funny thing. Jess had teeth that were movie-star perfect. Not what I would have expected in someone who eschewed any attempt to upgrade her image. Babette, ever the gracious southerner, did her part too.

"Come on in, honey," she said. "You need a hot toddy to perk you up, and I know just how to make it." Babette's restoratives were legendary among her social set, one of many unique skills that distinguished her from the common herd.

Jess leaned on me as she carefully unwound her legs and entered Steady Eddie. I barely knew the woman, but my duty was clear. Luck, chance, or providence had literally landed her in our laps, and it was the perfect chance to quiz her about that awful night when Bethany had died. Carpe diem and all that.

The inquisition was delayed for a bit by practical considerations. Babette bustled about making hot toddies, while Pruett turned on the low-voltage charm machine for our guest and I released the dogs. Jess was wary of men. Actually, she seemed distrustful of all humans, especially us. We sat in a semicircle, sipping our drinks and making cautious small talk that got us nowhere. Jess said very little. She clenched her fists and scanned each of us with narrowed, blue-gray eyes as if expecting an imminent attack. Babette, the perfect hostess, dished up crabmeat omelets and southern homilies that were comforting even though they made very little sense. Then, with superior canine logic that defied human comprehension, Guinnie crept up to Jess and jumped into her lap. That's all it took. Jess buried her head in Guinnie's soft fur and hugged the beautiful pointer. When she looked up, Jess began to speak in a torrent of fevered words.

"I had to see you," Jess said. "No one else believed me." Although the room was toasty warm, she shivered uncontrollably. Babette hastily placed a cashmere throw around her guest's shoulders and replenished the drink in her hand.

"There you go, sugar. Take your time. We've got all night."

Jess stroked Guinnie's fur as she continued. "I didn't kill that woman."

At times like this, Pruett became a telepathic metamorph able to mold himself to suit any occasion. He knew intuitively that Jess was frightened. Therefore, he powered down and allowed me to start up the party. The duplicity was staggering but effective.

"How did Bethany contact you?" I asked. "You weren't at Lee's memorial."

That earned me a snarl from Jess. "I'm no hypocrite. I hated Lee Holmes and his snobby wife. Still do. I found a note on the door in my motel room, so I went to the barn."

Babette jumped full speed into the fray. "Were you two pals? I know I tell Perri everything."

"I barely knew her. Mostly she acted like I wasn't even there." Jess choked back a sob. "They all do."

That answered one of my questions. Jess, the perfect dupe, had been set up by the murderer. It was a clever scheme designed to incriminate a recluse with known hostility toward both victims.

"Did you see or hear anything in the barn?" Pruett's tone was calm and matter-of-fact.

She shook her head.

"She was dying when I arrived," I said. "Did she say anything before then—anything at all?"

Another head shake from Jess. No one could ever accuse her of being a chatterbox. Guinnie nuzzled her hand, as if offering encouragement, while Keats and Poe formed an honor guard around me.

I decided to try yet again. "Bethany told people she knew who killed Lee. Did she tell you that?"

Jess hesitated. "No, but she said so in her note. That's why I went there. I thought...I wanted to be a big deal just that once. Make people like me." She bowed her head again.

Pruett leaned forward. "I know the feeling. Everybody wants that at least once. What did the cops say?"

Jess stayed silent as she fed egg scraps to Guinnie. "Not much. That woman told me I was guilty, and she'd prove it. The pretty guy just watched me. They finally had to let me go when I showed them the note." It was not surprising that Genna Watts had been the lead inquisitor. If she ever left the police force, a bright future in horror films or the gulag awaited her.

"How come they released you?" Babette asked. "That's one tough cookie. Wouldn't expect her to crumble."

Surprisingly, Jess smiled as she answered. "I ran into that Whit Wiley creep while I was walking over. The big clock was striking ten. I remember that. He even said something about me and Lee Holmes. How I was probably glad he was dead." She curled her lip. "Only time that creep ever helped me out."

I thought about it for a moment. Bethany had left the arena right before ten o'clock—9:45 or so, according to my watch. I had checked it before I slipped out to follow her. Twenty minutes later, she was dead. That narrowed the window of opportunity for the killer. He or she must have been waiting there, determined to silence Bethany and her loose talk forever.

Pruett didn't have to take notes. Among his many attributes was an eidetic memory that made note taking superfluous. Coincidentally, it also helped him sync alibis with any liaisons he had planned.

"Bethany had a lover. Any idea who he was?" His tone was casual, one friend to another.

I'd never heard Jess laugh before. After hearing it, I was just as glad. The sound had more cackle and croak than mirth. Maybe she hadn't had much occasion to use it.

"You don't get it, do you?" she said. "She was a slut! Bethany Zahn had tons of lovers, so why should this one be special? Ask your handler friends if you don't believe me."

I pondered that for a moment. If Bethany had witnessed Lee's murder, she made no attempt to hide that guilty knowledge. Someone—ruthless and decisive—had silenced her. It was probable that her lover had nothing to do with her murder. Another dead end, to make a very bad pun.

Pruett had a technique of listening—actually listening—to a woman. A rare enough talent anywhere, but in the political morass of the nation's capital, it was unheard of. That had helped him gain the trust of confidential sources. Come to think of it, listening played pretty well in a western Massachusetts dog show too. I was willing to wager that Jess had never experienced anything like that from a man like Wing Pruett or any male at all.

"Help me out, Ms. Pendrake," he said. "Who do you peg as the killer?"

She bowed her head as if the question were impossible. "Roy Vesco could have done it. That slutty wife of his was always in Lee's face. Come to think of it, she's mean enough to off someone too."

"Kiki?" Babette was appalled. "What a horrible thought."

Pruett and I exchanged looks. No need to mention how often women lashed out at their enemies. The Internet teemed with examples.

Jess bit her lip as if she had come to a difficult decision. "I lied before."

Pruett raised his eyebrows but said nothing. Fortunately, Babette was too dumbstruck to jump in.

"You asked if she said anything." Jess scrunched her eyes together as if the very thought was painful.

I nodded encouragement.

"Just one thing. Probably don't mean nothin', but she said, 'Cops!' Like she wanted me to call 'em." Jess's eyes filled, and she turned her head away. "Too late for that."

The energy in the room quickly waned as we processed the sad ending of Bethany Zahn. Too much alcohol and too little sleep muddled my mind. Maybe a nap would fire up the old synapses and promote rational thought. Apparently, I wasn't alone in thinking this. Babette was already dozing, and Jess looked almost comatose. Only Wing Pruett, man of steel, was ready to rock. "I'll walk you back to your camper," he told Jess. "Let you get some rest."

She agreed only after I emphasized the need for one final potty break for our dogs. Just mentioning them brightened her face, transforming her wan features into something approaching animation. To my surprise, Babette joined our little caravan as we headed toward the open fields of the Big E acreage. Although she'd never admit it, I suspected that my pal felt a tad uneasy with a murderer on the prowl. Safety in numbers, as they say.

"Who's taking care of your dogs, hon?" Babette put her arm around Jess.

"Mine are all ringside pickups," she said. "Easier for me that way, and they stay with their owners." Some handlers preferred to house and groom each of their charges, but others met the dogs and owners at the ring before showtime. Large breeds like shepherds required a lot of space, so it was no wonder that Jess, whose camper was minuscule, chose that option. On the other hand, there was no greater safety, if danger arose, than canine company. With Keats and Poe at my side, I felt perfectly protected. In view of all that had transpired, Jess might have welcomed the security.

Since she lacked Babette's bank balance, Jess's camper was located on the far side of the Big E in what was tactfully termed "Siberia." Handlers incurred plenty of expenses, especially for hotels, transportation, and meals. By hunkering down in a camper, Jess had saved herself a bundle. If Steady Eddie was a luxury behemoth, the pop-up camper Jess owned was an impoverished relation. Pruett remained impassive as we approached it, but Babette couldn't help but wrinkle her nose. Fortunately, Jess missed that reaction. The pop-up was hitched to a weathered truck that, like my own Suburban, had seen plenty of miles. Although it was humble, the camper served its purpose and presented a realistic picture of what many workers faced. We waited for Jess to enter it before leaving. She slipped inside without saying a word—no thank-yous or good nights from that guest. On the homeward trek, we stayed silent, and even Babette, the perpetual chatterbox, seemed chastened by the evening's events. As I adjusted the eiderdown on our bed, I thought of Jess and those like her whose finances were limited. Then Pruett folded me in his arms and banished those thoughts with something much more pleasurable.

Chapter 18

"We didn't get much last night," Babette grumbled. "Big waste of time." She poured Pruett and me a mug of espresso and passed plates of fruit, fried chicken, and waffles to each of us. A pitcher filled with steaming syrup graced the center of the table. After some coaxing, she shared her conversation with Yael Lindsay.

"I've been a widow before," Babette said, "so I know what I'm talking about." That was one of the understatements of the year. My pal had been widowed three times thus far and wasn't ruling out another go on the marital merry-go-round. "Mark my words. Yael was glad to be shed of Lee Holmes."

"Go on," I said. Babette loved me to tease information from her. I refused to play that game today, but Pruett had no such qualms. He placed his hands on the table and gave her his most engaging grin. Worked like a charm.

"Anyhow, Yael planned to dump his ass as soon as possible. Told me so herself. After a few shots of scotch, she said someone saved her a lot of trouble and expense." Babette was triumphant. "Top that one if you can, Perri."

I tried to be patient, but it wasn't easy. Babette's big scoop added nothing new to the equation and merely confirmed what we already knew or suspected.

She batted her eyelashes and launched into her coy act. "One thing more. Want to hear it?"

Pruett and I both nodded.

"I think she's already lined up his replacement. What do you think of that? Even I waited a while. Six months was my minimum. Anything less is indecent!"

That added an interesting wrinkle to the case. Perhaps Yael was less innocent than she appeared to be. Pruett must have had the same thought.

"Any idea who the lucky guy is?" Pruett asked.

Babette bowed her head in defeat. "Nope. We were swappin' bad husband stories, and Yael said next time she'd know better. Something about shared interests. That told me he was part of the dog show gang. No names, though." She heaped Pruett's plate with more food. "Eat up now."

To her credit, Babette was the ultimate hostess. That breakfast of chicken and waffles was simply too good to resist—so we didn't. It wasn't until our plates were cleaned that I added my two cents.

"The guys had a few things to say. For one thing, Lee Holmes cheated Rafa big-time on a land deal right around here. Some kennel property, apparently. That plus the vitamin scam adds up to a major motive."

Babette kept her composure as she poured our espresso. Her hand was steady—didn't spill one drop—but her eyes told a different tale. Rafa's story piqued her curiosity and maybe a bit more.

Pruett tilted his head. "Anything else?"

I shared the scoop about Rafa's brother and his nonexistent family. That won a smile from our hostess and a sigh of relief. The talk about Bethany and her checkered past raised a few eyebrows.

Pruett curled his lip in distaste. "Sounds more like a gossip session to me. Who ever said guys don't talk? Besides, men brag about their success with women, and nobody cares."

I raised one brow at that comment.

"You know what I mean," Pruett stammered. "Bethany got branded a slut for having an active social life. A guy with the same moves would be called lucky."

He had a point, even though I wouldn't admit it. "Moving on," I said, "what did you learn from your adoring female fans?"

He wrinkled his brow. I had to admit, it made Pruett look even more delectable, especially when a thick strand of hair fell across his forehead.

"Okay," he said, "the ladies had plenty of opinions about these murders. Most of them voted for a disgruntled business associate. Lee Holmes was notorious for destroying other people's lives, financial and otherwise."

I asked about the pet supplement Le Chien Champ. Punky had been closed-mouth about that, but I couldn't shake the feeling that she was hiding something. Babette gave Pruett the gimlet eye and pounced.

"You and Punky got mighty close, mister. I saw her sitting on your lap, just singing away. What else did she offer in return?"

Grown men don't often blush, but this one did. Pruett did an "aw shucks" routine and waved Babette off. "Come on," he said, "you're killing me. I did my part, just like we planned."

"And?" Babette put her hands on her hips.

"Apparently, this supplement business was a bigger mess than we thought. Lee dangled the bait in front of everyone, including the AKC and UKC, whatever that is. Signed up the American Handlers' Union too. Lots of high-level folks were involved, I gathered."

I explained that the UKC stood for United Kennel Club and was another large organization devoted to dogs and their people. Pruett made a face and continued his narrative. "Anyway, when things went south, all hell broke loose. Le Chien Champ LLC got sued big-time, and Lee got dragged into court. He was sued individually as an officer of the corporation. Yael too." Pruett coughed discreetly. "Apparently, he 'misled' the court when he testified and came damn close to being cited for perjury. That stuff contained additives from China. Phorate. I researched it, and, man, it is really bad stuff."

I had predicted the outcome of that story, and I was correct. The insurer backed out based on false and misleading advertising, and Yael waved her checkbook around and made things right. Once again, big bucks snatched Lee Holmes from the jaws of perdition.

"Money aside," I said, "some dogs were sickened or actually died. There's no compensation for that."

Babette nodded and hugged Clara for emphasis. Lord help anyone who messed with my pal or her beloved pets. Mine too, come to think of it.

Pruett hesitated. "One of the dogs that died was a poodle handled by Alf Walsh. Guess he took it hard and gave Lee a beating."

I shrugged. Lee Holmes deserved to be bloodied for what he did. Perhaps the use of those poodle shears was a type of poetic justice. That didn't justify Bethany's murder, but it certainly raised the stakes for Alf and Rafa as the prime suspects. All in all, Pruett topped our trio as a super sleuth. I lagged far behind.

According to Roar, they hadn't traced the murder weapons yet. Almost impossible to do around this place with the size and number of people going in and out. I'd bet that plough gauge was someone's discard—careless but not unusual in a huge area filled with horses and livestock. They had had more luck with the shears. Rafa had already admitted that they were his. Most had a number on the inside blade that would confirm ownership.

When I trotted out my theory about a professional killer, Babette had no reaction, but Pruett's eyes lit up. He was intrigued and wanted more.

"Bethany's murder is the key to this whole thing," I said. "Analyze that crime, and we'll identify the culprit."

Whatever she saw or thought she saw had imperiled the murderer and sealed Bethany's fate. She must have believed that she could turn a profit by toying with a killer. Bad move. Foolishness. Fatal, as it turned out.

I put aside my deerstalker the moment I checked my watch. Even Sherlock had to earn his living, and mine depended on keeping Creature Comforts open and fully stocked. Pruett did his part by loading up Guinnie's show gear and heading for Ring Ten, the next stop for pointers. If I knew the scourge of scribes—and I did—he would quiz Alf about the fracas with Lee Holmes and confirm the handler's alibi as well. For a man who was uncomfortable around animals, Pruett had made great progress. I spent a pleasant minute considering the rewards I would offer him before focusing again on the task at hand.

With Babette zeroed in on the agility competition, I had time to groom Keats and Poe and plan my next move. In four days, the show would conclude, whether or not the murderer had been apprehended. At that point, Roar Jansen and his trusty sidekick could solve the case or admit defeat. I sympathized with them since most cops, even unpleasant and obnoxious ones, hated ambiguity. They disliked letting a killer escape even more.

I busied myself with completing sales tax records and adjusting my inventory. By eight AM, a steady stream of customers with last-minute needs and plenty of side commentary filled the aisles. Punky sidled up to me, aching to reprise last night's festivities. I waved her off, promising to meet her at lunchtime for a quick bite. I quickly checked the food supply in my satchel. Not bad. It was crammed full of a thermos of strong coffee and several bottles of water. As a veteran of these events, I knew that the food was suited for fuel rather than appetite, heavy on chips, mayo, and fat. Better to forego them except in emergencies. Fortunately, Babette, the perfect hostess, had packed fruit, nuts, cheese, and grapes to sustain us throughout the day. I had enough to share with Punky if she wasn't too greedy, and I planned to use it as leverage. Food for facts or something like that.

At noon, I closed up my stall, crated my dogs, and headed toward the concession area. Punky was already there, sitting on the bench, tapping her toes. When she saw me, she waved and patted the seat next to her.

"About time, Ms. Perri. I'm in the ring in half an hour. Rafa's judging the group, you know, and he's very punctual."

I dangled sustenance her way. That earned me a big smile and a sigh of relief. "Thank you, ma'am. If I had to eat one more grilled hot dog, I'd puke." She pointed at the food stand with its rotating wieners. "That poor little soldier has bitten the dust. Reminds me of so many men I've known around here. No staying power, and not much to look at."

Punky grinned at her own joke, even though there was an element of truth behind the words. According to her, Lee Holmes had the physical attributes that attracted a loyal female following. Quality and quantity—a recommendation for a tryst but nothing long-term.

We arranged our spread before chatting, then got down to business. "Your guy Pruett was lively last night," Punky said. "Made the time fly by."

"He has that effect on people," I said sourly. "Mostly women." Punky took a sip of water and giggled. "Lordy, yes. He is fine."

"You looked happy enough dancing with Roar last night. Is that his version of the third degree?"

Punky gave me a coy look but remained silent. "Don't tell anyone, but we kind of got together afterward." She rolled her eyes. "I recommend it if you get the chance. That boy knows his stuff."

"Sorry. Not interested." I kept my tone light to avoid giving insult. Punky was harmless enough as long as she kept away from Pruett.

"Looked like Rafa scored last night too," she said.

"Yeah?"

Punky nodded. "He left with Yael right after you did. That's one thing I never saw coming. Whit Wiley went ballistic."

"Really?"

After snagging a wedge of cheese, she continued. "Little shit. Whit, I mean. What made him think any woman would want him, let alone one with big bucks? I thought he wasn't even into girls. Maybe he takes whatever he can get." She checked her watch. "Oops. Got to run." Punky galloped off to gather her dog and get an armband from the judge.

I stayed, transfixed by thoughts of Whit Wiley and false expectations. Had he eliminated Lee Holmes to clear the path to Yael Lindsay? Filthy lucre and the prospect of attaining it were among the oldest motives in the book. If Bethany had threatened him, Whit probably felt that he had little choice. Even a cornered rat will fight to the death. I just hadn't pictured him having the guts to physically confront anyone, male or female.

"Thought you had a business to run." No one could mistake the strident tones of Sergeant Watts. She stood at my side, hands on hips, with her perpetual sneer firmly in place.

I applied a liberal dose of sunshine and soft soap designed to annoy the heck out of her. "Good morning, Sergeant. Sorry. I didn't see you standing there. Care for some grapes?" No one could fault my letter-perfect smile except one venomous cop nursing a major grudge.

"We have unfinished business," she said. "Come with me."

Time to take off the gloves. No more nicey-nice with this vile creature. I gathered my refuse, stood, and stared her down. "I don't think so. If you want to arrest me, feel free, but be prepared for a major lawsuit. Otherwise, as you pointed out, I have a shop to run." I chucked the garbage into a nearby bin and gave this parting shot. "Just a bit of advice. Better check with your partner first before you arrest anyone. Roar and I had a nice chat last night at O'Doul's. We covered a lot of ground."

For a moment, I feared that Genna would implode or assault me. Fortunately, even the most combustible cops have their limitations, and I was spared. She spun around and stalked toward the exit doors without uttering another word. The taste of victory felt curiously flat, like champagne that had passed its prime. Instead of triumph, I felt a strange sympathy for the unlovely sergeant, who obviously adored her partner. My taunt had cut her to the quick.

"Stop moping around, Perri. Clara just won points in agility, and I want to celebrate!" Babette dispelled gloom with her air of boundless optimism as she slapped me on the back. Few could resist her, and I didn't even try. "Was that the Gorgon of the constabulary I just saw? She looked as steamed as a lobster in the pot."

"Follow me back to the shop," I said. "I want to hear about Clara's win. Then I'll tell you a thing or two I just found out."

"Sorry, kiddo. I'm meeting Rafa in five minutes. Don't worry. I promise to grill him like a hunk of beef." She tittered. "Beefcake, actually. I'll think up something else for dessert. Count on it."

I waved her off and hurried over to catch the finals of the pointer competition. Once again, Guinnie prevailed over a crowded field, including one of Yael Lindsay's prize pooches. She earned more Grand Champion points and a nose kiss from Alf Walsh. Pruett stood outside the ring, playing the proud but puzzled parent and no doubt missing Ella. I could relate since I also felt a void every time the little girl was elsewhere.

"Great stuff," I said. "You're really getting the hang of this dog show thing."

Pruett coughed. "I'm just doing it for Ella." His glistening eyes put paid to that lie immediately. "Alf said Guinnie's headed for the group ring, whatever that means."

I rolled my eyes at him. "She's competing against all the other Sporting breeds. If she wins there, it's on to Best of Show." I rubbed my hands together. "Exciting."

This time, it was Pruett who rolled his eyes. "My editor has been bugging me about the piece. You know, 'Death by Dog Show.' She wants a conclusion, something to knock their socks off."

I lowered my voice and mentioned that Roar and Punky had hooked up last night. That didn't shock him, but he raised his eyebrows when he heard about Rafa and Yael.

"She's at least ten years older than Rafa. Maybe more." Pruett, the sophisticated man about town, sounded scandalized.

I bit my tongue and avoided mentioning the obvious. If Rafa were older, no one—Pruett included—would think anything was amiss. Older men with big bank accounts often coupled with much younger women. In this instance, Yael had the bucks, so why not use them to attract a hottie like Rafa?

"But she just lost her husband," Pruett said. He pursed his lips like a prim schoolgirl.

"From what I gather, Lee Holmes wasn't much of a loss. Maybe Yael doesn't want to be a hypocrite."

Pruett made some vague sound of disapproval and pointed toward the group ring and Guinnie. Unfortunately, I couldn't stay. Several clients had contacted me about custom collars, and a number of mother-daughter combos had pre-ordered my belts. I'd already spent too much time away from my business.

"Later," I said, blowing him a kiss. When our eyes met, an electric charge radiated from my head to my nether parts, accompanied by a full body flush. It was totally unbecoming in a woman of thirty and quite a heavenly sensation. I floated on a cloud of blissful lust all the way back to Creature Comforts.

Chapter 19

After a profitable afternoon spent ringing up sales, I decided to reward myself with a temporary respite. Guinnie had won the group competition and was slated for the Best in Show ring at four PM. Her loving daddy pledged to film the proceedings and stream them for Ella that evening. Naturally, we both hoped against hope that Guinnie would be crowned Best in Show.

Yael Lindsay slipped into my store just as I extinguished the lights. Growls from Keats and Poe warned me of an intruder before she got very far.

"Anything you need?" I said. "You caught me as I was just closing up."

I noticed that she had ditched her widow's weeds for a becoming coral pantsuit and upped the makeup quotient as well. Nothing like a night of wanton sex to stir up the old hormones.

"Why were you stalking me?" she asked. Her tone was decidedly frosty.

For once I was totally gobsmacked. The most I could manage was a wholly inadequate "Huh?"

Yael narrowed her eyes and hissed. "Don't think you're fooling me, Ms. Morgan. Mind your own business. My husband's murder had nothing to do with you."

For once, I abandoned the good manners and deference to my elders that adults had drummed into me since childhood. Yael was old enough to be my mother. That earned her a modicum of civility, but that's where her rights ended. "Frankly, your husband's death doesn't really interest me, Mrs. Holmes. I found his body, of course."

She stepped back as if I had struck her. This doyenne of dogs was unaccustomed to a peasant purveyor like me having the effrontery to strike back. Emboldened, I upped the ante.

"I want justice for Bethany Zahn, though."

"She was a slut!" Yael's voice grew shrill. "No better than a whore."

"Perhaps." I kept my tone calm and unemotional, knowing that would enrage her still more. "She was blackmailing someone. I'm certain of that."

Yael Lindsay grew pale beneath her carefully applied paint.

"Makes one wonder," I said, "who around here had anything to lose. Most folks are barely making ends meet."

Yael sputtered and nearly collapsed against the counter. For a moment, I feared she would stroke out, but she regained her composure and staggered to the entryway, issuing a parting shot as she did. "I warn you. There will be consequences."

With Keats and Poe at my side, I followed behind and locked the door. "Yes. I'm positive of that."

* * * *

The Best in Show competition always thrilled me, even when I wasn't a participant. With Guinnie in the hunt, the thrill quotient expanded tenfold. I grabbed a seat on the bench next to Pruett and scanned the field. All the competitors were nice dogs, but two in particular stood out as threats to Guinnie: a sleek and sassy bichon frise and a charming petit basset griffon vendeen, or PBGV, as the breed is commonly known. Both were Silver Grand Champions, and the PBGV in particular was a crowd favorite. Guinnie's elegance and style might be an impediment if the judge preferred smaller, more popular breeds, although through my slightly biased eyes, she led the pack. Best of Show judge was considered a plum assignment in the conformation world, and this man, an unknown from Canada, certainly looked the part. His height and crop of thick white hair seemed more suited to a senator or Supreme Court justice than a magistrate at the Big E. If only his judgment bore that out as well.

Alf Walsh lounged at the entrance, speaking softly to Guinnie and stroking her fur. Punky, handling her black standard poodle, waved to me from behind them. Poodles were another breed that placed near the top at virtually every show. I never counted Punky out since a great handler upped her dog's chances for success in any ring. Punky was a winner who knew every trick in the book. Some said she even wrote that book.

"Well, look at that," Pruett whispered, nodding toward a black Newfoundland, accompanied by none other than Kiki Vesco. Devoted swain Roy waited in the wings, nervously cracking his knuckles as his dream girl joined the lineup. Apparently, Kiki had bowed to convention by at last heeding the informal dress code. She sported a conservative, black-skirted suit paired with sensible low-heeled shoes. Kiki still managed to look seductive, even in that attire, but I resigned myself to that. Some females exude pheromones at any age. Unfortunately, I'd missed that particular heavenly gift. Any allure I had was limited to a full-court press for wholesomeness. Rebecca of Sunnybrook Farm with a dog lead.

My eyes turned back to the ring and the business at hand. I adore Newfies and usually root for them but not with Kiki at the helm. That little heifer had plenty of years to learn her craft and way too much attitude for a novice. Early victories would only feed that monstrous ego and lead to more trouble. Besides, Guinnie deserved the win.

Pruett's hand shook as he adjusted his iPhone. I laughed, thinking how a man who had conquered mobsters, cartels, and assorted white-collar thugs could be reduced to a puddle of nerves by a seven-year-old child. Emmy Awards and Pulitzers paled in comparison to these high stakes for Pruett, the devoted daddy. I loved him all the more for his vulnerability.

"Want me to handle the filming?" I asked, patting his shoulder. "That way you can study things for Ella."

He pulled a macho act. "Nope. I got it."

As the judge waved the contestants around the ring, I noticed Whit Wiley lurking on the sidelines. Between lurking, slithering, and slinking, that guy had all the basic reptile moves covered. I hoped against hope that he was the murderer but realized that the possibility was remote. Wish fulfillment only works when supported by evidence, and thus far Whit was clean.

Yael Lindsay sat soldier straight in her personalized chair, watching every move the handlers made. Most pros brought their own chairs, emblazoned with the kennel name or their favorite pup's moniker. Yael's chair had a regal flair that looked more like a throne than the humble fold-ups the rest of the crowd favored. Not surprising. The Big E was her domain, and she was its monarch. The rest of us lived to serve.

Pruett suddenly elbowed me none too gently in the ribs. "Look!"

Sure enough, Sergeant Watts had slipped from the sidelines and crouched next to Yael. The cop covered her mouth as she whispered in the doyenne's ear, although her steely look never wavered. The message—whatever it was—caused Yael to curl her ladylike lip and hiss something I couldn't quite catch. I craned my neck to see if Roar was also on the premises. No such luck. It was hard to imagine any relationship between the regal Yael and a down-market cop like Genna, unless the latter was gearing up for an arrest. Anything was possible, but that seemed very unlikely unless West Springfield was prepared for one enormous lawsuit.

Meanwhile, the judge made his first cut, paring the field down to five dogs. I held my breath as Guinnie was selected to join the party. Her competition included Punky's standard poodle, the PBGV, the white bichon, and, belatedly, the black Newfie, with Kiki trailing behind. The other handlers stepped back as the fortunate five semi-finalists were ordered to go once around the ring.

"Be objective," I cautioned myself. "All are fine specimens of their breeds." I wished in my heart of hearts that Ella could have seen her beloved pet in real time. Guinnie was a queen, a show dog without peer—she owned the ring. Unfortunately, the judge didn't see it quite that way. In the end, he awarded Best in Show to the PBGV, with Guinnie snagging Reserve Best in Show. Not quite the prize she deserved, but still worthy of praise. Pruett stood with Alf and Guinnie as they received a handsome silver plate in recognition of the win. I recorded the big event on my iPhone, while spending a few moments mooning over the prime specimen of his breed that was Wing Pruett.

Sudden inspiration jolted me back to reality. Everywhere, professionals and spectators were recording the proceedings, just as we had. On the night Bethany was murdered, the same situation had prevailed. iPhones were thick as the proverbial fleas in an unmown meadow. I saw it happening, but it didn't register until now. Surely, that would help pinpoint where the principals were when Bethany left the arena. The time frame was narrow, and most dog enthusiasts savored every memory of their beloved pet's triumphs. Even though that evening had been ostensibly a remembrance of Lee Holmes, it was still all about dogs. I searched for Roar but saw only the gnarled features of his partner. No sense in sharing my thinking with her. She'd probably interpret it as an admission of guilt or something equally inane and drag me down to the station.

Pruett returned from the photo session flushed with victory. "Ella will love this silver plate," he said. "Guinnie was simply phenomenal. That Alf really knows his stuff."

I knew that he had already e-mailed a photo to his little girl, and who could blame him? There was plenty of cause for celebration. It would thrill Ella, who, unlike the adults in the room, now knew not to quibble about first versus second place. I shared my theory with Pruett about iPhone videos.

"Hmm," he said, stroking that cleft in his chin. If he was trying to distract me, it almost worked. "Good idea. I'll phone Roar right away. Of course, he's probably thought of that already." He sped off to commune with his buddy, while I hunkered down to visit the World Wide Web on my computer. My phone was way too cumbersome and inadequate to the task. Most people shared their triumphs and tragedies via social media these days with a worldwide community of similar interests. Dog people were no different, and in fact they tended to be even more obsessed. I scurried back to Creature Comforts and fired up my machine.

As I suspected, someone had devised a special tribute page to the late and unlamented Lee Holmes, complete with photos, flowery language, and completely specious accounts of his virtues. Fortunately, Lee's memorial gathering at the Big E was prominently featured. I scanned several photos, including a particularly hideous one of me and a glamour shot of Bethany Zahn displaying cleavage and a triumphant grin, pointing at someone or something. She seemed downright ecstatic, despite the somber surroundings and the subdued crowd. I consoled myself with the thought that at least her final moments were happy ones full of expectation. Knowing Bethany, that meant the promise of either sex or money. Maybe both. The photographer had snapped her standing alone under the large clock on the east wall. The time was clearly visible: 9:30 PM. I knew that she slipped out of the auditorium precisely at 9:45 because I'd checked my watch before following her. Twenty minutes later, she was dead.

Someone—someone she trusted—had left before us and was lying in wait. Bethany probably expected an assignation or a payoff. She ran quickly, joyfully, toward the Equine Pavilion unaware that a grisly fate awaited her. My stomach roiled as I studied the photo. I wasn't her friend, and I hadn't really liked Bethany. I thought she was harmless, but obviously that was wrong. She posed a threat to someone who was willing to ruthlessly eliminate her rather than risk exposure. That murderer was probably among the shining faces and sober smiles of my colleagues, hoisting a toast to Lee Holmes, the man who started it all.

Guilt was noticeably absent in the page's many Facebook photos. Yael was composed yet hardly disconsolate, balancing a plate of fruit on her lap and dressed in duds straight from Bergdorf's fall collection. Babette had spotted them right away and spilled the beans. I was no fashionista in fact, I had never set foot in Bergdorf's hallowed halls. Still, I couldn't help but wonder how in the world Yael had managed that. Dog show attire tended to be practical rather than trendy. Drool, excrement, and tuffs of dog hair blanketed the area as if they were weapons destined to destroy designer duds. I shrugged. Maybe she always packed an elegant little black dress in case Lee should do the gentlemanly thing by popping off. Perhaps there was a more sinister twist to the wardrobe question: she knew in advance that something bad would happen and had come prepared for the occasion.

Nothing of interest stood out in the other photos except a candid shot of Rafa and Alf Walsh, arms folded in front of them, scowling from the sidelines. Both wore heavy sweaters and dark jackets. Dark clothing would hide bloodstains, at least temporarily. I bit my tongue to infuse some sanity back into my thoughts. Half the men and women at the event wore dark clothing. Why single out Rafa or Alf?

Babette, Roy, Punky, and Whit were mere faces in the crowd, as was a glimpse of the police presence of Genna and Roar. Wait a moment! Against all odds, Genna must have blended seamlessly into the crowd. I recalled scrutinizing the participants during the ceremony and the social hour that preceded it. Nothing seemed out of order then. Roar was there, of course. He was always floating about, thrilling the ladies and exchanging high fives with the guys. I clicked on a video that one of Punky's pals had uploaded. It featured the postprandial nattering of a number of guests and appeared to be anything but funereal. As the camera panned the crowd, everything I saw looked jarringly normal—just dog people gathered in knots, drinking and exchanging greetings.

True to her word, there was no sign of Jess Pendrake. She might well be a murderer, but to her credit, she was definitely not a hypocrite. Pruett, on the other hand, was busy charming the socks off Kiki, the seductress at large. As he hovered over her chair, Kiki threw back her head, not unlike a cat that had just lapped up some superior cream. Funny. I had missed that scene on the fateful night. What else had slipped by me?

None of the videos showed the clock or caught any other image of Bethany. My brainstorm now seemed more like a trickle than a torrent. Any one of the principal suspects might well have slipped away and dispatched the psychic without anyone, including me, noting their absence. None of the snapshots or videos were conclusive on that point, and according to Babette, the gathering broke up well before eleven. The murderer had ample opportunity to steal back to the Better Living Center and re-join the party. Winter clothing could easily mask bloodstains or other traces of mayhem.

Keats and Poe leapt up to alert me that we had company. Since they didn't bark or growl, I wasn't concerned. It had to be someone they knew and trusted. True to form, Babette, accompanied by the ever-faithful Clara, flounced into my shop with the bloom of romance still flushing her cheeks.

"Wondered where you'd gone to," she said. "You sure move fast, girl."

I buttoned my lips and said nothing.

Babette strode over to my computer and rudely pushed me aside. "Whatcha got there? Oh, that's the Facebook page for Lee." She gave a derisive snort. "Bunch of BS, if you ask me. Outright lies." She pointed to the shot of me. "Smile for a change, Perri. You always look so serious. Like some kind of prison matron. And looky there. Pruett sure charmed the pants off Kiki. Smile looks like a darn Cheshire cat, the little hussy."

Although she tends toward the dramatic, Babette can often be useful. This was one of those times. "Hey," I said, "I didn't see Genna there, did you?"

She shook her head. "Nope. Couldn't miss that sourpuss. Probably out nailing drunks somewhere or rousting old ladies."

I pointed to the crowd shot featuring Genna.

For once, even Babette was stymied. Her eyes widened as she studied the glimpse of the intrusive Sergeant Watts. "Well. I'll be . . ."

It seemed unlikely, but I had to consider every angle. Genna had the skill and strength to wield those pretty pink shears or the lethal blade of the plough gauge. Frankly, she also had the attitude—mean. What I couldn't reconcile was motive. It seemed unlikely that a cop would embark on a murderous rampage for no reason. Unless...Lee Holmes was an infamous womanizer who sought quantity over quality. Jess Pendrake was certainly proof of that. Had he also romanced and discarded Genna? I shuddered as I thought of the consequences of that ill-advised action. If Bethany found out, Genna might have neutralized the threat decisively and emphatically.

"Yoo-hoo," Babette cried. "Anyone home in there, Perri?"

I quickly explained my latest theory and the evidence behind it. Babette wrinkled her brow and stayed silent for several minutes as she pondered it.

"Genna Watts? Gee, Perri, I don't know about that one. She's certainly mean enough." She shivered. "More than enough. Vicious. Unlikable too. But a cop as a double murderer? Doesn't seem right somehow. What did Pruett say about it?"

I admitted that we hadn't yet discussed the theory. However, the more I considered it, the more I liked it. Who better to cover up evidence than a cop? Not just any police officer, but one of those charged with investigating the crime. From the outset, Genna had bullied witnesses and accused everyone, including me, of complicity in the crime. Was that her normal behavior or a smoke screen? Only one person really knew Genna, and that was her partner. Roar would probably protect his colleague to the very end, although he was smart and dedicated enough to bring a murderer to justice.

"I have to talk to Roar," I said. "He'll set me straight or at least listen to my theory."

Babette folded her arms in front of her. "Better make sure he comes alone, honey bunch, or you'll be next on her list. I say wait for Pruett. That way you'll have backup."

I gave my pal the side-eye. "What about you? Don't you count as backup?" I knew that, despite her good intentions, Babette avoided danger whenever possible. She squirmed in her seat, then blurted out her feelings.

"Why risk your life over two people we barely knew? We'll be out of here in three days anyway. Let it go, for heaven's sake. Cops stick together. You know that, Perri. They'll run us right out of town. Besides, I still think that slimy Whit Wiley fits the bill. Look at it. He butchered Lee Holmes to get to Yael and her money. When Bethany became a problem, he offed her too."

Despite her use of lowbrow language, Babette's version made sense. Maybe more than my own theory. Based on the Facebook photos, Whit Wiley disappeared from the memorial service not long after I did. He made no secret about his feelings for Yael, and he was certainly a viper. I pounded the desk and shut down my computer in frustration.

"Calm down," Babette said. "Close up shop, and we'll go back to Steady Eddie." Her eyes glinted with mischief. "I need a stiff drink. How about you? Maybe Pruett has what you need, and it's not a drink."

I abhor vulgarity even when it hits the mark. Especially when it hits the mark! Tonight, as frustration mounted, and my patience ebbed, Babette persisted in pushing every one of my buttons. I grimaced, intending to scold my pal for talking like a third-rate gangster but, as usual, her sweet smile made me laugh out loud and forget my anger. Babette was one in a million—a good-natured soul with a generous heart and impetuous tongue. She would never change, and as her best friend, I had to accept that and value her as she was.

"What does Pruett think about all this?" Babette asked. "Seems like you two are miles apart lately." She shook her finger my way. "Men don't like that, Perri. Take it from me. I'm no genius, but I know how men think. Remember. I've had four husbands, and men are all alike. They have to be in the driver's seat, or think they are. Trust me on that."

Babette meant well, so I didn't bring up her last husband, Carleton Croy. That man was certainly in the driver's seat. He almost drove my sweet pal nuts with his lies and affairs. Having said that, Babette's comments about Pruett rang true. I refused to concede the issue, but there was more than a grain of truth in what she said. Whenever a hot story loomed, Wing Pruett was a bloodhound on the scent. Nothing deterred him—except Ella, of course. I wasn't a journalist or a celebrity. We weren't competitors or antagonists. It didn't mean we weren't a team. Did it?

Pruett's approach to most things was rational and balanced. I enjoyed swapping clues with him and testing my theories. We didn't always agree. In fact, we rarely saw things the same way. That was one of the strengths of our relationship, or so I thought. Was I deluding myself?

Babette propelled me out the door of the auditorium, narrowly averting a snowbank in her zeal. Most of the exhibitors and handlers were leaving, and the show was winding down for the day, with a profusion of dogs, crates, and assorted paraphernalia clogging the walkways. That's why I missed the danger signals until it was too late. Sergeant Watts was wearing a particularly insidious grin as she blocked my path, forcing me to stop. With Keats and Poe by my side, I wasn't particularly alarmed. Babette, on the other hand, came close to hyperventilating. She clutched Clara in a death grip and dissolved into a fit of heavy breathing. I was weary of gestapo tactics and fed up with the small-town antics of this cop. My rights counted too, and I intended to assert them.

I stepped forward and faced her head-on. "Yes, Sergeant. May I help you?"

At first, Genna seemed startled. She backed up a step and stood, hands on hips, with easy access to her weapon. "I've got a message for you, Ms. Morgan, and this time you better listen. Stay out of this investigation. Let the professionals handle things, or you'll regret it. Ever hear of accessory after the fact? You're getting pretty close to that, lady."

Babette gasped, but I felt calm and confident. "I don't know what you mean. Ever hear of police harassment? You're getting very close to that, Sergeant. As a private citizen, I can speak with whomever I choose." I scratched Poe's ear and launched a final zinger. "Perhaps you should brush up on police procedure and civil liberties." I flashed a friendly smile. "Unless, of course, you have something to hide."

Genna's mottled complexion changed from pale to puce as she digested my comments. For once, her threats and taunts had failed to intimidate. I pivoted and signaled to my dogs to heel. Babette trailed behind, but before leaving, she shot a few barbs of her own Genna's way. "Yeah," she said with a sneer, "my lawyer will make mincemeat out of you. He's not afraid of cops, and neither are we."

Chapter 20

Pruett was waiting for us when we got there, but he wasn't alone. His buddies Roar and Rafa were hunkered down on the couch, watching a football game on the big screen. A huge bowl of gourmet popcorn and several imported beers decorated the coffee table between them. They lounged about with perfect ease, while Babette and I stood awkwardly, like strangers in a strange land.

"Hey, you guys," Babette trilled, "glad that game is almost over. Need any more snacks?" Her voice always ascends an octave when she confronts eligible males. It's automatic, possibly a primitive throwback to her cave-dwelling ancestors.

The trio raised their hands in greeting but kept their eyes glued to the screen. For many New Englanders, whenever the Patriots play football, everything else fades into oblivion. That explained Roar's trance but not the behavior of the other two. Rafa wasn't even an American, for heaven's sake! It appeared to be an instance of male bonding gone awry, and I wasn't having any of it.

After the final touchdown, I broke up the gathering. "Listen, you guys, we need to talk." I established eye contact with Pruett to emphasize the urgency of the matter. Rafa leapt to his feet, chugged down the last of his beer, and headed for the door. "That's my cue to adios. Thanks for the company, guys. In Spain, we're more soccer fans, but this was fun." He bowed to Babette and me and vamoosed before we could stop him.

Pruett narrowed his eyes and patted the couch cushion. "Okay, Ms. Morgan. Have a seat and tell us what's so important."

"Want me to leave?" Roar asked. "If this is private . . ."

Babette grabbed his arms and pulled him to his feet. "Not so fast, mister. We need both of you to hear this. Help me fix some civilized drinks, why don't you, while Perri gets started."

I took a deep breath and launched into my theory of the dog show murders. It took delicacy and an unemotional recitation of facts, motives, and opportunity. After a character analysis of both the victims and the main suspects, I led slowly, inexorably to my conclusion. "Lee Holmes was loathed and hated by almost everyone. I haven't found one person, including his wife, who mourned his passing. He was a lying, unscrupulous philanderer who thought nothing of deceiving and destroying anyone in his path. I wasn't surprised when he was murdered. The only surprise was that it took someone that long to finish him off."

Pruett started to interrupt, but I held out my hand to stop him. "This won't take long, I promise. Plenty of people had motives to kill Lee Holmes, but Bethany's murder stumped me."

Pruett jumped right into the discussion. "I thought we agreed that Bethany knew something about the murder and tried to blackmail the killer." He shrugged. "Q.E.D.—it makes sense."

Roar nodded agreement, and even Babette began to waver. Once again, I plunged into dangerous territory. "Okay. We agree about the motive. What bothered me, though, was the brutality of her murder. That plough gauge was a bloody, painful way to end someone's life. Up close and personal for sure. It took a cruel, confident killer to do that, and some of those folks just don't fit the bill."

Pruett folded his arms, more foe than friend. "What's your point, Perri?"

I swallowed hard and forged ahead. "I mentioned this before to both you and Roar, but it makes more and more sense. I believe that only a professional could commit two murders without flinching. Someone familiar with weapons, physically active, and determined."

Roar exchanged glances with Pruett, transmitting a message that I didn't like. "Look, Perri," he said, "Wing mentioned your tip about the Facebook tribute page. That was a good, solid lead, and both Genna and I appreciated it."

I knew by the way he hesitated that there was a humongous "but" coming. Pruett knew it too. He averted his eyes and occupied himself by stroking Guinnie's soft fur.

"Okay. What did you think?" I was a big girl capable of withstanding rejection quite easily. If Roar had an objection, I wanted to hear it.

"Frankly, we didn't see much there. Nothing we hadn't gathered through witness interviews anyway."

"I presume you matched those faces to the timetable surrounding Bethany's death. The last time she shows up, she's pointing to that big clock, grinning like she just won the lottery." My voice stayed calm. Nothing defensive in my manner, no sir.

Babette threw me a life preserver, or her version of one. "I know that look," she said nodding. "Only two things that woman was thinking of—sex or money. Trust me on that."

Pruett got a puzzled look on his face. Other men look weird that way, but on him it was sultry. I gave myself a mental shake and focused on the murders.

"Wait a minute. Hold on. You think Bethany's lover was in that room?" He spread out his hands, palms up. "What's your proof?"

I hated to backpedal, but I did. "I don't know for certain, but she left the hall right about then. You can see from the look on her face that she was elated. That woman wasn't afraid to meet whoever it was."

They were losing interest. Probably thought I was some sort of obsessed female on a tear. They may have been right. I didn't need a clairvoyant to tell me that, but some things needed saying. It was time to unleash the nuclear option and damn the torpedoes. In the army, we used "Fish or cut bait" and a few less savory expressions.

"There's more," I said. "Let's fire up the computer and watch it."

Babette the hostess reasserted herself then. "Hold the phone, folks. Let's whip up a quick supper. We'll all think better with a full stomach."

The hospitality break defused tension and allowed everyone to relax a bit. I hoped it would take the edge off a very difficult conversation to come. No guarantees, though. We spent a pleasant thirty minutes talking about—what else?—dogs and the show world. Roar was surprisingly knowledgeable on the subject and entertained us with wry observations and anecdotes about the Big E. When Babette complimented him, he did an aw-shucks routine and attributed any wisdom to five years policing the complex.

Over an especially yummy dessert, I brought out my computer and nudged the conversation back to murder. "Bear with me on this. Please. Watch the faces at the memorial, and check the time when they appear. You'll note that Jess Pendrake told the truth. She never showed up for Lee's memorial."

Roar snorted. "So what? She still could have been there, waiting to kill Bethany. We know for sure that she was in that show barn, and that's what counts."

Persistence was always my watchword, and it came in handy now. "Several other people fit the bill, you know."

Pruett leaned forward, and Babette chewed on her nails. They knew that something big was bound to happen, and it wouldn't be pleasant.

Roar folded his arms and stared me down. Those eyes weren't dreamy anymore. They were ice shards. "Give me a name if you have one. Come on, Perri. Don't be shy."

He was trying to goad me. I knew that, but the time for delicacy had long passed.

"You want a name. Okay. Try this on for size. I think the killer was a cop. Your partner, to be precise. Right from the beginning, she's done everything possible to threaten and scare us off. Well, guess what? It didn't work. Genna Watts fits the killer's profile perfectly."

He rose from his chair, calmly and deliberately. "You're nuts, lady. Crazy as a coot. Why in the world would Genna commit a murder?"

Pruett moved closer to me in a gesture of solidarity. Babette backed up against the kitchen stove and shivered. She never believed in idle gestures that could alienate others.

"Power down, Roar," Pruett said. His tone had a hint of frost in it now. "Perri has good instincts. You need to hear her out."

Motive was the weakest part of my theory. Roar knew that and had zeroed right in on it. My conclusions had crater-sized holes in them, but they still made sense. Suddenly, I recalled the strange alliance between Genna and Yael Lindsay. Talk about the ultimate odd couple. That had to mean something. I knew that. It was up to me to convince two skeptics of its soundness.

I recalled the first briefing I'd conducted as an army sergeant. A roomful of guys with half sneers and folded arms sat on the edge of their chairs, just waiting for me to fail. I didn't. Facing Roar Jansen was a piece of cake after that.

"You asked about motive. Okay. There's one big one that springs to mind. Money. Yael has plenty of it, and I believe she got Genna to murder Lee and implicate Pruett or Rafa. After all, you said it yourself. You guys have been fixtures around here for five years. Plenty of time to observe the habits of the handlers and show people."

Pruett put his arm around me and squeezed. "Keep talking, Perri. This is getting interesting."

I continued my explanation, trying hard not to ramble. Anyone with exposure to dog shows knew that handlers tended to leave their supplies near the enclave they'd claimed with their friends and doggy clients. No one bothered their gear. It had no intrinsic value to anyone outside the show world, unless, of course, someone needed a particular weapon to commit a murder.

"Yael Lindsay wanted out of her marriage, but she refused to be crippled by alimony and property settlements. Massachusetts is famous for its punitive divorce laws."

Roar shook his head. "You mean Yael paid Genna to murder her husband. No way! I refuse to believe it."

Pruett interceded to avoid a shooting war. "Genna has been riding us pretty hard, Roar. More than normal with the cops I know."

"Yeah," piped up Babette, "I call them threats. Even today she cornered us. I have my attorney on speed-dial."

Roar blinked. "You don't understand her like I do. Genna can be rough at times, but she really cares. She'd never dishonor her badge. Never."

I rejoined the fray with a helpful suggestion. "Maybe you should check her bank account, or Yael's. Money can do strange things to folks."

The muscles in his jaw tightened like a violin string as Roar Jansen said, through gritted teeth, "I don't need to do that. Genna is the least materialistic person I know." He shot a look of triumph my way. "Besides. We plan to make an arrest tomorrow. Then you can forget sleuthing and focus on your dogs. That's why you came here, after all, isn't it?"

Babette slugged down a glass of wine before speaking. Fortunately, she chose not to prostrate herself before Roar and beg for information. Bad enough that she pleaded. "Tell me it's not Rafa. Please."

As the hot cop gathered his winter gear, he smiled ruefully. "Sorry. That's police business, Mrs. Croy. Need to know basis only." He nodded stiffly to us, thanked Babette for the hospitality, and sailed out the door without saying another word.

Pruett's expression was grim as he surveyed me and Babette. "What the hell was that all about? Did you expect him to give up his partner because of your theory, which I hasten to add was presented without a scintilla of proof."

Babette hung her head, but I fought back. "Thanks for all the support, Pruett. Glad you didn't choose sides. While you were having your bromance, we were trying to solve this thing. And don't forget that they were measuring you for handcuffs at one point."

Pruett and I had never really fought, but that was about to change. His eyes narrowed as he fought for self-control. "What you don't seem to get, Persephone, is the fact that this whole investigation is off-limits to you." His barely contained fury was evident in the tight fists that he made. "You have no business propounding ridiculous and frankly libelous theories that could harm someone's career. Not to mention that you're playing hide-and-seek with a killer. Butt out." He grabbed his coat and stalked out the door, leaving Steady Eddie a lonelier place by far.

"He'll be back," Babette whispered. "He's afraid for you, that's all."

I wasn't so sure. This was a new, angry side of Wing Pruett, one I was very wary of. Perhaps it was an insight into the dark recesses of his character. In fairness, I had to admit that springing my theory on him with Roar around was probably ill advised. Actually, it was downright reckless. Stupid even. Still...most men would have defended the woman they loved, even if they had their doubts. Lord knows, I'd had to defend Pruett many times from friends who thought he was a scheming sneak. Journalists were the most despised profession in every national survey—excluding politicians, that is.

"I think he's jealous," I said. "While we've forged ahead, Pruett was blindsided by this buddy group he joined. He looked damned cozy sitting on the couch with Rafa and Roar, sipping brews. Too cozy." I suspected that they were swapping tales about their conquests too, joining the sophomoric male ritual that was older than time. Pruett, chick magnet that he was, could certainly add to that discussion. The possibility bothered me. Had he betrayed Babette and me? Especially me. Journalists were trained to be professional skeptics, not cop groupies. On the other hand, perhaps I was the jealous one.

"What do we do next?" asked Babette, ever practical. "We've burned some bridges tonight, Perri. Roar probably hates you. I could see it in his eyes, and we know already how Genna feels about you."

Sometimes my best friend lacks tact. This was one of those times.

"Gee, thanks for the morale boost," I said. "If Roar were any kind of cop, he'd welcome new theories. He's too close to his partner to be objective. As for Genna . . ." I said a really bad word that shocked Babette. Anything that shattered her concept of genteel living shocked Babette.

We needed to go back to basics. Yael mentioned her new love, a person from the dog world. Frankly, eligible males were in short supply there, so our list of potential suitors was limited. A casual glance around the Big E confirmed that. She and Rafa became intimate the other evening at O'Doul's. Maybe he was the stud in question. Babette would really hate that train of thought, but so be it. I broke the plan to her cautiously, and as expected, it didn't go well.

"Why bother with Yael?" she asked. "Who cares if the old trout got some action on the side? Her cheatin' skunk of a spouse wasn't giving her any, and Rafa knows his way around women." She choked back a sob as she said that.

"Don't you see? Rafa fits the bill as the killer almost as well as Genna. He could really feather his nest if he hooked up with Yael. Let's not forget that the murder weapon was his."

"Yeah, but . . ." Babette paused for thought. "Not that leather thing. Besides, why would Bethany meet him?"

"You said it—sex or money. Or both."

She had no answer to that, so we took the dogs for one last romp, locked Steady Eddie up good and tight, and agreed to sleep on it.

Chapter 21

Pruett didn't return or call that night. As a result, I slept fitfully, waking periodically to check the clock and rue my tactical blunder. At five AM, I gave up. After showering and dressing, I fortified myself with an espresso and took Guinnie and the Mals out for a romp. Sunup was still an hour away, and the playing fields at the Big E were deserted. Ordinarily, I would have been on alert, but I was deep in thought, and the company of three dogs allayed my suspicions. A loud crunch in the snow made me whirl around. A shadow melted into the copse of trees behind me and vanished. Probably nothing, I told myself. Some guy who needed a quick bathroom break.

The dogs were well ahead of me, covering the ground in long, loping strides that were marvelous to watch. It was Friday—two days left at the show. In all probability, we would pack up on Sunday and leave the Big E without ever knowing the identity of the killer. I meandered through the grounds until I reached the Equine Pavilion. Returning to the scene of the crime was macabre even by my standards. I reconstructed that awful night when Bethany died, visualizing the leather tool slicing into that soft white flesh, watching the blood as it soaked into the hay. Horses were spooked by blood. Had the stalls been filled, there would have been pandemonium.

Dogs reacted differently, but they smelled blood long before we humans with our paltry senses did. Was the killer still there when I arrived, assuming, of course, that it wasn't poor, bedraggled Jess Pendrake? That was a fairly safe assumption since even the cops had released her for lack of evidence. I firmly believed in her innocence. She was certainly strong enough to do the deed, but underneath that rough exterior, I sensed a type of vulnerability that most murderers sorely lacked. Our culprit was a stone-cold killer. That was my assessment, and I was sticking to it. If Wing Pruett and Roar didn't agree, so be it.

I didn't open the barn door. The scene was still too vivid to face up front and personal. Bad enough reliving it in my dreams.

A litany of barks and growls startled me. Keats and Poe stood on alert, guard hairs bristling as they emitted their fiercest sounds. Guinnie joined in, but her contribution was half-hearted. Pointing to prey was more in her genetic code than guarding. I peered at the tree line. There was that shadowy figure again, just out of eyesight. This time I went on high alert. I called the Mals to me and gave them the Schutzhund command *Achtung*, meaning "watch and stay alert." If danger threatened, my next word would be *Fass*. That meant "attack," and Keats and Poe were primed to respond. I didn't know if the shadow person was friend or foe. That called for restraint, lest I injure an innocent citizen out for a walk. I had no plans to investigate the situation or draw any closer. Discretion appealed to me far more than aggression this time.

I shivered, even though the temperature had risen to a balmy thirty degrees. Some primitive instinct warned me that danger was imminent. If the attacker had a gun, we were in trouble. Otherwise, the distance between us gave me more than a fighting chance. I leashed Guinnie and cautiously retraced my steps, circling back toward Steady Eddie and safety. Keats and Poe stayed by my side, never losing sight of the potential enemy. I heard my name called as a dark figure—a man's shape—came from the other side of the Equine Pavilion and advanced toward us. Keats and Poe stayed poised for action, but Guinnie broke away and galloped toward the man. She flung herself into his arms and began to enthusiastically lick his face.

As he stepped into the light, I knew the reason why. Alf Walsh beamed his semi-smile and loped toward me. In his hand, he carried a rusty draw gauge, cousin to the instrument that had ended Bethany's life.

"Alf! What in the world were you thinking of? You scared the hell out of me."

He looked startled, not sinister. "Gee, Perri, I'm sorry. I saw you guys and decided to join you. Didn't mean to scare you." He nodded toward Keats and Poe. "Though with those two along, I'm the one who should feel threatened."

It made sense, but I wasn't ready to relax my guard. Alf had a motive for murdering Lee Holmes—a rather good one, in fact. Lee had virtually murdered a dog that Alf adored. A jury of pet lovers would exonerate him in a flash.

"Where did you find that draw gauge?" I asked, pointing at the weapon. It looked like a discard, with the blade rusted but still lethal.

Once again, he looked puzzled. "This thing? Found it in the weeds near the horse barn and figured I'd turn it in to the show organizers. Careless of someone to leave it like that. A dog or horse could have been hurt."

He was right, of course. A human had already been injured by the relative of that device. Either Alf was a consummate actor, or he wasn't too swift. Prancing around the scene of a grisly murder with a similar weapon could land him in a heap of trouble. Sergeant Watts would add one and one and get three. Who knew what Roar would think? Since opportunity knocked, I decided to question Alf about a few things.

"You were at Lee's memorial, weren't you?"

He nodded and snorted something unintelligible.

"When did you leave? I'm trying to establish a timeline."

Alf bit his lip. "Why? Not doing the cops' job now, are you, Ms. Perri?"

He caught me. I had no defense but the simple truth. "I have my reasons," I said loftily. "Bethany died in front of me, and I feel obligated."

"Let the cops handle it."

I was weary of lectures from imperious males who set limits for me. "The police haven't made much progress. Maybe they need a little help."

Alf chuckled. "Okay. I'll play along. I took advantage of the free booze and vamoosed around ten-thirty. Yael was still holding court, and folks were milling around."

I decided to push my luck. "Anyone absent who should have been there or vice versa?"

He wrinkled his brow. "Let's see. The cops left, but your friend Babette was there and most of the other handlers. Can't recall where Rafa or Whit were, though." Alf leaned down to stroke Guinnie's fur. "Today's a big day for this lady. I have a feeling she'll make Best in Show. No guarantees, of course." He walked away, carrying the blade gingerly by its tip.

* * * *

Babette was busily preparing breakfast when we returned. I played dog chef while she flipped flapjacks with blueberries. The portions were large enough to accommodate an extra guest should he arrive. He did not.

My scoop on Alf Walsh made her stop mid-pancake and gasp. "Could he be the killer? I never even considered him, but that blade thingy sounded ominous. Don't you go wandering off again by yourself, Persephone Morgan. You could have ended up just like Bethany."

I shrugged off any comparison to the dead psychic. Bethany had been careless, and she lacked my secret weapons—Keats and Poe. She obviously trusted someone and had been cruelly deceived. I wouldn't make the same mistake. After inhaling a second espresso, I summoned the pups and headed out to my store. Business was business, murder or not. Besides, work was a great tonic for mending a broken heart. With any luck, I wouldn't have time to even think about Pruett or his hasty exit.

The moment I opened Creature Comforts, a knot of frantic customers appeared. Between dishing up bait, hawking leads, and measuring collars, I stayed busy until lunchtime. Guinnie was slated for an early-morning appearance, and before joining her, there was some important business I planned to finish. I surveyed the crowd before venturing out. Despite my brave words, I had no desire to encounter the odious Genna today. No doubt Roar had briefed her on my theory of the crime and the identity of the killer. I had a notion that she wouldn't take that very well. I told myself to focus on Guinnie and be indifferent to Pruett, should he resurface. Everything was about the dogs—actual canines, not horndogs like a certain scrumptious scribe.

The Sporting Group was in Ring Nine this day. That meant a long, perilous walk past throngs of spectators and exhibitors and the possibility of encountering any number of hostile actors. As it turned out, my fears were groundless. The real problem occurred when I reached the ring. First, my name was called, and a pint-size missile launched herself into my arms.

"Perri," Ella said, giving me a vigorous hug. "I missed you and Guinnie, so Daddy let me come back."

Daddy Pruett stood at ringside, looking suspiciously guilty. One glance to his left told me the reason. Monique Allaire, famous photojournalist and mother of Ella, had already attracted a crowd of fans. No wonder. Amidst a mostly average crowd, she was a beacon of beauty and poise. I felt no envy. How could any mortal compete with a goddess? No way. At least not in the looks department. I admired Monique for capitalizing on her talent and forging an incredibly lucrative career in a tough business. Her ruthless nature and indifference to Ella were another matter entirely.

I smoothed my hair and wet my lips. No telling how I looked after a hectic day and sleep deprivation. Pruett slunk over and kissed my cheek. It was a brotherly touch, not that of a lover. "I hoped you'd join us," he said mendaciously. "Ella was going crazy. Come say hi to Monique."

I squared my shoulders and followed his lead. As usual, Monique gave me a vaguely startled look, as if she had no idea who I was. Two could play that game. I grinned as if we were besties and embraced her. That unexpected move set her back. She leaned toward Pruett and whispered something in his ear. Whatever it was—and I had my suspicions—caused him to flush. I moved toward the benches and found a perch near the judging area. Ella wedged her way in next to me.

"I saw Guinnie's movie," Ella said, "She won a prize."

"Indeed, she did," I said. "She's a superstar."

The little girl beamed. "Just like my mommy." Needless to say, my only response was to hug Ella and nod.

We hushed as the dogs entered the ring in a circle around the judge. I had to admit it was a beautiful assortment of spaniels, retrievers, setters, and Guinnie, a pointer. Ella squirmed in her seat, trying to contain her excitement as Alf Walsh paraded Guinnie in front of the judge. Other than our girl, I was taken by the spinone Italiano, and the clumber spaniel. Although each was very different, both were splendid examples of their breed. I focused on the stars of the ring, forcing myself to ignore Pruett and his ladylove. Dignity over desire was my mantra. Unfortunately, some slogans were easier to chant than fulfill.

"Scoot over, Perri. Don't hog the seat." That insipid voice had to be Whit Wiley. I made room for him, wishing mightily that he would descend into the depths from which he came.

"I see you have competition today," he sniffed. "Hard to compete with a superstar."

"Right. I think you've met Ella, Pruett's daughter." I pointed to the little girl, who beamed her perfect smile his way.

Whit produced a grin that had more snark than smile. "Who are you cheering for?" he asked.

"Guinnie." Ella gestured toward her dog. "She's a pointer, and Mr. Alf is her handler."

"Nice," Whit said. "By the way, Perri, I suppose you've heard the news about Rafa."

I caught my breath, waiting for the blow to fall. Roar said an arrest was imminent, and he must have made good on his word. To annoy Whit, I feigned indifference.

"Nope. We've been swamped by dog stuff all day. No time for gossip."

He curled his lip. Clearly, I had spoiled his conversational gambit. Meanwhile, Ella grabbed my arm as Guinnie was waved in to join the final four competitors. The kid had quite a grip on her for a seven-year-old, as my arm could attest. We watched breathlessly as the spinone Italiano, clumber spaniel, and a stunning Irish setter strutted their stuff. During Guinnie's turn around the ring, we cheered lustily and clapped until our hands stung. When the judge anointed Guinnie as Best of the Sporting Group, I heard Pruett's baritone leading the cheers. Ella jumped up and leapt into her father's arms. Even Monique managed to look passably pleasant. I stayed in my seat as the three of them joined Alf and Guinnie for a photo session.

"Feeling left out?" Whit asked with synthetic charm. "I know I would."

I treated the vile creature to my brightest Brownie smile. "Why should I? That child is with her parents and dog. It doesn't get much better than that when you're seven."

Whit grinned. "As I was telling you, big doings today."

"Yeah?"

"Yael and Rafa formed a partnership. Announced it just this morning."

Naturally, I was curious. "Personal or professional?"

He patted my hand. "Both, sweetie. Yael bought that kennel land nearby for a breeding program. Rafa agreed to run it." His eyes narrowed. "They've gotten close since Lee died, you know. Inseparable. Lots can happen when you concentrate on breeding."

That inference and its progenitor sickened me. I try to be neutral, but sometimes I regress. "You must feel dreadful about that, Whit," I said matching his feigned friendship. "We all thought that you and Yael...well, you know."

His color rose, and Whit stifled a cough with his handkerchief. "Certainly not. I merely comforted her as a friend, nothing more." He mumbled some sort of excuse and made a rapid exit.

Score one for the mean girl! The sick thrill of triumph that I felt was unworthy of me, but I didn't regret it one bit.

I rose from my chair and found Pruett standing behind me, looking distinctly uncomfortable. "Hey," he said looking down at his feet, "that was pretty great, wasn't it? Ella went crazy." He brushed aside a lock of his thick black hair, a nervous habit that was a dead give-away. "Listen, we're going to grab some lunch. Want to join us?"

When I begged off with some feeble excuse, his relief was palpable. Apparently, Monique and Ella planned to stay until the Best in Show competition at the end of the day. No word on their sleeping arrangements. I quickly shared my earlier encounter with Alf and Whit's bombshell about Rafa and Yael.

"Wow," Pruett said. "Talk about motive! You may have been on the right track all along. Just had the wrong suspect."

"Perhaps," I said. My voice had a slight edge to it.

"Babette will feel bad, though," Pruett said.

I summoned my mean girl self again and delivered this zinger. "She'll be fine. After all, men come and they go. There's always another one hanging around."

Chapter 22

I hustled back to Creature Comforts to find Babette. She had to know the truth before someone else spread the news about Rafa. As her best pal, I owed her that. Punky, accompanied by her standard poodle, was hovering around the door when I got there. I could tell by the look on her face that she had news she couldn't wait to share.

"Have you heard?" she asked. "Can you believe it?"

"If you mean Yael and Rafa, someone beat you to the punch." I gritted my teeth as I delivered that message.

Punky tilted her head. She was clearly puzzled by my response. "That's old news, sugar. We all figured that out when they disappeared from O'Doul's. The business part was just icing on the cake. I'm talking about the arrest."

I gaped at her like the fool on the hill.

Punky's expression went way past smug. "Come on. You're the detective. Can't you guess?"

I clutched her wrist. "Nope. I'm a bad guesser. Help me out."

"Chill, for crying out loud. The hot cop and the hag came out and arrested Roy Vesco for both murders." She pulled away and flexed her fingers. "I don't buy it, though. He's probably covering for Kiki."

For once, I was too stunned to speak. Roy Vesco was the last suspect on my list, despite the depredations of his ex-wife. Besides, he had an alibi for Bethany's death—my best friend.

"What made them arrest him now?"

"Who?" The door swung open, and Babette peeked her head out. "Who got arrested?" She turned to me. "Not Rafa. Tell me that's not true, Perri."

Punky couldn't wait to share her news with someone else. "I heard that someone saw Roy with those shears the night of Lee's murder. Plus, he slipped out of the memorial service at just the right time."

"Who told them that?" Babette asked.

Punky's grin was a mile wide. "Ask your buddy here. She put them on to Facebook. Someone videoed the whole thing."

"He was with me," Babette cried. "Ask anyone."

"Apparently, he slipped out at just the right time to finish off Bethany." She laughed. "Roy likes to smoke, and smokers always take little breaks. No one thinks anything of it. Guess it's harmful to your health, after all!"

My head felt muddled and all at sea. That couldn't be right. Roar must have something more that implicated Roy Vesco. Talk about circumstantial evidence! If only I could contact Pruett. His running buddy probably spilled every sordid detail about the arrest to him. I couldn't do that. It wasn't possible, and I had to face facts. Pruett had made his choice. I had to respect it and hope we could still be friends—colleagues, not lovers. Then we could salvage the best part of our relationship. I missed him more than I could bear to admit.

Rafa and Yael's big romance seemed anticlimactic after that, but I broke the news to Babette as gently as possible. To my surprise, she shrugged it off as if it were no big deal. "We never really clicked, if you know what I mean," she said. "Rafa was an illusion—a sexy one but never anything solid." As she turned away, I glimpsed the tears filling her eyes. In moments like this, I take solace in planning my next move. Two more days left in the show week. That meant a golden opportunity to sell my wares and expand my customer base. I'd agreed to conduct a free seminar for puppy owners on Saturday, a fun event that boosted sales of leads, collars, and incidentals. Besides, who could brood when surrounded by a group of puppies?

"You need cheering up," I told Babette. "How about a session in O'Doul's to perk us both up? After Best in Show, we'll feed the pups and sneak over there."

Babette pulled a sad face. "Nah. Maybe I'll watch TV for a while."

"Oh, come on. It'll be fun. No one lights up a room like Babette Croy!"

Flattery always works with my pal. Almost against her will, she smiled and nodded agreement. "I'm surprised you're going to Best in Show. The Lucrezia Borgia of the photo world will be there with her boy toy."

"Might as well get used to it. Besides, we'd disappoint Ella if we skipped it. I have a feeling that today is Guinnie's big day."

We agreed to meet at Ring Nine promptly at two PM. While I did some bookkeeping, Babette and Clara ambled over to the agility competition for one last go at a title. Things would gradually settle down now that I had faced the truth about Pruett. I'd skipped all the way from grief to stage five of Kubler-

Ross—acceptance. Surely that deserved a pat on the back and an "Atta girl."
When Pip passed, I had veered between denial and depression until Babette
hauled me up by the bootstraps. No more wallowing in self-pity for this girl.
No siree! I hunkered down at my computer doing Quick books, while a few
customers browsed. I detested accounting, but keeping an accurate balance
was a necessity for a small business owner like me.

I suddenly looked up, sensing someone hovering over me. Kiki Vesco,
with clenched fists, ravaged cheeks, and smeared lipstick was a picture of
distress. Although Keats and Poe stayed vigilant, they apparently sensed no
danger from her. Maybe they gave all dog handlers, even angry ones, a free
pass. I reminded myself that Kiki was immature despite her wanton ways. I
had an obligation to help her if possible.

"Hi Kiki," I said, "Need anything special?" My voice was
impersonal but friendly.

Her lip quivered as she faced me. "It's your fault," she said, pointing a
finger my way. "You got Roy arrested."

Keats and Poe quietly rose and surrounded my chair. They didn't growl,
but their bodies tensed. I rose slowly, shooed out a stray customer and locked
the front door. "You're wrong," I said. "The police made that decision."

"He was framed," Kiki said. "Just 'cause he clobbered Lee." She bowed
her head and sobbed. Actually, the sound was more reminiscent of a howl.
"He didn't do it. I know he didn't. He wouldn't."

I didn't kid myself. Kiki was a thoroughly unpleasant person, selfish and
hyper-sexualized, not above lying or twisting facts to suit herself. Still...I
empathized with her loyalty to poor downtrodden Roy Vesco. Unless, of
course, she was hiding her own complicity in the crimes.

"What do you want of me?" I asked. It was a reasonable question, although
Kiki didn't think so. She reared back and bared her teeth. Hopefully Kiki had
gotten all her shots. When dogs show teeth, you brace for trouble. I held my
ground while considering my next move.

"Get him out," she said. "We don't have money, but they'll listen to you
and your boyfriend."

The poor deluded soul had no idea how wrong she was. Roar Jansen
rebuffed my theories, his partner actively hated me, and Pruett had already
moved on. My influence was less than zero. Still, my curiosity was aroused.

"Why did they arrest Roy? The police must have had evidence."

Kiki stopped wailing long enough to curl her lip and sneer. "They said he
killed Lee because of me, and the fortune-teller knew about it."

"Were you involved with Lee Holmes?" I asked, hoping I had broached
the subject with enough delicacy and ambiguity to keep her talking.

Kiki bowed her head. "Nope. He tried to kiss me a couple of times, but that's all. Roy didn't even know about that."

"What about Bethany? You know, the fortune-teller?"

I could tell that Kiki was hiding something. In this instance, silence was the best weapon. After a few moments, she sniffled and gave a slight nod. "We were friends. She was fun to talk to. Didn't treat me like a stranger, you know. We mostly talked about interesting stuff."

I tilted my head and waited for an answer. "What kind of stuff?"

"Sex. She knew lots about that." Kiki was on a roll now, proud to flaunt her superior knowledge. "She had a new boyfriend too. They did all kinds of weird shit." She looked unabashed as she said that, and I was too cowardly to ask for specifics. Besides, it wasn't relevant.

"Really."

Kiki's face glowed as she reminisced. "She wanted to marry him. Said she had the magic potion, whatever that meant."

I refused to be sidetracked by the excursion into the seamy side of life. "So, what did that have to do with Roy?"

"Nothing. The ugly cop said he had a 'track record,' whatever that meant."

When my iPhone beeped, it scared the stuffing out of me. Best in Show was only five minutes away, and I had some thinking to do.

"Look, Kiki. I'm sorry about Roy, but they can't hold him without evidence. His lawyer knows that."

She bristled like an angry terrier. "I knew you wouldn't help. Your kind never does." Kiki flounced out the door, leaving me to ponder that last sentence.

* * * *

A crowd converged around Ring Nine, awaiting the start of the Best in Show competition. This wasn't Westminster, and all four days had their own Best in Show event. Still, it gave me a secret thrill to watch Guinnie lined up with the other group winners, awaiting her chance for glory. Babette had snagged two seats on a long bench facing the judge, so we settled in with fingers crossed. Pruett and his family were seated on the opposite side in special chairs monogrammed with Guinnie's name. I angled my body out of their line of sight and ignored them. In a move guaranteed to thrill the boys, Monique crossed her long shapely legs and leaned back. I sat soldier straight.

Babette's sharp elbow pierced my side. "Check that out," she said. "She looks like the queen of Sheba. What a snob. Pruett keeps staring at you though, Perri."

I swallowed hard and stayed silent as Kiki's words reverberated in my head. What did she mean "my kind?" I was no elitist. Far from it. I'd worked hard for everything I ever got or hoped to achieve. And what was this noise about Roy's track record? If he had a police sheet for violence, Pruett probably knew all about it.

On the other side of the ring, Yael sat on her throne with her new consort, Rafa, nearby. The recently deposed Whit Wiley was nowhere to be found.

The group winners made their initial pass around the ring. At first glance, Guinnie had some formidable competition: a Rhodesian ridgeback, cairn terrier, Akita, Pembroke Welsh corgi, pug, and, of course, Punky, with her standard poodle. In my judgment, they couldn't hold a candle to Lady Guinevere, but I had to admit to some bias.

Alf gave Guinnie a nose kiss and squired her around the ring in a perfect gait. She stacked beautifully for the judge, showcasing her exquisite head and shoulders. As Guinnie trotted around the ring, Pruett and Ella clapped lustily. Monique remained stoic, untouched by her daughter's joy. I considered the parallels between Guinnie's turn for the judge and the media circus that Monique attracted. Maybe she was bored because she wasn't the center of attention. Maybe I was wildly jealous.

The judge eliminated half the field, leaving Guinnie, the ridgeback, and the pug still standing. Finally, it happened. Lady Guinevere was awarded Best in Show, to the exultation of her handler and one very happy little girl.

"Let's go," I said, grabbing Babette's hand. "Let them bask in the glow." Naturally, there were pictures in the offing and, due to Monique's fame, a no doubt fulsome interview in the *Springfield Gazette*. I fled to my store, taking refuge in my dogs and simple things like leads, leashes, and collars. Thirty minutes until closing, I told myself. Shape up.

Babette was floored when she heard about Kiki's visit. She stopped grooming Clara and uttered several expletives that no upper-crust lady should even know. "That little hussy's involved in this. Mark my words. Run like hell if you see her with a pair of shears!"

How easy for everyone to blame a down-market type like Kiki. She had no defenders. Her behavior was rude and impulsive, just the kind of traits that might cause her to plunge shears into Lee Holmes. Once again, it was Bethany's murder that gave me pause. Kiki said they were friends, and I believed her. Kiki's speech and manner softened when she spoke the psychic's name. Bethany had no cause to blackmail Kiki, no hope of reaping a reward. Roy Vesco was devoted to his ex-spouse. His every action confirmed that, and he would do anything, including murder, to defend her. Once again, I recalled the sheer brutality of Bethany's murder. Slitting a throat was a bloody, messy endeavor that required a cool head and a cold heart. Roy Vesco had neither. My theory about a professional hit gained traction every time I thought of it. Too bad no one else saw its brilliance.

At closing time, Babette and I sprinted back to Steady Eddie to repair and refresh our appearance before hitting the bar. While I led our three canine charges on a brief run, she prepared their dinner. It felt strange without Guinnie in the pack. I knew Ella would take loving care of her pet, and Pruett—gutless wonder that he was—would never neglect the pointer, even if Monique urged him to. That was unfair. Although Monique looked like Aphrodite and acted like Medusa, I had no evidence that she would mistreat Guinnie or Ella. She regarded them both as bargaining chips in a high-stakes game with Pruett. Thus far, she was way ahead.

Babette looked like a million bucks, or at least several hundred thousand. She'd paired her paisley cashmere twinset with a smart wool skirt and killer boots. Naturally, her makeup was pristine, and her hair was fluffed beyond belief. I was a poor companion to such magnificence.

"Get a move on, Perri," she squawked. "Happy hour's on at O'Doul's, and the music starts at seven. Punky and the gang will all be there."

The temperature had risen to thirty-six degrees, with only a hint of snow in the forecast. I celebrated by breaking out my favorite velvet tunic over leggings. My hair and makeup required only the lightest touch-up.

"Red's your color," Babette said, "But for crying out loud, use some blush. You look like a ghost." She dove into her makeup bag. "Here. Let me help you." After dabbing and blending, she held a mirror up for me to inspect the result. I feared the worst—would I resemble a desperate dame or a harlot on the make? I was pleasantly surprised. Babette had shown restraint and a touch of artistry this time. If Pruett happened to show up, he would see a winner, not a wan castoff. If Monique accompanied him, he wouldn't see me at all.

We crated the dogs and made tracks for O'Doul's. Without Pruett's Porsche, it was slow going through the crusty snow. Fortunately, a weathered van stopped, and the side door slid open.

"Don't worry, ladies," said Alf Walsh. "You're safe with me. Besides, you're just too purty to walk in all that slush."

Babette leapt inside before I could stop her. Alf was still a possible suspect, although not a viable one. Caution had to be our watchword. Telling that to a woman with a pair of Prada boots on was wasted effort. I thanked Alf and slid in next to my pal.

The tavern was filled with merrymakers that evening. Most of the dog show crowd filled the seats, while a few townies lingered at the bar. Among them was the toothsome form of Sergeant Roar Jansen. Tonight, he was a testament to the power of jeans so tight they left nothing to the imagination and even less room to stow his weapon. His weapon...talk about your Freudian slips! I felt my face and at least one other body part grow warm. I was not that type of woman, was I? Perhaps this was Pruett's legacy to me—perpetual arousal.

Roar beckoned to me immediately. "Hey, Perri, come on over." He patted a stool. "Got a seat saved just for you."

I should have ignored him. No man who looked that good drank alone unless he'd planned it that way. Waves of women were already eyeing Roar, waiting for any overture. There was nothing special about me. I couldn't delude myself about that. Still, my curiosity propelled me forward against my better judgment.

"The joint is jumping tonight," he said. "I hoped you'd show up."

"Yeah." My response wasn't elegant, but it was succinct.

He caught me in the beam from those blue eyes. "Guess you heard about what happened."

Once again, I played it cool by nodding without comment.

Roar grinned and ordered me a drink. "Scotch okay?" he asked.

"Sure." This game was getting interesting.

He patted my arm. "Sorry about last night. I overreacted, and I was wrong. But Genna—she's like a sister to me. I know her, and she's no killer. You floored me by accusing her."

It was time to get the conversational ball rolling. "Roy Vesco. What made you arrest him? He's volatile but not a killer. At least from what I've seen of him."

Roar was proficient at this game of cat and mouse. In fact, he was better at it than I was. "He has a record, Perri. Assault with a dangerous weapon. Both times he put the other guy in traction." Our drinks arrived, and Roar clinked glasses with me. "Still think he's not violent?"

I gave that some thought. Roy might well be a brawler. Kiki said he stopped drinking last year, and I suspected that his prior problems were fueled by alcohol and angst. I shared my reservations with Roar.

He slowly sipped his scotch before responding. "There's more. Genna found blood on one of his neckties. Covered with gore it was. Waste of a nice piece of silk. He stuffed it underneath the carpet in his trunk where he figured we wouldn't find it."

There was more. I knew it but decided to let him go first. "The blood on that tie matched Bethany Zahn's. That's why we waited for the DNA results before charging anyone." His smile was dazzling. "We try our best to be professional, Ms. Morgan."

I decided to push my luck. Any man that confident could withstand a bit of prodding. Roar reminded me of Pruett in so many ways that it tugged at my heart. No need to dwell on the past. Eyes forward, as my old drill sergeant used to say.

"Okay. What about motive? Leave Lee Holmes out of it for a minute, and focus on Roy. He had no reason to kill Bethany."

Roar's smile was way too smug. There was more to this tale, and he was bound to share it. "We think he had one dandy motive for murdering Bethany."

I prayed that he wouldn't ask me to guess. Things had progressed way beyond that by now, and I felt testy.

Roar took pity and dangled some bait my way. "Vesco loves his ex-wife, wouldn't you agree?"

"Yeah." I had no idea where he was going with this, but I knew I wouldn't like it.

"We think there were two murderers involved. Lee Holmes's death was a crime of passion. Ms. Zahn's was one of necessity."

I closed my eyes, willing him to go elsewhere with this theory. He was wrong. I knew it, and nothing would change my mind. When I stayed silent, Roar continued. "We agree that Kiki is passionate and impetuous. She stabbed Lee in a fit of jealousy and was somehow seen by Bethany Zahn. That left Roy to clean up after her."

"Bethany was her friend. Kiki told me so."

His laughter verged on rude. It was clearly disrespectful. "Excuse me, Perri. If Kiki said so, it must be true. No killer ever lies." He signaled to the bartender for another round of scotch.

I'm not adverse to alcohol, but it tends to cloud my mind. I swirled the rich mahogany liquid in my glass without drinking. Time to bring out the big guns, and damn the consequences. My appetite for destruction grew exponentially.

"Sounds like Genna did most of the leg work on this. Did it ever occur to you that she might have planted that bloody tie? Easy enough to do since handlers leave their stuff lying around. Cops have access to all kinds of incriminating material, including blood. Ask anyone. You'll find that Genna has been all over the Big E ever since this show began."

I folded my arms in front of me and faced him. There was a touch of defiance in my stance, and I didn't really care.

Roar took a deep breath before responding. When he spoke, it was with that easy cop cynicism that he did so well. "Hmm. I guess we're at an impasse here. I hoped since Pruett was with his family, you and I might get together tonight." He swallowed his drink in one gulp. "Guess not."

His comment stung, but I masked the pain with a sunny smile. "Think again, copper. I'm still looking for a hit man—or woman—while you rest on your laurels. No time for anything else."

Roar pivoted gracefully and walked away, shaking his head as he did so. He never once looked back.

Chapter 23

Babette was in fine form. She loved dancing and had had plenty of practice over the years. Tonight, she pranced from partner to partner, kicking up her heels with abandon. I stayed by the sidelines cheering her on. No need to dampen her spirits just because I was alone. Besides, there were plenty of people to chat with about Roy Vesco's arrest. It was literally topic number one on everyone's lips.

Punky and her pals hovered around a large table, sharing a pitcher of beer. When I walked by, they scooted over and made room for me. I could tell by the pity in their eyes that word of Pruett's defection had already spread. Bad news travels at lightning speed in the Big E.

"You look awful perky tonight," Punky said. She slapped me on the shoulder. "Good for you, girl. Keep that head up high."

She meant well, but I never fancied playing the role of the wronged woman. Self-pity was simply not my style. Still, it might work to my advantage with a group of women who were all too familiar with romantic misadventures. I shared a few tidbits about my conversation with Roar.

"That's crazy," Punky said. "Roy's not the sharpest knife in the drawer, but he's no killer. Sounds like that Watts woman went on the warpath."

I tried to be noncommittal. "Maybe he's an easy target. They have to be feeling tons of pressure to find someone."

Another handler piped up. "You know, Roy looked real nice for a change that night. Course, that string tie wasn't great, but still . . ."

Something clicked in my mind. Roar described a fabric soaked in Bethany's blood, not a string tie. The guy probably owned only the one tie. Sounded more and more like a setup, with Roy as the hapless victim. I made a mental note to review that Facebook video as soon as we got home.

When Babette finally wound down, we hitched a ride back to Steady Eddie with Alf. I was too exhausted to do more than peel off my clothes and fall into bed. It wasn't until morning that I turned on my cell phone and read Pruett's text:

Perri—don't give up on me. It's not what you think. I miss you so much I can't even think straight. Meet me tomorrow, and I'll explain everything.

That message cheered me more than I cared to admit. He was probably spinning a tale, knowing how much I wanted to believe him. I decided not to seek Pruett out. At least I had that much pride intact. Creature Comforts would be open for business at eight AM, and he was well aware of its location. I intended to wring an explanation out of him too. What was his real connection to Lee Holmes and the other actors in this murderous play? Although Pruett was no murderer, the police considered him a viable suspect. Roar seemed friendly enough, but Genna openly accused Pruett of involvement. She was the one whose motives I questioned. Kipling had said it well: "The female of the species is more deadly than the male."

Babette, the eternal romantic, had a different reaction. She flung her arms around my neck and rhapsodized about the reunion to come.

"He loves you, Perri. Told you so." She gave me a smug wise woman of the Western world look. "I don't know how you ever doubted him."

I came down from the clouds just in time to remember my question. "You helped Roy with his wardrobe the night of the murder, didn't you?"

Babette scraped toast crumbs from her plate. "Yes. But don't blame me for everything. He insisted on wearing that stupid string tie." She smiled. "Kind of endearing, actually. Plus, I think it's the only one he owns."

Roar Jansen was so sure of himself. How would he react to this blockbuster bomb in his airtight case? Obviously, the silk tie in question had been planted in Roy's vehicle for Genna Watts to find. Conveniently placed, I might add. Perhaps the object and the person who found it were one and the same. I couldn't wait to share that bit of news with Pruett. Good sense suddenly returned, and with it the realization that despite his text Pruett was no longer my partner—professionally or otherwise.

"We have to tell Roar," Babette said. "Not the Gorgon. She'd probably put a bullet in our brains rather than admit to planting evidence." She fluffed her hair one more time. "Besides, lookin' at Roar is pure pleasure. His mama and daddy sure knew what they were doing when they combined gene pools."

I looked at my watch and jumped to my feet. "Oops! I have ten minutes to get over to Ring Ten for the puppy demo. Think you can hold down the fort while I do that?"

Babette loved a challenge. "Natch. Your shop will be in good hands." As I sailed out the door, she stopped me cold with this question: "What should I tell Pruett when he drops by?"

"If he drops by, tell him to have a nice day." It was a paltry response but the best that I could do under duress.

It didn't faze my pal one bit. She blew me a kiss and closed the door behind me, mumbling something I couldn't quite hear.

* * * *

Puppies, puppies everywhere but not enough to pet. I never got enough of those wiggling bundles of fur and fun, no matter how many times I conducted these sessions. Most of the students were adults accompanied by their pet progeny, but a few kids Ella's age and over also joined the group. One common bond united us all: canine love.

After reviewing some ground rules for raising a pup, I demonstrated basic techniques, using Keats and Poe as my assistants. Their performance was letter perfect, although mine suffered when I glanced at the crowd and saw Pruett and Ella standing on the sidelines. I'd done these so often that I could conduct these classes on autopilot, a useful feature when my mind was otherwise engaged. After a spirited exchange with the audience and demonstrations with the students, I concluded with a mild pitch for the custom leads and collars available at Creature Comforts.

I planned to slip silently away before encountering Pruett. It was better for all concerned that way. The plan was derailed when a pint-sized missile hurled herself into my arms and hugged my neck.

"Perri, we missed you," Ella cried. "Guinnie looked everywhere for the other dogs."

Who could resist such a captivating child? I couldn't, and I didn't even try. "What time does Guinnie go into the ring?" I asked, although I knew her schedule by heart.

Pruett eased into the conversation. "Eleven. Do you have time to grab a coffee before then? I promised Ella a soft-serve."

"Sure. I need to exercise the dogs first." No sense in being disagreeable. After all, we had started out as friends and could be that again. He put his arm around Ella and lightly touched my neck with his fingers. A jolt of electricity traveled down to my toes, proof positive of how pathetic I was when confronted by the sexiest man in DC.

"I'll help," Pruett said, brave talk from a man who was still skittish about operating in the canine world. "Ella too."

We formed a sextet, half-canine, half-human, and braved the bracing wind and chilly temperatures outdoor. Keats and Poe streaked to the outer fields, but Ella kept a tight rein on Guinnie.

"You got my text?" Pruett asked. His voice was subdued, almost timid. I liked him that way for a change.

"Yeah. This morning." I plastered a pleasant smile on my face and kept my cool. It was his move, and I wasn't about to preempt that. Pruett sent Ella ahead to throw sticks for Guinnie and turned to me.

"I really blew it. Can you ever forgive me?" His eyes blazed into mine with an intensity that was quite unlike him.

At times like this, the truth will out. "I don't know what to say, Wing. Your life and mine are on different tracks, it seems."

He grasped my arm and pulled me close. "No. Don't ever say that. I love you. We belong together. You, me, and Ella—we're a family."

I seldom cried under any circumstances, especially around a man. Generations of unenlightened females used tears to manipulate men. Emotion was a power ploy, a tool used by the powerless to control the clueless. I never operated that way and never would. A drop of moisture formed in my eyes, and I quickly turned away.

Pruett knew the value of silence. He drew me to him again and held me tight. We stayed that way until Ella returned and my Malinois were back at my side.

"You heard about the arrest?" I asked him as we sipped a double latte. When he nodded, I shared the rest of the story, particularly the part about the string tie.

"You're sure?" Pruett asked.

"Check out the Facebook video. There's no doubt."

The wheels were spinning in his journalist's head as he wrote and rewrote the lead to his story. Suddenly, "Death by Dog Show" had a different, even more sinister headline. Had the police deliberately falsified evidence, or was a clever murderer still on the prowl?

"What did Roar say?" Pruett asked.

I spread my hands in a hapless gesture. "We parted ways before discussing that. Roar was convinced that Kiki and Roy were the culprits." I couldn't help adding a final touch: "Incidentally, Genna was the one who discovered the so-called evidence."

Pruett quickly shed his lover's pose and went full-bore writer. "This is big. Maybe your hit man theory isn't so far-fetched, after all. Let me check into it." He pointed to Ella and Guinnie. "Can you watch these two while I make a few calls?"

"One minute, writer-man. Time for you to come clean. What were you really doing at this show?"

Pruett knew by my tone that I was serious. Dead serious. "Okay," he said. "I was tipped to a story about money laundering at different venues. Dog shows were one of them. Unfortunately, I couldn't find any evidence to corroborate the charge. I planned to interview Lee Holmes the night he died." Pruett spread his hands. "You know how that turned out."

It made sense. When he pursued a story, Pruett was sneaky and secretive and suspicious of everyone. Too bad that murder became the headline for his newest article. Money laundering seemed tame in comparison.

"How about it?" he asked. "Watch out for Ella? Please?"

He knew the answer before I said a word. Pruett dashed off on his quest, while our pack, now a quintet, sauntered back to my shop. Ella wore Guinnie's Best in Show rosette pinned to her jacket, along with the belt that I had made for her. An eclectic look, but she managed to pull it off as only a moppet could do.

At the store, Babette proudly totaled up the day's take. I had to admit, she had reason to crow. The puppy session had inspired plenty of pet parents to pony up for collars, leads, and other frippery for their new babies. After thanking her, I hastily reviewed my notes before a conference call with a potential buyer—an upscale store with a dash of panache—that was interested in my belts. While Babette and Ella freshened up, I got down to business. Guinnie's ring time was coming up, and I wanted to be there front and center to show Pruett that I was still in the game. No word on Monique's part in this charade. If she showed up I would fold my tent and slink off into the night.

An unexpected visitor stumbled in just as my call concluded. To my surprise, Jess Pendrake looked almost cheery in a navy pantsuit with red piping. Unless I was mistaken, she had also applied a smidgeon of cosmetics and blown out her hair. Wow! Babette would have been on this like the best scent hound. Even I knew that a man was somehow involved.

I greeted Jess with a friendly smile. "Need anything special?"

She cast her eyes downward instead of meeting my eyes. "Nope. Just wanted to thank you." For a moment, I feared that she would weep. If a bastion of strength and defiance like Jess broke down, what hope was there for the rest of us? She gulped and finally raised her head. "I know you took up for me. Nobody's ever done that before."

"You were innocent. Right?"

"That cop tried to bully me. Told me to plead guilty."

Genna Watts again. Would that woman ever stop? Her excessive zeal was rapidly morphing into something far more sinister.

"Don't worry. She has another victim in mind now."

Jess wrinkled her brow in confusion. "What?"

"They think Roy Vesco murdered Bethany. He's been arrested."

"No!" Her loud shout caused Keats and Poe to come to my side. "Roy couldn't kill anyone, especially a woman."

Devil's advocate was a role at which I'd excelled in the military. "Why not?"

Jess knelt down and stroked Poe's silky head. "His mom. Her boyfriend beat her to death when Roy was a kid. He would never hurt a woman." She jumped up and bolted toward the door. "I gotta tell them."

"Wait. Stop, Jess!" She ignored my feeble effort as if she hadn't heard a word. It was too late to stop her, so I spent some time pondering this new insight into Roy, a more complex character than I had envisioned. On the night Bethany died, Babette squired Roy and Kiki around like prize poultry at a county fair. To be accurate, Roy had exited for a least one smoke break, and knowing Babette the social butterfly, she had lost track of time. By hoofing it over to the Equine Pavilion, Roy could have murdered Bethany and still rejoined the others. It was possible but in my opinion not probable. Only a soulless psychopath could slit a woman's throat and then calmly rejoin a social gathering. That buttressed my theory about a professional killer. Roy was volatile, but no one would call him a criminal mastermind by any stretch of the imagination.

By a stroke of luck, I made it to Ring Two just as Guinnie and the other specials entered. There were eight competitors, five dogs and three bitches, including entries from Yael and Whit Wiley. In my opinion, there was no real competition. Guinnie outclassed every one of them.

Alf Walsh kept his eyes trained on Guinnie, although he subtly checked out her rivals as well. Yael employed a professional handler from Manhattan, but Whit showed his own dog. On the opposite side, Ella, Babette, and Pruett sat in a tight bunch ready to cheer on Guinnie to victory. That other show bitch, Monique Allaire, was noticeably absent.

Each dog did a preliminary turn around the ring and stood for examination by the judge. I scrutinized each, noting whose gait was smooth and frictionless, as ordained by the breed standard. On all counts, Guinnie emerged as the winner—at least in my eyes.

"Nice lineup." Rafa Ramos slid next to me on the bench and patted my back. His smile seemed a bit forced. "Mind if I join you? You're not saving a seat, are you?"

I matched his smile with a sprightly one of my own. "Heavens no. What about you? I heard congratulations were in order."

He nodded toward Yael, enthroned on her special chair across the ring. "Thank you. I am a lucky man indeed."

The judge instructed Alf and Yael's Manhattan guy to run their dogs around the ring yet again. Whit Wiley was waved to the back of the line.

"She won't win, you know." Rafa's words had an unpleasant edge to them. I deliberately chose to misinterpret his message. "I thought Yael already won."

"I meant the dog, Perri. Lady Guinevere."

"Oh?"

Rafa's response reeked of smugness. "Guaranteed. I know that judge. Bitches never win with him."

The subtext to the conversation was hard to miss. I confronted it head on. "Bitches sometimes win, Rafa, if they have the right attitude."

He immediately switched to charm mode. "Forgive me, Perri. My English sometimes fails me." We maintained a companionable silence until the judge made his final decision.

Guinnie was not the victor.

Chapter 24

"We were robbed," Pruett said. Like all parents whose child loses a prize, he fumed about the injustice of it all. In this case, he fumed sotto voce in case Ella got too close. No need to set a bad example for a child.

"Cheer up. Guinnie still got two points," I said. "Besides, it was preordained." I repeated Rafa's comments about the judge and his predilection for male winners. Pruett shared some choice words about both Rafa and the errant judge, none of which bore repeating.

"Was Rafa threatening you?" he asked. "Sounded like it. Be careful. The world around here's gone totally crazy. When this thing ends tomorrow, I for one will be very glad."

He was right, of course, but I still railed against the injustice of it all. Bethany Zahn had her faults, but she didn't deserve her fate. Lee Holmes had almost begged for his, but murder never solved anything, even when it was warranted. Both crimes would probably go unavenged after tomorrow. Roy Vesco's arrest was fraught with problems and would no doubt be invalidated. What would the outcome be then? I closed my eyes, envisioning a slow, steady slide into the oblivion of the cold case file.

"Come on," Pruett said, putting his arm around me. "Ella needs her dinner."

"I get it. Tonight is another Applebee's night. Buffalo wings, here we come."

Pruett planted a sweet kiss on my forehead and nudged me toward the exit.

* * * *

Our dinner was surprisingly festive and tasty as well. Alf and Babette joined us as we chowed down on Ella's favorite wings and fries. No sign of the photojournalist. I giggled thinking how outraged Monique would be if she saw her child eating peasant fare.

"Too bad about Roy," Alf said later as we shared a drink at Steady Eddie. "He's a little rough around the edges but basically a good guy."

Babette launched into an impassioned defense of Vesco and a stinging indictment of Sergeant Watts and the authorities in general. "I'm so disappointed in Roar," she said. "He must be afraid of that partner of his."

"Could you blame him?" Alf asked. "Woman's a menace if you ask me."

Pruett grinned but said very little. He probably had sworn a blood oath with his buddy Sergeant Jansen—fealty to the bitter end.

No one mentioned Yael, but I knew that she held the key to solving the entire puzzle. While murder, blackmail, and intrigue made great fodder for Pruett's article, they also formed a solid link leading squarely to the dowager queen of the Big E. Without access to police sources, I had no idea whether or not Yael's bank records had been checked for a hefty payout to a possible assassin. Maybe it didn't matter anyway. Soon some other tragedy would come along and sweep the seamy details of these crimes from public notice. That didn't mean I had to give up, of course. In the next twenty-four hours, I might be able to tie up a few loose ends.

"What did Roar say about the string tie?" I asked Pruett.

"Not much. There's no proof that it wasn't Roy's. The silk tie, I mean."

Babette laughed. To be accurate, she guffawed. "Men! Don't know diddly about clothing. I recognized the tie in that crime scene photo. Bought one like it for my nephew only last month."

"So?" I knew she was leading up to something big. Even Pruett went on alert.

"It wasn't just any silk tie. That was Tom Ford, baby. Two hundred and fifty big ones at Neiman's." She gave us an evil grin. "Do you seriously believe that Roy Vesco would lay down that kind of money for a tie he'd never wear?"

Alf gulped. "Do ties really cost that much? I wouldn't spend that much on a suit." He seemed scandalized at the very thought.

Babette pinched his cheek. "Make Guinnie a Silver Grand Champion, and I'll get one especially for you. A good luck show tie."

Pruett furrowed his brow, a look that enhanced his already sexy self. Leave it to Babette to ferret out a vital clue. That gore-soaked tie, steeped in Bethany's blood, belonged elsewhere, certainly not in the closet of fashion-challenged Roy Vesco. On the other hand, it was no big deal for the likes of Yael Lindsay. The closet of her late, unlamented husband was probably filled with designer duds, including high-end ties.

"Think you could watch Ella for a while?" Pruett asked Babette. "I'd be grateful. Perri and I have something to do. Shouldn't take long."

Babette faced us with hands on hips. "You two are up to something. What is it?"

Pruett's move mystified me as well. Was it related to the case or something personal between the two of us? I planned to confront Yael tomorrow at the show, not now. Frankly, I had no clue where the doyenne of dogs housed herself in West Springfield, unless a nearby palace was vacant.

"We need some alone time," Pruett said, squeezing my hand. "You understand."

His appeal to her love of romance scored a home run. Babette wagged her finger at us and smiled. "Okay. Just don't do something crazy like elope. I want to catch the bouquet."

Pruett flashed a rakish grin her way but stayed silent. I was too overcome to even comment. "See you soon," he said, herding me toward the door. "We'll leave the dogs here too."

As soon as we climbed into his Porsche, I demanded an explanation. "What was that all about?"

"Time to confront Mrs. Lindsay," Pruett said. He sounded determined, ready to resolve things immediately—or, as Babette would say, ready to rumble.

"I don't even know where she's staying," I said. "Springfield's a big place."

Pruett looked smug, way too sure of himself. "I know," he said. "She's at the same hotel where I've been staying. Got a penthouse suite." He winked. "Of course, if you prefer, we can follow Babette's suggestion and elope."

I skipped right over that remark. The issue was unsettling and way too delicate to discuss so casually. "Down boy," I said. "Focus on the mission."

He turned the heater up full blast. "You're no fun at all, spoilsport. With Ella as our flower girl and Babette playing matron of honor, we'd be all set."

I saw the humor of the situation. "Keats and Poe could give me away, but who would be your best man?"

"Roar, of course. He'd do nicely."

I shook my head and returned to the matter at hand. "How do you want to play this with Yael? Guaranteed she'll blow up big-time."

Pruett programmed the GPS for downtown Springfield. "You go first. After all, you figured out that tie business. I plan to study her reaction." He shrugged. "She won't admit anything, but guaranteed she'll react. They always do."

I believed in planning and strategy, but Pruett was more prone to spontaneous action. Maybe that explained the difference between us. Was it an unbridgeable gap or a felicitous mix? Only time would tell. Meanwhile, Yael Lindsay, entitled patrician, would rail at anyone who accused her. She'd probably toss us out or have some minion do it. Anything was possible.

Pruett tossed the car keys to the valet and hustled me into the lobby. "Change of plans," he said. "I'll tell Yael I'm winding up my article and want to do some fact checking. Maybe ask for some on-the-record quotes."

"What about me? Do I sit there like the proverbial potted plant?"

"Clever girl. You play observer. If I drop the ball, jump in. Okay?"

It wasn't perfect, but Pruett's plan was far superior to anything I could dream up. Yael might actually answer the questions of a reputable journalist like Pruett. I had no official standing whatsoever.

Fortune favored us. I fumbled in my purse, pretending to search for the key card to the penthouse floor, while Pruett folded his arms and fumed. Another couple in the crowded elevator used their passkey without ever questioning our cover story. Pruett thanked them and rolled his eyes, while I feigned embarrassment. In everyday life, I was an orderly soul who never lost keys, cards, or anything else. For undercover work, I could play any part needed. Babette was another story entirely. She lost anything that wasn't tied down and a few things that were.

We hesitated after leaving the elevator and might have been stymied if a familiar face had not exited a nearby suite. Rafa Ramos had never looked so good, dressed to the nines in a handsome pinstriped suit. I elbowed Pruett and whispered. "Check out his tie."

We exchanged greetings, using Pruett's article as our excuse for being there. Rafa frowned. "Yael didn't mention an appointment with you," he said. "Rather late, isn't it?"

Pruett leapt into the breach with a careless shrug. "I'm on deadline, and she was kind enough to help me out."

I stepped closer to Rafa and fingered his tie. "Boy, do you look sharp! That tie is fantastic. Tom Ford, right?"

The fuss about his appearance disconcerted Rafa. "I don't know much about ties," he said sheepishly. "It was a gift." He exchanged men-of-the-world grins with Pruett. Normally, that would have set my teeth on edge, but in this instance, it was a lifesaver.

"We won't keep you," Pruett said. "Don't want to presume on Mrs. Lindsay's time any more than I already have." They shook hands and parted ways. Meanwhile, I sprinted toward suite 10-D, the one Rafa had just exited. Pruett was close on my heels. He knocked on the door while I stood out of the way. Yael Lindsay, wrapped in a kimono of scarlet silk, responded immediately.

Her eyes widened when she saw the two of us. "Oh. I thought you were someone else. What do you want?"

Pruett immediately turned on the charm machine and launched into a string of lies that were so plausible even I believed them. Mr. Mendacious, aka Wing Pruett.

Yael was female enough to appreciate the attention of a handsome male, no matter how dubious his story was. Unfortunately, her good humor didn't extend to me.

"What's she doing here?" Yael asked. "She's no journalist." Her tone was unfriendly, bordering on hostile. Naturally, that didn't faze Pruett one bit. He patted my shoulder and chuckled.

"Perri's my fact checker. You know how cautious the press has to be these days. So much fake news being spread all over the place. My publisher hired her to help with this story. Keeps me on the straight and narrow, I can tell you."

Yael curled her lip but waved us in and offered refreshments. Both of us declined. In novels and mysteries on the big and small screens, every time someone accepted food or drink from a suspect, bad things happened. Not tonight.

Pruett consulted his notes and asked a few perfunctory questions about her husband. The widow Lindsay answered them directly, with very little emotion and even less embellishment. Finally, Pruett eased into the main event. His technique was understated and soothing, designed to lull the widow into complacency.

"Were you surprised when Roy Vesco was arrested?"

She shook her head. "Not really. His kind can be violent, and I understand he's got a criminal record."

Pruett pulled out his iPad and frowned. "Just one thing puzzles me. I want to get it right for the article."

Yael stayed silent but nodded.

"The tie. Sergeant Jansen said it was soaked in Ms. Zahn's blood." He grimaced. "Ugh. I saw the crime scene photo, and that thing was full of gore."

I scrutinized every move that Yael made. Beneath her carefully applied makeup, she grew very pale. That was not surprising, in view of the subject matter, but interesting nevertheless.

"I don't know anything about these things," Pruett lied. "But Perri tells me it was a very expensive article. Well over two hundred bucks."

Jump in, I told myself. Keep her guessing. "It was a Tom Ford tie, Mrs. Lindsay, the kind your husband wore." I painted a sympathetic smile on my face. "We just saw Rafa Ramos wearing the same brand. That's a very generous gift."

I had to admire Yael's composure. She neither quaked nor faltered. "Indeed," she said, reaching for her drink. "Are you sure you won't join me? I adore champagne, and Veuve Clicquot is my favorite indulgence."

Pruett has expertise in all things French. He picked up an empty glass and raised it in a toast to Yael. "Ah, Veuve Clicquot—the Widow. How appropriate. Your taste is impeccable, Yael, and the Grande Dame is the best of the best."

I don't know champagne from cola, but Yael was clearly pleased by Pruett's compliment. She sipped daintily at the pricey brew as he continued the conversation.

"Here's the part that puzzled me," he said. "According to my notes, the police found that tie hidden in Roy's pickup."

Yael didn't move a muscle. She'd make a heck of a poker player.

"Thing is," Pruett continued, "Roy wore a string tie that night. Supposedly the only one he owns. He's all over Facebook wearing it. How do you suppose the fancy tie full of Bethany's blood got into his truck?"

Full marks to the widow. She stayed as cold as ice. "I have no idea, Mr. Pruett. Ask the police." She handed him her cell phone. "Here. Call them. Then we'll both know."

Pruett never shrinks from a challenge. He pulled his iPhone from his pocket and dialed Roar's number. "No problem," he said. "Sergeant Jansen's on my speed dial." Unfortunately, the call went straight to voice mail. When Pruett looked up, Yael had replaced her drink with something more potent—a shiny Glock sub-compact pistol.

I'm no gun nut, but like most military vets, I know weapons. This was a Glock 42, top of the line, billed as the smallest, most easily concealed product that company had ever made. The media buzz touted how suited the 42 was for "smaller hands," a subtle but obvious pitch to women. Yael looked comfortable enough handling it, so perhaps the hype was accurate for once. Either way, I knew just how deadly and accurate that pistol was.

I slid slowly to the edge of my seat, poised to spring at her. Yael surprised me by swiveling to the right and pointing that lethal weapon straight at my heart. "Don't move," she said. "I thought you might be trouble. Not the simple tradesman that you pretend to be. Luckily, I am an excellent judge of character and an even better shot."

Pruett eased back into his seat. "What's this all about? We'll leave if we upset you."

Yael's laughter rang out in the cavernous room. "Nice try. I hoped it wouldn't come to this. Tomorrow the show ends, and we'll all go home. At least some of us will."

Her superior airs were starting to annoy me. That leavened any fear I felt with anger. "Why resort to murder? I presume you paid someone to do your dirty work."

She cautiously reached for her phone and dialed a number. "Come right over. We have some visitors who need taking care of."

I knew immediately whom she had called. Genna Watts, Jill of all trades and hired assassin. Genna would dispatch us coolly and professionally and enjoy doing it. Suddenly, I felt the first quiver of panic. Nothing crippling, just mildly disquieting.

Even with his life imperiled, Pruett remained a journalist on the hunt for a big story. "Why risk killing two people? Divorce seems simpler."

"Really? That leech stole enough of my money. My money. He contributed nothing but heartache. Do you think I'd pay alimony to him too?"

I congratulated myself for having great deductive powers that rivaled those of Sherlock Holmes. Problem was, my genius would die unappreciated, along with me and Pruett. Not quite the outcome I had envisioned.

"Okay," I said. "But answer me this. Why murder Bethany? She was harmless."

Yael fixed her patrician glare on me. "It's none of your business, but since we have some time, I'll tell you. I had nothing to do with Bethany's death. Not that it bothered me. She was a slut, just as I told you before. No. Bethany saw something and tried to blackmail my partner. A big mistake."

"Pretty smart to have a cop do your dirty work," Pruett said. "Tie up all the loose ends and plant suspicion on a poor slob like Roy Vesco."

Yael smirked. "You're right. It was worth the price. Always get the best, I say."

A rap on the door startled us. Yael answered it, all the while covering both of us with her Glock. "About time," she said. "We have to deal with two of them now."

Sergeant Roar Jansen sauntered into the room, wearing his trademark smile and lugging a bulging carryall.

Chapter 25

At first, I felt relieved. Finally, someone would save us from this homicidal hag. Then I saw Pruett's face. Yael hadn't bothered him much, but clearly the situation had changed. Both of us had made a mistake that might well cost us our lives.

"Give me that before you shoot yourself," Roar said, grabbing the gun from Yael's hand. "We've got ourselves a real situation here." He turned toward Pruett and me and shook his head. "Sorry it came to this. I've gotten to really like you two." He pointed his gun toward me as he threw Pruett his handcuffs. "Help me out, Pruett. Truss her up good and tight. Then it'll be your turn."

He used plastic ties, or flex cuff restraints, as the purists call them. They were more comfortable than metal cuffs, but that was no relief to someone awaiting death. Roar restrained Pruett himself, an action I considered somewhat sexist but largely irrelevant under the circumstances. He pushed us down on the sofa and poured himself a flute of champagne.

"Sorry I can't serve you," he said. Funny. Those dreamy eyes held the same twinkle they had in happier moments.

"Stop wasting time," Yael growled. "Get rid of them."

He didn't like that. Roar pressed his lips into a tight line and ignored her. "I guess you have some questions, don't you? Too bad that article won't get finished, Wing. I was looking forward to reading it."

"Why?" I asked. "Was it all about the money—or something else?"

For once, Pruett had no questions. He locked eyes with Roar as if he already knew the answers.

"Sorry, Perri," Roar said. "I could invent some high-flying excuses, but I have none." He swallowed his drink and dabbed his mouth with a napkin. "Truth. The oldest motive in the world is money. Filthy lucre. I plead guilty to coveting it." He crossed those long legs and leaned his head back on the chair. "Never have enough of it. Not on a cop's salary, so I got a second job." Finally, Pruett spoke. "How much does a hit job pay these days, Roar?" The response was matter of fact. "Mrs. Lindsay here paid one hundred grand. Oh, she was cagey about it. Set up a dummy corporation, all nice and legal." He smiled once more. "Course I took a loss on Bethany. Had to do that one for free."

"Cost of doing business, I guess." Pruett's reaction was tinged with bitterness and a bit of sadness. His affection for Roar had been real.

Now I knew where that cashmere sweater and Roar's other toys came from. Blood money. "Why kill Bethany? She was harmless enough." Maybe if we kept him talking, some miracle would occur.

"Bethany, sweet sexy Bethany. Unfortunately, she saw me do Lee that night. What were the chances? Anyway, she wanted more than I could pay."

"Asked for money, did she?" Pruett almost seemed to enjoy the exchange.

"Hell no. The dumb broad wanted to marry me. Can you believe it? I couldn't let that happen. She would have stuck to me forever."

Yael's store of patience had been exhausted. Her voice rose to screech level. "Stop this chatter and finish them off. Use the service elevator if you have to, but get rid of them."

"No problem." Roar drew his own gun and attached a silencer on it. The correct term was noise suppressor, but why quibble when it's pointed your way. "Nope. Too risky. I got a better idea." He turned to Yael and shot a neat hole in the middle of her forehead. The pop of the silencer sounded more like the slamming of a door than a gunshot. Nobody noticed.

"Never did like that bitch," he said. "She and Lee deserved each other."

As a thin stream of blood trickled down Yael's face, both Pruett and I gasped. Would we be next? I surmised that Roar would arrange the three-way murder scenario to account for our bodies, with Yael shooting both of us before being slain herself. It was tricky unless you were the cop who arrived first on the scene. Easy to manipulate evidence that way and account for your presence. Besides, Pruett had called Roar and left a message, asking for his help. So had Yael. Reputable witnesses like Babette, Rafa, and Alf would attest to our presence in Yael's suite and our belief that she was a double murderer. Neat and tidy, just like Sergeant Roar Jansen, the friendly local cop. He might even pin the blame on Genna, if the need arose. That gave me inspiration.

"Was Genna part of this?" I asked.

He scoffed. "Hardly. Despite your brilliant detective work, you got her wrong. Genna is a straight arrow. Every so-called clue you found pointed to me as much as Genna, but you were blinded by prejudice. I knew every corner and crevice of the Big E."

"Made things easy for you, I bet." Pruett kept his cool, although I knew he had to be thinking of Ella and worrying.

Roar enjoyed boasting. I'd never seen that massive ego of his unleashed before, but it was on full display now. He was right—prejudice had blinded me to the evil behind a handsome face and great body. My bad, as they say.

"I grabbed those shears of Rafa's first thing," Roar said. "Just in case I needed to set him up as a fall guy. Holmes was too busy bragging to even sense the danger." Another chuckle from the lying lips of Roar Jansen. "Take it from me, Perri, that German steel is top notch. It did the job with no problems whatsoever."

I managed a smile. "Good to know. I'll be sure to stock more of them."

He wagged his finger at me. "Good one. Always did like a sassy woman. Too bad inventory won't concern you anymore."

Pruett flexed his knees, a move that caught Roar's attention. "Cramps."

"Don't worry. You won't suffer for long." Roar checked his watch. "I'm waiting for the band downstairs to start. Things get noisy up here then. Easy to mask any sounds." He pointed to the sagging corpse of his employer. "She bitched nonstop about it. She bitched about everything and everyone. Quite the princess, that one."

In death, Yael looked anything but regal. Corpses seldom do. I resisted picturing Pruett and me in the same pose. Ghoulish and unproductive. Better to devise a plan—any plan—that might save us from that fate. Pruett locked eyes with me, infusing me with his strength and, yes, love. I resolved to gamble on Roar's need to brag. Shrinks called it grandiosity, an unrealistic sense of superiority.

"I was fooled by your looks," I said. "Most women would be, even Genna."

That appealed to Roar the narcissist. He snickered and nodded. "I figured that. If he hadn't been around"—he pointed to Pruett—"we might have made sweet music. Too bad."

Pruett joined the game. He raised his eyebrows in disbelief. "Surely, you didn't—I mean Genna?"

"Nah. I have my standards. Besides I didn't need to. She adored me from the start. Probably one of the reasons she hated Ms. Perri here."

"But she hounded us," I said. "Genna did everything she could to annoy us."

Roar pointed my way. "Yeah. That was funny. She was trying to protect me. Trying to throw you off the scent."

"So she did know you murdered them." Pruett whistled. "Wow. No wonder she planted that tie and framed Roy Vesco."

Our conversation was surreal, so banal that it made my head spin.

"She never planted evidence or did anything wrong." Roar seemed angered by slurs on his partner's integrity. "I told you about that tie and you believed me. The tie business was one of Yael's little touches. A mistake. I knew it immediately when you found that Facebook footage." He sighed. "Oh well. Next time I'll be more cautious."

Next time! "So you plan to continue your side job?" I asked.

"Sure. Word gets out when your work is good. Don't worry. I have plenty of customers lined up."

To my dismay, the band started an initial tune-up. Roar was right. The volume was already high. When the music reached its zenith, the noise would be deafening. More than enough to disguise the pop, pop of a silenced Glock.

"Showtime, gang," Roar said. "Let's see. Stay seated. That way I'll pretend that Yael shot you where you sat."

"How do you explain that?" Pruett asked pointing to Yael's body.

"Easily. I responded to your call, got here just a bit too late, and downed the murderer." He walked over to the door, making sure it was ajar. When it came to scene setting, the man was a genius. Nothing left to chance.

"Ladies first," Roar said, pointing the Glock at me. I closed my eyes, waiting for the pain as that steel projectile penetrated my body. The shot sounded louder than I expected, yet I felt nothing. I opened my eyes and saw the reason.

Genna Watts, gun in hand, burst through the open door and shot her partner. Tears streamed down her face and her hair stuck out in tufts. Never had a woman looked so beautiful.

Chapter 26

When "Death by Dog Show" went viral, our adventures quickly became the talk of the nation. Pruett's handsome mug appeared on network television, cable news, and podcasts around the world. No one could dispute the veracity of his tale since that clever writer had recorded every word of our deadly encounter on his iPhone. No wonder he'd insisted on using it to contact Roar.

I resisted all calls to appear with him despite the pleas of Babette and Pruett himself. The body count was too high for me to profit from my part in the whole mess. I also knew that media attention was a two-edged sword that both gave and took away. I valued my privacy too much to become public property, subject to dissection on blogs, Facebook, and Twitter. It simply wasn't worth it.

Not everyone agreed. Rafa Ramos profited immensely from a codicil in Yael's will. He planned a palatial poodle breeding operation with some of the proceeds and welcomed any chance to discuss his role in the dog show deaths. My pal Punky had already signed up to work with him. I assumed the relationship was professional, but with Punky, who could say?

Rafa's looks and charisma served him well in those endeavors on the big stage. On the other hand, Whit Wiley's bid for attention fell flat. Every overture made by the little weasel was rebuffed by news outlets, and he was reduced to self-publishing his own highly colored version of the events. Sales were extremely slow.

True crime books pay well. Despite my decision to remain incommunicado, my business saw a substantial sales surge after Pruett's book was published. I gratefully accepted that outcome and laughed all the way to the bank. In another positive development, Guinnie became a Silver Grand Champion in short order and was invited to participate in the forthcoming Westminster

Dog Show with other canine superstars. She deserved it, and Ella's happiness warmed my heart.

Babette basked in reflected glory, especially since she was publicly credited with providing the vital clue about that pricey tie. The designer sent Pruett several of his products to wear during the media tour, and I must say that Pruett represented them well.

I haven't returned to the Big E since the murders, although the facility continues to host dog shows. I doubt that I ever will. Too many ghosts prowled the area; too many lives were destroyed.

I avoided the limelight, telling myself that a quiet life with my pets, friends, and business was good enough for me. Despite the brave talk, I had to admit that our brush with death had been exhilarating. Pruett, Babette, and I made a formidable if unorthodox team that got results. We weren't superheroes, and yet justice triumphed and a ruthless killer had been vanquished due to our efforts. That was pretty heady stuff.

When the media frenzy subsided, I quietly rejoined the show world. After all, there were leashes to make, collars to craft, and bridles to fashion. Who knew when our next adventure would call?

Acknowledgments

To my agent, Sharon Belcastro, for her diligence and sage counsel, and to breeder/owner/handler Juli-Lacey Black for her insights into the intriguing world of canine competition.

Homicide by Horse Show

Perri Morgan will return in the next Creature Comforts Mystery . . .

Keep reading for a special sneak peek!

A Lyrical Underground e-book on sale October 15, 2019.

Chapter 1

"It's an outrage! Morally indefensible! Outright murder." Babette Croy swept her arms in an arc as she built up a head of steam. When it came to outrage, Babette was second to none. However, on the issue of animal welfare our passions aligned. Her big brown eyes bulged with emotion as she ticked off the moral failings of her affluent neighbors in Great Marsh, Virginia. "All they care about is property. Their rights. What about the horses? They'll go to kill lots and be slaughtered for dog food. Those selfish prigs don't give a fig about the horses' lives." Tears welled up in her eyes, threatening several thick coats of mascara.

Despite the protests of citizens like Babette, our local town council had recently sanctioned the removal of Cavalry Farms, a forty-acre facility devoted to rescuing horses. The official excuse was community safety, but no one believed that, even after a prominent landholder claimed that the stench and runoff from waste products had polluted her well and contaminated her drinking water. No one had much sympathy for the citizen either, a perpetual whiner who had far too much time and money at her disposal. The local newspaper had been filled with tart comments about her, some of which had bordered on libelous.

Our little community valued property above all else and paid exorbitant taxes to prove it. Quite simply, the rescue facility infringed on those most sacred tenets of upper crust society—status and raw profit. It occupied one of the most coveted spots in town and drew what some referred to as a disreputable crowd, particularly on weekends. Certain Great Marsh residents prided themselves on the exclusivity of their enclave and paid big bucks to maintain it. Businesses and property owners had coalesced into a massive interest group that touted constitutional freedoms and vowed to "re-home" the horses and their rescuers in a more suitable spot, preferably in another universe. Eminent domain was the official tool for change, a tricky strategy that was subject to scrutiny and legal challenge. Several local attorneys argued on both sides of the issue, but to a simple soul like me, equity and compassion superseded everything.

Babette and I commandeered a choice slot in the local coffee house that abutted the town square. She was a regular there, so her histrionics were shrugged off and regarded as nothing special, just a normal part of the scenery. Our server carefully set a cup brimming with espresso next to her and fled. No one, no one sane that is, wanted to tangle with Babette on the issue of animal welfare. I leaned across the table and patted my friend's hand.

"Maybe we can mobilize public opinion," I said. "Most people in Great Marsh love horses. After all, we have all kinds of organizations devoted to equestrian stuff. Plenty of little girls and their mamas involved." The equine industry and all the attendant suppliers was a billion-dollar bonanza in Virginia and constituted a good part of my business.

Babette closed her eyes and raked her manicured fingernails through expertly highlighted tresses. She was no dilettante but a serious person who also cared about her appearance and had the money to indulge her needs. She didn't look her age—not at all. Facials, floppy hats and the occasional shot of Juvéderm preserved Babette at a perpetual thirty-nine rather than her actual forty-eight. She always described herself as "thirty-nine and holding on for dear life."

I sported a tailored look more suited to my needs. No manicure. That would be wasted on a leathersmith who spent her time crafting items for dog and horse enthusiasts. Minimal makeup made sense too, although I still had enough girly impulses to apply blush and lip-gloss each day. My one point of vanity was my hair, a thick chestnut mane not unlike those of my equine clients. I usually tamed it in a French braid or a twist but on formal occasions it cascaded down my back in a blaze of glory.

"You don't get it, Perri. It's a status thing. They say they love horses but only a certain class of them. You know, dressage, jumping, competition thoroughbreds. Cavalry Farms rescues draft horses, farm rejects—nothing that would show up in those glossy magazines they love. These so-called horse lovers see their animals as fashion accessories. Lesser specimens are candidates for dog food or the glue factory."

Babette's sympathies were aroused by almost any animal cause and her perspective wasn't always balanced. Some opposition was indeed based on property values and class distinctions, and while many of my friends and neighbors genuinely loved all animals, they differed on this issue. I'd heard the same arguments applied to dog shows by the "adopt don't shop" crowd. Babette and I were both devoted to animal causes, but we also were enthusiasts of purebred dogs and attended shows all over the country. As a purveyor of custom leather goods, my livelihood depended on well-heeled people who spent lavishly on their four-legged friends both equine and canine. Balance was the key to getting things right but there was no sense in telling that to Babette.

She chattered on, happily making plans. "You're so right! I'll showcase it on my next program. Pictures and first-hand accounts. That should throw a spanner in the works." She clutched her cup and sipped greedily. "You can help me, Perri. People listen to you. After all, you're a veteran."

Babette was the eternal optimist but unlike me she didn't have to support herself or worry about offending customers. That gave her the luxury of time and the illusion that throngs of people actually watched her local television program. Unfortunately, reality differed sharply from perception. Community television shows tended to air at odd hours when most folks were fast asleep.

"I'll do what I can. You know that." My response was weak and feckless but as a small business owner, I had nothing else to offer. Creature Comforts wasn't booming but at least it was operating in the black. That could change in a flash if my clients—the canine and horsey set—turned away from me. High-end leashes, bridles, halters and collars were luxury items affordable to only a few of them or their doting spouses.

"Maybe you should court controversy," I said. "You know, invite the opposition on your show and have a debate. That might stir things up."

Babette drained her cup and gave me a caffeinated grin. "Like who?"

I was playing with fire but what the heck. "What about Glendon Jakes? He certainly has a point of view and he's pretty well known around here."

I hunkered down, waiting for an explosion, but Babette's silence was even more ominous. Jakes was her sworn enemy, a buttoned-down biologist whose popular hunting blog, Bag It, took every opportunity to excoriate Babette and the causes she espoused. She folded her hands and sighed.

"I get it. Meet the enemy. Bring him into the tent and fight mano a mano. Crafty. You're a genius, Perri! Never met the little creep face to face but I've read enough of his posts to last a lifetime. I'll get right on it. Better still, I'll have Ethel handle that." Ethel, her long-suffering secretary, was a demon of efficiency who could conquer any task.

My cowardice immediately kicked in. Babette operated more on emotion than intellect, but she was a kindly soul who would help any creature, human or animal. I did not want to see her hurt or humiliated by a snarky PhD with a penchant for satire. The sticker prominently displayed on his truck said it all: "I love animals. They taste good."

"Maybe you should wait a bit," I said. "You know, build your case. Marshall the facts."

She bared perfectly capped teeth. "Wait? That may mean a death sentence for those horses. Re-home—that's the term they always use. Sounds so much nicer than slaughter. Face it, Perri. Who wants to adopt those old bags of bones, loveable though they may be? Land is expensive anywhere you look."

Before I opened my mouth, Babette continued. "Look what happened at that county animal shelter last year. We picketed, pleaded and blocked the roads like well-behaved citizens but nothing stopped them. Bloodthirsty bastards gassed most of the dogs rescued from Katrina."

Babette dusted off her slacks and jumped to her feet. "Well, it won't happen this time. No sir."

I made a rapid Hail Mary pass, hoping to slow her down. "What about Carleton? He's a good tactician. Maybe he'll have some ideas." Unfortunately, the reference to her former husband had the opposite effect. Babette narrowed her eyes and glared at me, hands on hips.

"Carleton has no interest whatsoever in my activities. My causes. That's what he calls them. Can you believe it? Like I'm some silly teeny-bopper crushing on a rock star."

"Sorry. I didn't mean anything." A shroud of invisibility would have come in handy at that point. Anything was preferable to inserting myself into a nasty ex-marital spat.

Babette grabbed the check and patted my hand. "It's not your fault, darlin.' Things haven't been peachy keen between Car and me for some time. It's probably my fault. When the wife holds the purse strings…" She shrugged. "I should've kicked him out when we got divorced but he was so pitiful. Begged to stay until he found another place. That was two years ago and countin'."

Carleton Croy had impeccable academic credentials, a prominent ego and a perpetual look of gloom. Several of my clients considered him a hunk although the reasons for that eluded me. It wasn't necessarily his appearance. His features were pleasant enough, his body looked fit, and his thatch of fiery red hair gave him an air of distinction that was probably merited. As head guidance counsellor and drama coach at the prestigious Hamilton Arms School, he held a responsible post and by all accounts was quite good at it. Unfortunately, while pricey institutions charge whopping tuition they seldom share the spoils with their staff. Thus, every conversation with Carleton was studded with references to his days at Yale and his many well-heeled pals. The air of entitlement and dashed dreams that surrounded him was almost stifling.

For someone like me, who had scraped by paying tuition at a public university with scholarships, loans, and GI benefits, Carleton was an enigma.

I was a product of the foster care system. Through luck, hard work, and sheer stubbornness, I had beaten the odds in more ways than one. Despite having a rough start, I felt gratitude at my lot in life. Things could have gone worse—much worse.

"Are you listening to me, Perri?" Babette fished her keys from her purse and nudged me toward the door. "I'll have Ethel make a few calls. Let's plan to meet up tomorrow morning. My house about nine a.m. Okay?"

I hated to disappoint her but there was no alternative. "Tomorrow doesn't work for me," I said. "Not the morning anyhow. Got a meeting with a potential client."

Babette's eyes brightened. "What's up? Something lucrative, I hope."

"Could be. A vendor saw some of my belts on Facebook and he's interested. Thinks he could sell a slew of them to the right buyer." I crossed my fingers. "Wish me luck."

She threw her arms around me. "No one can beat you, darlin.' Every time I walk my Clara, people rave about her collar and lead. Stop on over after you finish. We'll have our pow-wow then and toast your success. By the way, give me some more of your cards. I'm fresh out."

Babette was both my biggest booster and biggest challenge. She meant well even when her antics consumed every molecule of air in the room. Three years ago we had bonded instantly at a charity event for retired military canines. I admired the zeal of this socialite with a conscience. She was fascinated by my army career and begged for scraps of information. None of my anecdotes were particularly memorable, although after three years in the military I had learned a thing or two about human nature and the use of firearms. Babette had never wielded a weapon more potent than a pen or a credit card. To her my life was as exotic as the plot of her favorite thriller. Our friendship had blossomed built on shared values and love for all living creatures, but our circumstances were very different.

"By the way, Perri, I got great news today. You'll die when you hear it. You will not believe it. Guess." Babette steered me to the parking lot where her shiny Mercedes nestled alongside my battered Suburban.

I paused, waiting for the bombshell she was dying to share. "You know I'm a terrible guesser. Come on. Put me out of my misery."

She shifted from one foot to the other like a gleeful imp. "We did it! Finally got the attention of the mainstream media."

"You're kidding!"

"Nope. Wing called me about it yesterday. That man is just amazing!" Every sentient being in greater Washington DC knew the name Wing Pruett. You couldn't escape him if you tried. The airways were saturated with sound bites and the handsome mug of the investigative journalist. Oversaturated in my opinion. Naturally I was prejudiced, since Pruett just happened to be my private passion and main squeeze. His name evoked both lust and fear in many of the nation's trendsetters since he had news sources all over the globe. I was solidly with the lust brigade when it came to Pruett.

"He's covering this protest? I thought he only handled political corruption cases or mob hits. Stuff like that. Things that would get him his next Pulitzer. We're pretty small potatoes to a famous reporter." I kept a smile on my face but inwardly I fumed. Why hadn't Pruett mentioned this to me?

Babette's grin showcased a fetching set of dimples. "I saw him at that benefit for Hamilton Arms last week and I buttonholed him." She fluttered her lashes. "You know how persuasive I can be."

I did know and frankly I didn't care. A recent profile of Pruett in the Washingtonian had described him as the city's most eligible bachelor, a darling of the J School set and per the writer, a man whose social calendar was jam-packed. In my book, he deserved those accolades and more. We kept our relationship on the low burner, but the flame burned brightly just the same.

After animal welfare, Babette's next passion was finding a suitable mate for me. She had wed enough times for both of us, although to be fair three of her four spouses had succumbed to old age, with a smile on their faces as she always joked. Until she found Carleton, she'd had the foresight or dumb luck to choose extremely wealthy men who doted on her, showered her with cash, and made her rich.

Dating, especially dating a babe-magnet like Pruett, had been the last thing on my agenda until we connected two years ago. My expectations were low since I assumed that he would never be interested in a rather ordinary soul like me. I was above all a realist who adjusted my expectations to attainable goals. That philosophy didn't entail pining for the affections of a society darling like Pruett. I was self-sufficient and determined to stay that way. No ticking biological clock or marriage anxieties engulfed me. I was content with my lot in life. Very sensible until I fell hard for him and his adorable daughter, Ella. Now I buried my misgivings and focused on enjoying every minute I spent with them.

"It's time, Perri." Babette patted my arm. "And a few highlights and some makeup would do wonders for you. After all, it's been four years since you lost Pip. I loved him too, but life goes on. Time you stopped dodging Pruett and settled down. Competition is fierce out there, you know."

I turned sideways, ambushed by a sudden mist of tears. Babette meant well but she had no concept of what I had shared with my fiancé or the gaping chasm his death had created in my life. Philip Hahn, "Pip," had been the love of my life, a shy veterinarian with a million-dollar grin and a big heart. Melanoma, a cruel and stealthy killer, had taken him from me so fast that at times it still didn't register. What a rebuke to the champion athlete and avid outdoorsman who had shared my life and still consumed my thoughts. Pruett and Ella helped to salve that wound, but it still ached at times.

"Oh honey, I'm sorry." Babette seemed close to tears herself. "I never learned to keep my big trap shut. Forgive me?"

I gave her a quick hug and clutched the door handle of my truck. "It's okay. I'll call you after my meeting."

She sped off in her sporty red car oblivious to oncoming traffic or impending disaster. I shook my head, never dreaming what our future would hold.

Meet the Author

Arlene Kay spent twenty years as a Senior Federal Executive where she was known as a most unconventional public servant. Her time with the federal government, from Texas to Washington, DC, allowed her to observe both human and corporate foibles and rejoice in unintentional humor. These locations and the many people she encountered are celebrated in her mystery novels. She is also the author of the Boston Uncommons Mystery series as well as Intrusion and Die Laughing. She is a member of International Thriller Writers. Visit her on the web at arlenekay.com.

Made in the USA
Columbia, SC
29 May 2019